MYSTERY

AT

LITTLE

BITTERROOT

*They say dead men tell no tales
but do their spirits?*

Also by Felix F. Giordano

Montana Harvest

For more information go to:

jbnovels.com

Mystery

at

Little Bitterroot

The Second Novel in

The Jim Buchanan Series

Felix F. Giordano

Red Road Publishers

Ashford, Connecticut

RRP

Published in the United States by Red Road Publishers, PO Box 460 Ashford, CT—www.redroadpublishers.com
Copyright © 2016 by Felix F. Giordano

First Edition 2016
All Rights Reserved

Mystery at Little Bitterroot, a Jim Buchanan Novel

Cover photo: State Hwy. 28 where it crosses the Little Bitterroot River on the Flathead Indian Reservation by Felix F. Giordano
Front and back cover art: plbmdesign.com

ISBN 978-0-9905684-2-1

Registration Number, U.S. Copyright Office: Txu 1-740-696

Library of Congress Control Number: 2015951031

Printed in the United States of America
Available from Amazon.com and other retail outlets
10 9 8 7 6 5 4 3 2 1

For Jeff, my son
Your knowledge of aviation
and meteorology is impeccable

A very grateful thanks to Jordon Pecile, the members of Jordon's Twelve, Eileen Albrizio, all my Montana friends, and my colleagues at MCC

The ground on which we
stand is sacred ground
It is the blood of our ancestors

--- Chief Plenty Coups, Crow, 1848-1932

·1·

Driving his Cedar County Sheriff's Department issued SUV upland toward the Little Bitterroot River, Sheriff Jim Buchanan felt the darkness seep inside. He turned to his passenger, Elijah Sizemore. "Show me exactly where you found it."

"There." Elijah, a Native holy man and elementary school teacher from the Flathead Indian School pointed toward the river.

Jim slowed the SUV to a crawl. He pulled onto the grassy area alongside the road on a rise south of the bridge that crossed the Little Bitterroot. Jim flicked on his roof strobes and clocked the time of arrival. He grabbed a roll of tape labeled <u>SHERIFF'S LINE DO NOT CROSS</u>, a few metal stakes, and a rubber mallet from the back of the SUV.

In doing so he pushed aside his backpack and recognized the jangle from inside. It was the rattle he had purchased nearly a year ago for his then unborn son and it placed a heavy burden upon his heart. It had only been four months since Kate delivered her stillborn baby. Jim breathed a heavy sigh and followed Elijah past the livestock gate and down to the river.

Jim glanced at the area where Elijah pointed and spotted a scavenging coyote. Elijah bolted toward the animal's apparent discovery and raised his arms above his head broadcasting the red plaid colors of his long-sleeved shirt. Jim ran after him and grasped Elijah by the arm. The coyote wavered, and then dove into the tall buffalograss.

"Are you trying to get yourself killed?" Jim, a Mixed-blood Native asked.

"Little Hawk, the coyote was after the body."

"Show me."

Even from a distance, the stench of decay sucked the breath from Jim's lungs. He dug into his front pocket, pulled out a handkerchief, and covered his face. When they reached the coyote's find, Jim recognized the shape of a femur protruding from a blackened mass of bloated tissue.

Elijah pulled a bandana over his nose and shooed away a hovering hoard of flies. "Here it is."

Jim dropped the tape, stakes, and mallet as his law enforcement instincts kicked into high gear. He grabbed a pair of latex gloves from his back pocket and pulled them on. Crouching, he brushed aside the soil.

Elijah asked, "Is it human... maybe one of our ancestors?"

Jim snatched the tactical knife from his duty belt and used it to scrape away more soil. "It's a thigh bone and it's recently buried."

"Do you know what happens when someone dies at the hands of another?"

Jim craned his neck at Elijah. "Yes, it's my job to bring the killer to justice."

"No, it's the *malyè es šeyiɬk.*"

"What do you mean by spirit memories?" A chill raced up Jim's spine. He knew those rarely spoken words.

"Little Hawk, when a person dies a violent death and there is still flesh on bone, it drives the spirit to seek revenge."

Jim snapped the knife shut. "The tribal elders' intentions were to frighten the children and keep them out of trouble."

"They are not stories... it is the way of the *malyè es šeyiɬk.*"

Jim noticed the heavy spring rains and snowmelt eroded the high ground above the south river bank and exposed the underlying soil. He realized the swollen river threatened the downstream reservation homes.

A quick burst of lightning followed by a booming roar of thunder caused Jim to fixate on the threatening sky. He stood and faced Elijah. "This is a crime scene. If we're lucky we can get a forensic team here in an hour or two."

"What about the tribal council?"

"Call them and I'll contact Police Chief Walkabout."

Jim gazed at the land. A livestock fence that ran for miles and a solitary gate were all that separated them from the highway.

The rolling brown hills, sprinkled with fir trees, and traversed by one set of power lines that followed the highway and another set in the distance parallel to an abandoned logging road dominated Jim's view. He saw no sign of evidence of whom or what was responsible for this apparent homicide.

Jim roped off an oversized area around the corpse with the crime scene tape. He felt the weariness in his six-foot, five-inch frame as he trudged back to his SUV and sat in the driver's seat. He grabbed his radio and called the Cedar County dispatcher.

"Martha, Sheriff Buchanan here. Be advised I have a 10-79 where the Little Bitterroot crosses Route 28. Dispatch Rocky and have Chief Medical Examiner Hank Kelly follow him for an extraction. Tell them there's a body on the Flathead Reservation and I have a member of the tribe with me. The Taylor Police Department should know about this too, contact Captain Stevens."

Jim signed off and looked out the SUV's open window. The humid morning breeze carrying the powerful sweet fragrance of the bitterroot blossoms permeating the heavy air slapped his face and drove him into action.

Wiping the sweat from his cheeks, he gathered a forensic fluid resistant body sheet from his evidence kit behind the back seat and returned to the river. Jim covered the body, drove the stakes into the ground and secured them to the body sheet eyelets with nylon rope.

Jim and Elijah then settled inside the SUV and waited. Within minutes, the sky darkened and the rain poured. While Elijah phoned his tribal council, Jim documented the event on his daily log sheet. He called Tribal Police Chief Jacob Walkabout and agreed to meet him at the sheriff's office in Taylor.

Nearly two hours later, Jim heard a wailing siren competing with the rhythm of the rain on the roof of his SUV. He recognized a sheriff's department patrol car followed by a State Crime Lab forensic recovery van and Hank's county issued sedan. At the back end of the foreboding parade was a dark blue unmarked Crown Vic.

Jim told Elijah to wait inside the SUV. He stepped outside and held his hat against the pelting rain. State Medical Examiner, Hank Kelly and Cedar County Coroner, Leon Madison got out of the sedan while a county evidence response team jumped out of the van. Everyone was dressed head to toe in raingear.

Through his rolled down patrol car window Deputy Rocky Salentino asked Jim, "What'cha got here?"

"Elijah reported a body on the riverbank below the flood line where the storm eroded some soil. I came out to the Rez, picked him up and we found a corpse... probably buried at least a week... a coyote was nibbling on it."

Jim's attention was distracted by Hank. "Let's get to work," Hank said clapping his hands.

Hank gestured to Leon who in turn signaled four members of the county evidence response team. They carried equipment down to the riverbank while Rocky got out of his patrol car and placed traffic cones alongside the road.

The driver's door of the Crown Vic opened and a man stepped out. Jim walked up to Rocky. "Who's that?"

Rocky turned his head. "Not sure. He's with Hank."

"Paul, come over here." Hank walked back to the van.

Jim watched a tall black man with a shaven head, neatly dressed in a gray suit, remove his sunglasses, and pull on his raingear. Jim walked over.

Hank introduced him. "Jim, today was my annual meeting with reps from the FBI's Salt Lake City Office. I was reviewing cold cases with Agent Paul Harris."

"You must be Sheriff Buchanan. I'm Agent Harris, temporarily assigned with the FBI Evidence Response Team Unit."

Jim reached out and shook the agent's hand. "Are you here to assist?"

"Observe... at Hank's request."

"Great, let's get going."

Jim, Hank, Rocky, and Paul tailgated. Hank estimated it would take a few hours to complete his extraction and another hour or two to search for physical evidence in the immediate area. Hank, Leon and his crew threw on forensic garments.

The rain subsided allowing Hank to remove the protective body sheet. He then opened the evidence kit inside the van and snatched an SLR camera. He snapped pictures from a variety of different angles, and then put the camera away.

Two interns from the county evidence response team set up a crime scene waterproof canopy to protect the body and then removed six stakes and a roll of string from the evidence kit.

Hank placed the stakes around the body, then took the length of string, connected it to each stake, and marked an area six feet square. Then the senior members of the team along with Hank knelt on the muddy ground.

Jim watched them search for evidence. He knew that bloodstains, hair, fibers, anything that looked foreign to the riverbank would be fair game.

They dug a small trench around the perimeter of the marked area with a mini-pickaxe and then widened it with a small shovel. Digging around the bones they left a few inches of soil as a buffer.

At Hank's command they stopped every few seconds to ensure they were not damaging or disturbing any flesh or bones hidden beneath the ground. Hank personally used a whiskbroom and gently brushed aside grains of subsurface soil from the bones.

With most of the body exposed, Jim's eyes caught something new. Between a few bones and the folds of decomposed skin that remained were clumps of black soil. This new discovery contrasted with the riverbank's light brown, sandy clay. Jim had seen that black soil before when he was a child on his father's farm. Why it was here confused him.

Jim swatted at a few coffin flies that emerged from a rotted hole on the corpse.

"Grab masks from the kit so you don't breathe in any bacterial spores from these flies," Hank said to Jim and Paul.

The team positioned a body bag on the ground and then lifted the corpse onto the open bag.

Jim turned away from a swarm of blowflies. He coughed as the stench of decay flooded his nostrils.

Leon zipped the body bag closed and the team carried it to the van. The eerie silence of the riverbank prompted Jim to cast a final glance at the waterside tomb. Gazing at the sky, he noticed the threatening weather front creep across the darkening landscape.

Jim walked past the <u>Taylor 120 mi </u>sign and up to his SUV. He opened the driver's door and stuck his neck inside. "Elijah, we're done here."

"This is holy land."

"I realize that."

Jim stared past the unrecognizable once spindly river, its banks fully engorged, to the distant field with its buffalograss swaying in the wind. Jim recalled the story that took place more than a hundred years ago at the Battle of Bitterroot Valley. The United States Calvary accepted Chief Red Moon's surrender but they massacred him and his warriors anyway. Yes, Jim knew it was holy ground christened in Native blood.

Elijah said, "The spirits who died here will make the *ḿalyè es šeýiłk* stronger. That body has to be turned over to my tribe soon so they can bless it and send its spirit on its journey to the long quiet."

Then as if on cue, a sharp lightning bolt split the sky, followed by a rumble of thunder. Then the rain burst from the clouds.

Guiding the SUV onto the highway, Jim collected his thoughts. Could the Battle of Bitterroot Valley and the way of the *ḿalyè es šeýiłk* prove Elijah right about this cursed land and a tribal superstition?

When they reached U.S. Highway 228, Jim headed west past the towns of Horace and Big Stump, then onward to the State Crime Lab in Taylor where an autopsy awaited.

·2·

Distant thunder accompanied Jim and Elijah on their ride to the Cedar County Sheriff's Office in Taylor. Being a patient man, Jim enjoyed the quiet solitude of driving through Montana's wide open spaces but every ten minutes or so he heard Elijah mutter the words, *ṁalyè es šeýiłk*.

Finally, Jim had enough. "Stop repeating the words, spirit memories."

"*Issaxchí-Káata*, you know better."

Jim hesitated responding to Elijah's challenge. It wasn't often that people referred to Jim by his Indian name, Little Hawk and even less to his spoken name in the Crow language. "Why did you call me by my *Apsáalooke* name?"

The holy man of the Flathead Nation stared back at him. "Little Hawk, if you ignore my warnings, there will be consequences that even your daughter with all her shaman wisdom and healing powers will be unable to prevent or reverse."

Jim pulled into the Cedar County Sheriff's Office parking lot just as his emotions were about to boil over. "Stay in the car," Jim instructed Elijah. "This will take a few minutes." He hurried inside. "Martha, is Tom in?"

"Yes, he..."

Before she could finish, Undersheriff Tom Hyde, a middle-aged man with a blond crewcut opened the door from the secure side of the building and asked, "Jim, I heard the news. What happened?"

"There's a body."

"Who found it?"

"Elijah Sizemore. He's waiting in the car."

"Where did he find it?"

"On the Flathead Reservation, the south bank of the Little Bitterroot." Jim's voice struck a serious tone. "Let's meet in my office."

The former frontier jail's wooden floorboards creaked with his every step. Jim pulled a set of keys from his pocket, unlocked the door, and entered his office. Tom was right behind. As Jim shuttered the window blinds one by one, Tom closed the door and sat in one of the office chairs.

"How did he find the body?" Tom asked.

"Fishing." Jim took a deep breath. "I don't have a good feeling about this one. It reminds me of a drug cartel execution."

"You mean missing head, hands, and feet like the one we found in their abandoned safe house in Big Stump three years back?"

"Exactly." Jim eased into his chair. "However, Elijah thinks the body could be a member of his tribe."

"Just be careful what he tells you."

Elijah's warnings flooded Jim's thoughts. "Why?"

"The year before you took office, he filed a discrimination lawsuit against the county."

"I know. The tribal elders coerced him to litigate."

"That's exactly what I mean. I don't want to see another lawsuit."

Jim exhaled deeply, his thoughts grounded in reality. "Elijah is waiting outside and agreed to act as a liaison between our department and his tribal council."

Tom leaned back in the chair. "See… see what I mean. Already, we're making accommodations."

"I made the decision to bring Elijah along and that's how it's going to be."

"Jim, please reconsider. Maybe the cartels are active again up here? We can request assistance from the Feds down in Arizona like we did the last time."

"Until we know the who, why and how about this body, we treat it as a possible tribal member. Elijah stays in the loop."

"All right, you got it. You're the boss."

"Bring Elijah inside and take his statement. Then have a deputy escort him to Lucy's Luncheonette. Give them meal vouchers. I'll complete an incident report. We'll assign case number 96-F-023," Jim said.

"Is that it?"

"Should be... anything else?"

"Actually, there's something I've been meaning to tell you."

"What's up?"

"One more course, then the state exam, and I'll have my DVM license."

Jim nodded. "So the rumors are true, you're going to become a veterinarian?"

"It'll still be a few years before I start a practice."

Jim held out his hand. "I know you'll do well. We'll miss you, but it's a good career move."

"I hope so. I love treating animals." Tom shook hands with Jim. "Thanks for your understanding."

When Tom left the office, Jim called Rocky on his cellphone. "Where are you?"

"Ten minutes and we'll be at the crime lab. Want me to wait for you?"

"Please. I'll be there in a half hour. Just continue the security detail for Hank."

With Elijah at Lucy's and Jim finished with his incident report, he filed the paperwork and climbed back in his SUV. When he pulled onto River Road, commonly known as Warehouse Row, the storm had grown in intensity.

The Cedar County Office of the State Crime Lab, the newest building on the campus adjacent to the old morgue, loomed in the distance. This state of the art facility, sat next to the Burlington Northern railroad tracks that hugged the Clark Fork River.

Jim carefully drove past an ongoing construction site for the new morgue building. He backed into a front parking spot next to Rocky's patrol car. Jim then raced through the raindrops toward the doorway of the State Crime Lab, past the security desk to the elevators and then down to the basement tunnel that led to the neighboring old morgue building.

Jim slowed his pace when he approached the sign that read, <u>General Examination Room</u>. He noticed Rocky, posted outside the door, wearing his Cedar County Sheriff's Office one-year anniversary pin. Another county deputy was with him.

Jim nodded to both of them and patted Rocky's shoulder as the stocky, muscular man, standing nearly six-feet tall opened the door for him.

Jim went inside and stood next to a wall lined with numerous cabinets and an expansive stainless steel countertop, a fume hood, sink, and an emergency eyewash station. Leon, dressed in a cap, gown, slippers, gloves, and a mask directed Jim to a large stainless steel table with a sheet-covered body that stood front and center and cornered Jim's attention.

"Buchanan, are you ready?" Hank walked into the room dressed in forensic garments and took his place next to Leon at the autopsy table. Hank handed Jim the required forensic clothing. "Here put this on." After Jim complied, Hank lifted the sheet covering the body.

Jim looked over Hank's shoulder at the corpse. He thought its physical condition resembled a ghoulish Halloween front yard prop.

Hank lifted a toothed forceps and a scalpel from the neat row of autopsy instruments and spoke into a microphone headset connected to the portable tape recorder attached to his belt.

"State Medical Examiner's Office, May 10, 1996, 14:48 hours. Autopsy conducted by Henry Kelly, Chief State's Medical Examiner with Cedar County Coroner Leon Madison and Cedar County Sheriff James Buchanan in attendance. The body before us is that of an unknown individual found at approximately 8 a.m. today in Cedar County, Montana near the Little Bitterroot River on the Flathead Indian Reservation. A preliminary review indicates the corpse is nude and incomplete."

Jim listened as Hank determined and recorded the body's measurements. Then the autopsy got down to the important details and Jim devoted all his attention to Hank's skillful verbal delivery.

"A microscopic exam is to be performed later to detect hair or other fibers that may still be on the body. Relative to the skeletal structure, the skull is missing as well as the hands and feet. This does not appear to be associated with decay or scavenging since those areas have remarkable cuts made by a presumably sharp instrument. Part of the radius bone is denuded and displaced. This does appear to be a result of scavenging."

Hank continued, "The thoracic area is also exposed and most of the internal organs below the diaphragm are missing. The external sexual organs are intact and the body is that of an adult male. The race of the body is indiscernible at this time due to discoloration of the skin. There appears to be some insect activity outside the body. Inside the body cavities, we find adults, pupae, larva, and egg cases. Their physical activity is subdued due to the autopsy room temperature. There is the presence of adipocerous on the abdomen which indicates the body was buried in moist soil for at least a few weeks."

Jim cupped a latex-gloved hand over his mask to stifle the autopsy smells. The pale green walls with their random chemical spills appeared to close in around him.

Hank set down his autopsy instruments, then paused the recorder. "Are you all right?"

Jim wiped sweat from his forehead. "I saw the autopsy performed on the Hopkins boy a few years ago before you got here. It was a drowning. He was only under for a couple of hours but I've never seen anything like this." Jim's thoughts began to wander. "What do you think happened to the skull?"

"The head might be buried somewhere else. We don't know yet. Leon, hand me those rib cutters." Hank pushed the play button on the recorder.

After cutting, sawing, extracting, and weighing, Hank stopped the recorder again. Jim noticed him staring at the grains of black soil.

"How long do you think the body's been dead before it was buried?" Jim asked.

"It depends on the soil it was buried in, the temperature and the humidity. We can't even be sure the body wasn't moved from somewhere else."

"What makes you say that?"

Hank looked up. "I have to consider everything. I leave nothing to speculation."

"I've seen that black soil before."

11

"Where?"

"When I was a teenager my dad planted potatoes and that soil was on his farm."

"Now I'm confused," Hank said. "Do you mean that soil is…"

"It's not common to find it down by the river," Jim continued, "the soil by the Little Bitterroot has a different consistency and color."

Leon added, "Then the body must have been moved."

"Seems like it," Hank said. "At least according to what Jim is telling us." Hank stepped away from the autopsy table and pulled off his gloves. He motioned to Jim and Leon. "Let's talk in my office."

Leon put the body away and then the three men removed their forensic garments, washed up, and left the morgue. Jim stepped into the hallway and gestured for Rocky to follow leaving the other deputy to stand guard. The four men walked through the tunnel and into the State Crime Lab building.

Hank opened the door to his office and flicked the light switch on. "I hate this office, too antiseptic for my likes but they tell me I better get used to it because it's only a matter of months before they shut down the old morgue and my temporary office. Everyone have a seat. Jim, tell me more about this soil."

"When I was in high school I worked the fields on my dad's farm bordering Little Bitterroot Lake. The soil there was fertile, not like the ground on reservation land."

"But you grew up on the Crow Reservation not the Flathead Reservation."

"Hank, most reservation land is the same. It's not good for farming, only for the gas or oil that's hidden beneath it."

"So we should check the soil on your dad's spread?" Leon asked Jim.

Hank interjected, "Yes we will but we should also check other farms in the area. It seems this person was murdered, his head, hands, and feet severed with precision and then the torso, arms and legs buried in the riverbank along the Little Bitterroot."

"Sounds a bit like a mob killing to me." Rocky sat forward in his seat.

Hank replied to Rocky, "Plenty of those went down in New York."

Jim pointed out. "This isn't New York. Things like this don't happen here."

"Let me get this straight," Hank said. "If that soil were found on farms in the area, would it also be on other land in that same area? The murder could have taken place anywhere."

Jim stood up. "My guess is that because that black soil was loose on the body and not smeared, the murder must have taken place in a farmer's field soon after it was tilled this spring."

"Your dad's farm?" Hank asked.

"No... after my dad died five years ago, he donated his farm to the county in his will. There was talk the county was going to lease the farm to Taylor University for their agricultural program." Jim walked to the panoramic window in Hank's third floor office and gazed at the rushing waters of the Clark Fork River running parallel to State Highway 200 and the railroad tracks on the westward journey toward Idaho.

"Did they?" Hank asked.

Jim turned back to Hank. "Not to my knowledge. It's still owned by the county. They don't know what to do with it."

"Leon, have one of the interns examine the composition of the soil. Have them look for anything foreign like chemical fertilizer, types of manure, lime, seeds, and paint or metal shavings from farm equipment. If we find something in these soil samples maybe we can pinpoint it to the actual farms that use these additives or equipment." Hank then returned his attention to Jim. "If we're going to find out what happened, we also have to go back to the burial site to perform a further examination of the area."

"Do you think we missed anything?" Rocky asked.

Hank replied, "I'm not sure but I want to examine it with a fine-toothed comb."

Jim shook his head. "Hank, if you haven't noticed, it's been pouring. We'll have trouble finding more evidence."

Outside, the rain maintained a driving rhythm against the wailing wind, swelling the Little Bitterroot again, eroding more riverbank soil, revealing new secrets waiting to be discovered.

·3·

The rainstorm deteriorated into a full-blown downpour as Jim and Rocky left the State Crime Lab. When they returned to the sheriff's office, Martha told Jim that Elijah finished giving his statement to Undersheriff Tom Hyde and needed a ride back to the reservation. Jim quickly volunteered.

Jim drove less than a city block when his eyes caught movement in the shadows between the warehouse buildings. He slammed on the brakes.

"What's wrong," Elijah asked.

"Stay here."

Jim backed up, opened the door, and ran into the alleyway between two factory buildings. On the steps of one of the buildings sat a hunkered down Sam Clayton.

"Sheriff, I didn't do nothing. I'm just trying to stay out of the rain."

Jim looked at the brown bag tucked under Sam's arm. "I see your toting your medicine again." Sam tried to push it behind him but Jim snatched it up. "I want you to report to Saint Joan's Covenant otherwise you'll spend the night in jail. Get sober and stay out of trouble."

Sam stood up and brushed himself off. He nodded to Jim and wobbled toward the street. Jim followed and when he saw Sam headed toward the soup kitchen, he climbed back into his SUV.

"Is everything all right?" Elijah asked.

Jim shook the rain from his Stetson and then put the SUV into gear. "It's not your concern."

Just outside of town on a deserted stretch of road, Jim noticed a tow truck headed toward them. It slowed down and Jim stopped his SUV alongside the truck.

"Busy today?" Jim asked the tow truck driver as the diatribe from the conservative talk radio show spewed from inside the truck and lingered outside Jim's SUV.

The driver took a drag from his cigar, then dropped his hand outside the door and flicked the ashes onto the street. With the other hand, he stroked his goatee, and then smiled. "Just listenin' to Roy Lewis on KCHM on my way back from Ledge Flats."

"What business did you have in Ledge Flats?"

"Storm business."

"Stick around. I may need you. Elijah, have you met Jack Morton?"

Elijah leaned over. "Never had the opportunity, my name's Elijah Sizemore, your name's Jack?"

Jack puffed on his cigar. "Jack's the name, towing, car repair, and construction's my game."

Jim tipped his hat to Jack. "I'll call you later if I need you." They each continued on their way.

On U.S. Highway 228, a few miles out of town, Jim received a call on his radio.

"Sheriff Buchanan, this is dispatch. Are you there?"

"Martha, I'm here. What's up?"

"We just got a call from the power company in Kalispell. There's a washout on Route 28 near Lonepine, a fifty-foot section of the road just north of the bridge. They can't get by the washout and they need to restore power south of there."

"What else did they tell you?" Jim asked.

"They said a regulator bypass switch got hit by lightning from last night's storm. It blew the regulator, burnt the pole down, and tripped the circuit. They said there's more than two-hundred customers out of power."

"Did they say what they needed from us?"

"More flaggers... they've got a couple of contractors working the roads but it ain't enough. They're trying to reroute traffic from both directions."

Jim breathed a heavy sigh. "Get Jack Morton on the phone. I just saw him a few minutes ago. Let him know what happened and ask him to get a road crew together. Tell him I'll be at the washout. Send Rocky and a few deputies up there. Tell them I'll meet them once I get back. Keep the office under control." Once he ended the call he turned to Elijah. "I'll get you back home first. We'll have to go the long way."

After Jim dropped off Elijah, he doubled back in weather that worsened into a complete mess. The rain eventually settled into a light early evening mist when Jim saw flashing blue lights ahead.

People congregated on the shoulder of the road next to their cars, talking, smoking cigarettes, and arguing. The source of the flashing blue lights was a car from his office blocking the road. One of his deputies stepped out and waved to Jim.

"Where's Rocky?" Jim asked.

"He's a few hundred yards north of here. We rerouted southbound traffic to Route 93. We're using that old logging road north of the bridge as a turnaround area. We're lucky it runs so close to 28. South of here we got northbound cars and trucks turning around in Lonepine and we're sending them to U.S. 93 too."

"Good man. I'm going to check on Rocky. Stay put, call me if anything happens."

"Will do."

The deputy moved his patrol car out of Jim's way. Distant, flashing yellow lights marked where the bridge crossed the Little Bitterroot. As Jim drove closer, he noticed a section of road past the bridge was gone. It was close to where he spoke with Elijah that morning. The river undermined and eroded State Highway 28 leaving behind a six-foot wide section of roadbed and a mudslide gully dipping at a thirty-degree angle.

Jim parked his SUV and walked across the bridge and what remained of the pavement. On the other side, five line trucks and two pickup trucks from the local power company flashed their emergency lights. Jim walked up to Rocky and a man who wore a yellow hardhat inscribed with the power company's insignia. The man held a coffee in one hand and a doughnut in the other.

"Glad you made it." Rocky extended his hand to Jim. "Sheriff Donovan from Lake County helped reroute traffic north of here."

"Thanks." Jim shook Rocky's hand and then addressed the lineman. "I'm Jim Buchanan, Cedar County Sheriff. Are you in charge of these line crews?"

The man gulped on his coffee. "No. You'll want to speak with Charlie." He pointed with his doughnut to one of the line trucks.

"Thanks." Jim turned to Rocky. "Make sure no one gets hurt while I find out what's going on." Rocky nodded as Jim walked toward the line truck.

"*Issaxchí-Káata*."

Jim heard his Indian name called. He recognized the officer with his braided, black ponytail peeking out from under his Stetson. It was Flathead Tribal Police Chief Jacob Walkabout. The men were of equal height, but unlike Jim, Jacob had a daily weakness for fast food and it plainly showed.

Jim asked, "We agreed to meet in Taylor to discuss the body. When did you get here?"

Jacob pointed the butt of his flashlight at Jim. "Change of plans. I was first on the scene after the road gave way."

"We'll open it to reservation traffic as soon as we can."

"That's not my main concern."

Jim folded his arms. "What is?"

"That body."

"Hank Kelly is working on the autopsy. When I have some info I'll fill you in."

Jim tried to walk past Jacob but the tribal police chief placed his hand on Jim's chest. "If that body's Native we want it back."

"I know."

"If that body is not purified, the wrath of the *ḿalyè es šeýiłk* will be upon us."

"I went through that with Elijah. It's a myth."

Jim again tried to walk past but Jacob's hand on his chest held him in place. "Don't cross the council," the tribal police chief said.

Pushing Jacob's hand away, Jim said sharply, "I heard you. What about the Rez boys, how do they get their booze?"

Jacob spat tobacco juice on the ground and wiped his lips with the back of his hand. "You do your job. I'll do mine."

They exchanged sharp glances, nodded, and parted ways. Jim stepped up to the line truck. He noticed the silhouette of two people through the rolled up passenger window. Slapping his hand repeatedly on the door of the truck, he asked, "Which one of you boys is Charlie?"

The person in the passenger seat rolled down the window then took off her hardhat and safety glasses. "I'm Charlie."

Jim backed away when he saw the long brown hair fall from under her hardhat and replied, "I'm sorry. I thought..."

"Yeah, I know. Who are you?"

"I'm Sheriff Buchanan of Cedar County."

"Well, Sheriff Buchanan. If you don't get this road opened soon, my crews are going to be on rest time before they even get a chance to work on line restoration."

Jim stared at Charlie. "Unfortunately, you'll have to turn around, follow 28 to 93 south to 200 west and then pick up 28 north."

Charlie slammed her hand against the outside of the passenger door. "I've heard enough excuses for today. My men have been working all day. They're tired and we ain't driving a hundred-fifty miles out of the way just to get twenty miles south of here to repair a blown regulator. Just open the damn road."

Jim's face grew warm all over. Maintaining his authority, he said, "You listen here. I don't give a crap how long you've been working. I've been through hell and back in the last twelve hours and I'm in no mood for any of your lip. There's a construction crew on their way and until they get here, you'll just have to settle your butt in this truck."

Charlie stared at Jim and then turned to her driver. "Lou, go over these schematics. Trace out the 21Y7 circuit and mark where it's jumpered." She opened the door to the truck, placed her feet on the steps, and leaped to the ground. Folding her arms resolutely, she said, "I hate this shit. It's been a long day. My nerves are shot."

Jim said, "If we don't cooperate, nothing will get done."

"Okay, I'm sorry. We're a bit edgy. Storms will do that."

Two linemen walked up to the truck. One yelled, "Hey Chief!"

Charlie wheeled around. "What do you boys want?"

The younger of the two linemen, a grizzled man with a black beard halfway down his chest, slapped his work gloves in his hand. "Hey Charlie, me and Pop were having a smoke by the washout. What we saw scared the living shit out of us."

"Armand, what are you talking about?" Charlie asked.

Pop, a man with a weather-beaten face said in his finest Midwestern drawl, "I been 'round this county for near forty year. Ain't seen nutin' like this afore."

"If I was alone, I'd say I was seeing things," Armand added. "Who's this?" he asked staring at Jim.

Charlie extended her palm. "This is Sheriff... I forgot your name."

"Buchanan."

"Sheriff, I think there's something you'd want to see for yourself," Armand said. Jim and Charlie followed the two linemen to the washout. "See, over there. But now it looks like it's rolled over." Armand pointed to a spot amid the raging river.

Across from where they were standing, Jim saw something. It was about a hundred feet from where Elijah had found the corpse.

"I've got to go down and take a look," Jim said.

"No," Charlie reached out to grab Jim's arm but he eluded her grasp and stumbled down what remained of the riverbank. Charlie yelled to Jim, her voice competing with the sound of the rushing water. "If you're not careful, you're liable to end up in Idaho."

She tossed a yellow nylon rope. Jim grabbed it and tied it around his waist. He waded into chest-deep water to the far side of the washout. Something resembling a branch was stuck in the river, caught in debris.

Jim reached for it but just when it was in his grasp, the swift current caused him to fall backward into the water. The branch and an object attached to it fell on top of him. Jim found himself face-to-face with a torso. The branch that he held onto was human bone, its flesh stripped clean.

"Old Man Coyote!" Jim shouted as he struggled to regain his footing. Charlie, Armand, and Pop pulled on the lifeline. They managed to get Jim and the torso onto the riverbank. Jim collapsed as he inhaled and exhaled long, deep breaths.

"Grab a hold of my hand." Armand reached for Jim and pulled him up the river bank.

Jim untied the rope. "What do you have for line trucks?"

Charlie frowned. "Three buckets, a digger, and a hundred-foot man carrier."

"Does the hundred-footer have a bucket?"

Charlie put her hands on her hips. "It's for transmission work. I've got a job to do. You are not... taking any of my trucks."

"I have to go up in that one-hundred foot bucket and take a look around."

Charlie tapped her steel-toed boot on the ground. "Dammit. Armand, see to it that the Sheriff gets what he wants."

"The T-Rex? Okay boss."

Before Charlie could turn away, Jim called to her. "Charlie?"

"What now?"

Jim tipped his hat to her. "Thanks." He walked with Pop and Armand to the T-Rex and instructed them to park the vehicle alongside the washout.

Pop lowered the outriggers for stability and set up the bucket. Jim ran back to his SUV and grabbed a pair of field glasses. They extended the hydraulic boom to its full height to ensure that the bucket would be safe while it was in the air. Then they lowered the bucket so that the men could climb aboard. Pop then harnessed Jim and Armand in the two-man bucket.

Positioned almost one-hundred feet above the river, Jim scanned the area with the binoculars. He looked up and down the river until he saw something across from the washout on the far end of the riverbed about five-hundred feet upriver.

"Rocky! Look over there, across the river," commanded Jim through a headset. He held the field glasses in one hand and pointed with the other.

Jim watched Rocky walk to the edge of the river and look past the raging torrent.

Through a two-way radio Rocky replied, "I don't see anything."

Jim's eyes searched through the binoculars, "In the water, stuck to that clump of sage grass. See it?"

Rocky replied, "I still don't see anything. There's nothing there."

Jim noticed Charlie lower her pair of binoculars and heard her shout from her cab. "I see it. There's an arm and part of a shoulder. There may be more under the water."

Jim yelled to Rocky, "Call Hank on your cellphone. Tell him we found two more bodies. Get him up here right away."

·4·

After a few hours, slumped in the driver's seat, his clothes still damp from his river encounter and his Stetson covering his face, Jim awoke from his deep sleep. It was almost 8 p.m. and he could hear the growing roar of trucks barreling toward him on Route 28.

His right knee buckled as he climbed out of the SUV and stepped onto the roadway. He stood and gazed at the convoy of six, fully-loaded dump trucks some with trailers carrying track loaders and excavators. The air brakes on the first truck squealed as the driver brought the vehicle to a sudden halt. The remaining trucks stopped one by one.

"What do you have here, Jim?" Jack stuck his glossy, shaven head through the open driver's window as he massaged his goatee.

"Thanks for getting here so soon on such short notice." Jim pointed toward the washout. "I need a temporary fill between the shoulder and the gulch. Then we can reopen this road."

"No problem. We'll be done in a couple of hours."

Jim nodded and waved to Jack. "Thanks. If you need me I'll be in my truck."

As he reached for the SUV's door handle, a deep voice startled Jim. "We need to talk."

He turned and again saw Jacob Walkabout. "What now?"

Jacob's bronze skin contrasted with his gray uniform. He pulled the Stetson from his head and spoke in a mocking manner. "You know what I want. The *ṁalyè es šeýiłk* is already at work. Now we've got three dead bodies on reservation land."

Jim said, "I've got a hundred people pulling at me from all directions. Don't piss me off."

Jacob spat tobacco juice on the pavement. "We've known each other a long time. Keep me in the loop and I'll share with you what I know."

"When I hear from Hank Kelly I'll call you."

"No. I want a complete autopsy report in person from Hank and recovery of all three bodies. I'll come to him, just see that it gets arranged." Jacob again spat on the ground and walked to his patrol car.

Jim opened the door to his SUV. The minute his body sunk into the driver's seat the sound of another vehicle garnered his attention. A white van with a <u>State of Montana Medical Examiner</u> insignia on the side doors parked behind his vehicle.

"What do we have here?" Hank Kelly asked. Jim sat up in the seat, opened the door, and slipped to the pavement. He braced his fall with his hand on the inside door handle. Hank continued, "You need to go home and get some rest. I brought Leon and a couple of interns with me. They'll place the bodies in our van. We can handle this. Tomorrow, I'll need your help with these autopsies."

"I'm staying."

"Jim, go home. Your deputies can cover for you. Are you all right to drive?"

Jim ran his fingers through his hair. "I'm okay. Before I go, I want to show you where the bodies are." Jim walked with Hank to the washout. They reviewed the locations of the two bodies and then Jim asked, "Can I help you remove them?"

"No."

"Don't you need anything from me?"

"Yes, a promise to go home and get some sleep."

"All right… all right. There's something I need to do before I leave."

Hank shook his head. "Hurry up then."

Jim watched Hank gather tools from the van for the transport of the bodies. "Leon, let's go. We've got a lot of work to do."

Jim placed a call on his cellphone. "Tom, I'm on Route 28 near where Elijah found the body yesterday… Martha filled you in on the two bodies from today? Good. I'm done here and Rocky left a while ago but Hank just got started... I know, I know, but hold your horses for a minute. Look, this will make the papers and the TV. Don't provide any information before we know what we have. And Tom, bring Chief Peters up-to-date on what's going on. I want things kept quiet... Good. I also want you to work with Hank and treat this as a crime scene. Let's get ahead of the curve before we get buried in paperwork."

Satisfied that everything was in order, Jim turned and waved to Hank. He climbed into his SUV and his cellphone rang. It was Kate.

Upon hearing Kate's voice, Jim's tone sparkled. "Hi dolly, I know it's late. I'll be home soon." Jim suddenly froze as he listened to Kate. "What do you mean life or death? Tracy wants me to drop by now? I know she's your sister-in-law but your brother and I aren't exactly on speaking terms. All right, I'm going there now."

·5·

Jim turned onto Rockland Road, near Taylor High School just as a cloudburst erupted. He glanced at his wristwatch; it was a few minutes past 10 p.m. He parked his SUV and grabbed a battery-powered lantern from the backseat. His eyes focused on the two-story home a few hundred feet away. The sound of droplets beating on his Stetson plus the rhythm of his boots hitting the wet sidewalk played a two-part harmony that Jim despised.

It was a neighborhood of about a dozen tidy residences. Jim's focus remained on the yellow house with the white picket fence. He walked up the Nelson's driveway past the manicured shrubs bordering the neatly edged lawn. The aroma of freshly blossomed azaleas infiltrated Jim's nostrils. Three knocks and the door opened a crack.

"I'm glad you're here."

"Where's Matt?"

"He's at a church meeting."

Tracy opened the door and Jim stepped inside. He removed his rain-laden coat and hat and handed them to her. She hung them to dry in the guest bathroom.

"When will he be back?"

"Around eleven."

"Is Josh asleep?"

"He went to bed an hour ago. He was so tired from his Little League game."

"Tell me about this life and death situation that Kate spoke about."

27

Tracy placed her hand against her temple and cried. Jim massaged her shoulder. "What's the matter?"

"I wouldn't be telling you this if you weren't here in person."

"What is it?"

"I don't know where to start."

"Just spill it out."

"It's... Matt."

"What do you mean?"

"He's been real angry, plain mad at the world. I think that hate talk Roy Lewis spews on the radio has something to do with it. I should have told you sooner."

"It's never too late. Just get it out."

"Tonight he took his guns with him."

"To church... why?"

"It's gotten real bad lately. He's been talking about secrets. Saying that he can't live knowing what he knows and that he wishes he were dead. Last week I found a paper in his bureau drawer with names on it. It wasn't in his handwriting."

"Whose names were on the list?"

"You and Kate, your deputy Rocky, and some names I never heard of before."

"Can I see this list?"

"I left it in the drawer because I didn't want him to know that I found it. Today it was gone."

"I want you to write down the names of every person you remember on that list." Tracy collapsed into Jim's arms, her brown hair cascading onto his sheriff's uniform, her face pressed against his chest. "Don't cry." Jim patted her back. "Why was Kate on the list?"

Tracy looked up at him. "Matt was never happy that she married you."

"I know. Kate told me he said he'd never speak to her again."

"When Kate almost died last January, he said you were to blame."

"I don't need to get into this right now."

Jim tried to turn away but felt Tracy grab his arm.

"Please help us. Look in on Matt for me."

Jim exhaled deeply and then nodded to Tracy. "I'll do it for you and Josh."

"Thank you."

Jim glanced at his watch. "It's ten-thirty. If you're afraid for yourself and Josh, call me. You know my cellphone number. I can get you into a shelter tonight."

"I can't, that might push him over the edge."

Jim stepped into the guest bathroom, grabbed a box of tissues, his hat and coat, and walked back to Tracy. "Dry your eyes. Call me if things get worse. It doesn't matter what time it is."

"You'd do that for me?"

"You're my sister-in-law."

Jim gave Tracy a hug and left.

It was a short drive to the Church of the Revelation on West Street. He parked a block away, and then walked among the shadows to the church parking lot. Next to Matt Nelson's car were vehicles belonging to Cy Taylor the fire marshal, Harold Porter the town attorney, and Jeb Peck, owner of Cedar County Real Estate, three of Taylor's most outstanding citizens, along with nearly a dozen or so other cars and trucks.

Jim crept alongside the foundation of the building. From behind a bush and at an angle, Jim crouched and peeked into one of the back windows of the illuminated basement meeting room.

He noticed Matt seated at a table with at least six other men in camouflage fatigues. Rifles, shotguns, and pistols decorated the front desk. A draped banner on the wall in red letters spelled, Guardians of Doctrine. Jim heard a muffled voice from a hidden corner of the room as the men stood and extended their right arms with a straightened hand salute. The words on the blackboard were as plain as day.

WE ARE GOD'S ANSWER
MUD PEOPLE = DEATH
ARYAN RACE IS THE ONLY RACE
LONG LIVE THE WESTERN IMPERIUM

Jim got up and brushed himself off as images flowed throughout his mind. The stockpiled weapons, the anger Matt had for him, it all made sense. Could the recently discovered bodies also have something to do with this? Every time Jim came up with a theory, another question begged for an answer. He slipped back to his SUV, climbed in, grabbed his cellphone from the glove compartment, and called Tracy.

"Hi... yes, I found him. He's meeting with some townsfolk at the church... don't worry. I'll look into it. Everything will be all right... Of course, I'm sure. Don't say anything to Matt about this and don't tell Josh either." Jim ended his call and drove away.

With the increased perception of constitutional civil liberties, even a white supremacist organization has their First Amendment rights. Through strict investigation Jim knew he could ensure the public safety. He planned to warn Chief Peters and Captain Stevens about this. Undersheriff Hyde needed to know too.

Jim's thoughts centered on Tom Hyde heading an investigation with Agent Harris embedding a surveillance operative. He decided not to get involved since his name was on that list. Besides, the bodies from the Little Bitterroot River were enough to keep him busy.

Jim's cellphone rang. It was Kate. He pulled to the side of the road and put the phone on speaker.

"Jim, are you coming home?"

"Yes. I looked in on Matt and I've got it covered. There's nothing to worry about."

"Then what about today? You were up before sunrise and you're still working."

"Elijah found something and Hank had to get involved."

"What did he find?"

"It's police work."

"Jim, I'm not a little girl."

"Kate it's only been a few months since you left the hospital. I'm still worried about you and now this doesn't help."

"Jim, I know you've got a lot on your plate. I never want you to neglect your duty as county sheriff on my account."

"You know how stubborn I am."

"I also know how much you mind my advice," Kate said.

"You know I do."

"Then come home now... before the weather gets worse."

·6·

Jim drove along U.S. Highway 228, through the town of Taylor, and then north up Route 56 into the Cabinet Mountains. Heading up Cross Creek Road and then turning right near a rock outcrop that resembled an eagle's head, Jim gazed at the town stretched out below.

When the paved surface ended and the dirt road wound through the southernmost edge of the Cabinet Mountain Range, Jim slowed his truck to a crawl stopping at a flat, open area halfway up the ridge in front of a modern post and beam home cut into the hillside.

Inside the extra-wide garage, Jim parked his county issued SUV between a white Ford F250 four-wheel drive diesel pickup truck, and a Vietnam era deuce-and-a-half. Kate's 1962 blue and white Volkswagen Samba Bus sat in its familiar spot.

He stepped inside the house and with the flick of a light switch, the living area offered Jim its plush furniture but he turned down the invite. A geothermal system warmed the entire heating requirements and photovoltaic solar panel arrays on the roof provided the home's electrical needs.

Jim placed Angel's bowl on the large kitchen island and filled it with jingling kibble. He heard the sound of the sixty-pound German Shorthaired Pointer run down the steps and roar into the kitchen. She sat in front of Jim and patiently waited.

"Here you go girl." Jim set the bowl on the floor. As Angel buried her muzzle in the food, Jim retrieved a can of seltzer and a pre-wrapped sandwich from the refrigerator. He read aloud the Chinese proverb written on the sticky note stuck to the plastic wrap. "The longer the night lasts, the more your dreams will be."

Jim smiled and mirrored the young Asian girl's image in his mind, Taiwanese, long black hair, deep olive eyes.

Jia Li had just celebrated her twentieth birthday and Jim hired her when Kate returned from the hospital. They needed a housekeeper and someone to help Kate with her activities of daily living or ADLs as Kate's nurse called them. Jia Li had done such a good job the first few months of Kate's recuperation it convinced Jim to retain her services.

Jia Li came to the United States on a working visa just two months before Kate's ordeal. She lived in a third floor, four-room apartment over Billy's Bar in Taylor.

"Looking for a husband in America," she once told Jim. He knew it was only a matter of time before some lucky local hitched up with her.

He reflected on a recent question she had asked. "Mista Jim, why you and Missa Kate live alone? Nobody see, nobody talk. Very lonely, no?" He reminded her that they were happy the way things were. "Oh Mista Jim. No good for couple to live alone. Jia Li be very happy to stay with you. Clean place all time, not just once a week. Cook too, every day, be like second daughter." He remembered her giggling.

She was right, he thought, she would make someone very happy someday.

Jim finished his meal and headed upstairs to the second floor media room. A Gibson acoustic twelve-string guitar rested on the floor against the stereo. Jim placed a finger on the bridge of the guitar, slowly ran it across the rosette, up the fingerboard, and onto the head where he let his finger drift away from Kate's prized possession. He curled his fingers into a fist and bowed his head.

Breathing a heavy sigh, he headed toward the master bedroom down the long corridor. Resting his right palm on the doorframe, he pressed his head against the dark grainy surface of the wood. His long hair fell across his cheeks as he reached for the doorknob.

Opening the door, he pulled off his shirt. Collapsing onto the bed next to Kate, he then pulled the pillow over his head. He felt Kate stir and the touch of her hand on his back. A tear slid down his left cheek. Jim heard a sigh as Kate's arm caressed his shoulder. He peeked at her from under the pillow and saw the sleepiness in her eyes.

"When did you get home?" she asked.

"A few minutes ago. When did Jia Li go home?"

"Right after I called. Are you all right, dolly?" she asked.

Jim pulled the pillow off his head. "It was only a couple of years ago that I was easing into the job, learning the ropes from Sheriff McCoy. I met with city leaders and got to understand the issues in Cedar County. We still had enough time together to enjoy the things we love to do."

Kate kissed Jim's upper arm. "I'm still here for you."

Jim hugged Kate and pulled her closer to him. "I know but today was bad."

Kate nestled her head on Jim's upper arm. "Do you want to talk about it?"

For a moment, Jim felt the release of accumulated tension only to have it whiplash back. He propped himself up on his elbow. "Last year the craziness began and it's only been four months since you lost the baby."

"You can stop protecting me."

"Kate, you were kidnapped, you almost died, and now you're a state witness. Expect a certain level of protection. Plus you're still recuperating." He glanced at Kate, her body still thinner than usual from her ordeal. He answered her thoughts. "It's my job." Jim rolled onto his back. "I wish we could just move away."

"I know that you're still reconciling with Alma Rose. She's your daughter and you promised to spend more time with her. Thanks to her, I didn't die."

Jim lay back on the bed. "Kate, she is only a shaman in training. The Crow Tribe did not sanction her healing ways."

"Tell me what's bothering you. I can't help if you don't confide in me."

"It looks like all hell is about to break loose."

"What do you mean?"

Jim told Kate about the bodies at the Little Bitterroot. He even mentioned the black soil but he dared not speak of her brother's participation in the white supremacist meetings.

"Now do you understand how serious this is? I almost lost you because of my job. I won't allow it to happen again."

Jim noticed a smile stretch across Kate's gaunt face.

She spoke with earnest, "A long time ago I learned from Uncle Henry that a father should never put his job ahead of his family."

Jim nodded. "I know you're right."

"He's coming for dinner tomorrow and he'll ask about Alma Rose. Will you be ready for that?"

"I'll do what I can."

"My cousin Karen invited me to New York. I'm on leave from the university until the fall."

"That's out of the question. It's too soon for you to travel on your own."

"Doctor Donnelly said I'm healthy I just need to put the weight back on. When will Alma Rose be done with school? I did promise to take her to New York."

"Next month."

Kate gave Jim another hug. "Will it comfort you if Alma Rose goes with me or does she need to stay with your sister?"

"Cousin Becca is helping my sister get back on her feet after her liver transplant. I guess if Alma Rose wants to…"

"I'll call Alma Rose in the morning."

They kissed goodnight. Lying on the covers, Jim descended into a deep sleep.

·7·

The threatening weather finally cleared as the morning sun poked its dancing rays through the windows of the master bedroom in the Buchanan home. The warmth invaded every corner enveloping Jim and Kate in an aura of rejuvenated well-being.

Jim was up early. He called to Kate. "I'm going to drop in on Hank. It's Saturday but I know he's working."

Kate rolled over on her back. "I'll give Alma Rose a call."

"It will be good for both of you to spend time together," Jim said.

He showered, threw on jeans, a tee shirt, and boots. When he caught Angel staring at him, he said, "Don't give me that sad-eyed look. I can't take you." Angel whimpered and lifted her paw. Jim took her paw in his hands. "All right, come on." She pulled her paw back, wagged her tail, and licked Jim's hand.

Angel bolted outside and ran after a group of blue-headed vireos selectively picking at insects. From the doorway, Jim watched them elude Angel's half-hearted alpha response. Stepping onto the front porch Jim caught the morning breeze carrying the scent of the bitterroot blossoms permeating the air. He inhaled deeply recognizing the familiar aroma. Although early May, the white and rose-colored flowers heralded spring's welcome return after a long, cold winter.

His cellphone rang. It was Alma Rose.

"Dad, I just hung up with Kate. She invited me to New York for three weeks next month."

"Will you go?"

"Cousin Becca will care for mom. I'll go."

Jim's voice took on a deliberate tone. "Please take care of Kate for me."

"I will… I had another vision."

Jim switched the phone from his right ear to his left. "About what?"

"You ran into a field of buffalograss. You were bleeding. Then there was the letter A three times then the letter A again before something terrible would happen."

"What does it mean?"

"All I know is what I see."

"Write down everything you remember about your vision and email it to me."

"I will. Is something wrong?"

"Nothing's wrong. I want to read it when I have the time. I have work today." They ended the conversation and then Jim placed another call. "Good morning Hank, were you able to complete those autopsies… Sure, I can be there at seven-thirty… See you then."

Stepping into the garage, Jim helped Angel inside his SUV and then drove away. Passing through Taylor, he noticed the storm's legacy of partially flooded streets and parking lots. Approaching Lucy's Luncheonette, Jim scrutinized the typical Saturday morning crowd headed inside. He surmised that the rest of his day would be less predictable.

After breakfast, he returned to his SUV and gave Angel a paper plate of special-made scrambled eggs from Lucy. He drove to the State Crime Lab where he spied seven news vans in the parking lot. He told Angel to stay and stepped out of his SUV. Broadcast masts extended into the sky like trees in a pine forest as a half-dozen reporters quickly accosted him.

"Sheriff Buchanan. Can we have a word with you?" asked one female reporter followed by a camera operator.

"Franklin, I don't have time for this."

Staring at the camera using Jim as a backdrop she said, "This is Julie Franklin, KTAY's Chief Investigative Reporter for Channel 2 News outside the State Crime Lab in Taylor." She turned to Jim. "Sheriff Buchanan, can you provide us with any information about these bodies so that the residents of Taylor can rest comfortable in their beds tonight."

"I have no news," Jim replied.

Another reporter looked at his associate, "Roll it."

Jim stopped abruptly in front of the small crowd. "I have nothing to say."

"Private sources report that you found all three bodies. Is that true?" A reporter shoved a microphone in Jim's face.

Jim glared at the reporter. "No comment."

Another reporter turned to his camera operator, "Did you get that?"

Jim stepped up to the door, slid his cardkey through the reader, and walked inside. He pushed the door closed against the throng of inquisitors. A half-dozen people milled about the lobby, law enforcement officers, professionals wearing badges affirming their clearance, and a few civilian employees like receptionist Millie Lawson.

"Sheriff Buchanan, how are you and Kate?" Millie asked.

"We're fine."

Millie pointed to the register on her desk. "Hank told me you were coming." She glanced at her wristwatch. "Right on time too." When Jim finished signing in, she handed him a lanyard with a visitor's badge. "You're good to go. Do you know your way?"

"Sure do. See you later."

Jim rode the elevator to the third floor, walked down the hallway, and knocked on the door with the nameplate, <u>Henry Kelly, Chief State's Medical Examiner</u>.

A voice from inside answered, "Door's unlocked."

Hank sat behind his desk while the aroma of fresh brewed coffee spiced the air. Hank spoke without glancing up, "You get any sleep?"

"Enough." Jim reminded Hank. "Don't forget you and Mary are coming over for dinner tonight."

"I wouldn't miss it for the world."

"Good. Tell me what you have."

Hank swept up a folder from his desk then leaned back in his chair. "I finished the write-up on the first body and Leon assisted with the autopsies on the two bodies you found yesterday. He worked all night. I knew you'd want answers this morning."

Jim sat in one of the two chairs facing Hank's desk. "Any conclusions?"

"Here's a copy of the report for you."

Jim quickly thumbed through the folder. "I can't understand half this stuff. Explain in layman's terms."

Hank stood up and wrote a list on a white board that hung on the wall next to his desk. "We have three bodies in various stages of decomposition, a real mess. All three were naked, headless, with missing hands and feet."

"Are they Native?"

"The DNA results won't be back for at least a week. I pulled a few strings and requested priority handling. It appears that any identifiable marks, tattoos, piercings, scars, and ethnic characteristics were either carved or chopped off the body."

"What do you make of it?"

Hank put the folder away in his file cabinet and stared at Jim. "I heard a rumor that people on the reservation think this is the work of a demon."

"The ḿalyè es šeýiɫk."

"What is that?"

"It's a superstition among a few plains tribes."

"Tell me all about it."

Jim elaborated. "Some believe that when a person dies a violent death and the body is not given a traditional burial, then that spirit roams the Earth seeking revenge destroying everything in its path until it finds who's responsible for its death. That way, it achieves peace before its journey to the long quiet." As Hank stood frozen in place, Jim tried to put things into perspective. "Hank, it's just an old story... from the 19th century told to the young to frighten them and keep them in their tipis at night."

"Jim, I saw a lot of things in my career that can't be explained. I've worked with psychics and saw people who should have died but survived for some unknown reason. I don't dismiss anything that I can't prove."

"Hank, let's not give any credence to this myth. It'll be a distraction."

"You're probably right but I'll accept any tips or information that'll come my way. If this were New York, I'd say it was the work of organized crime. Being Montana, my gut feeling is it's a serial killer."

"What makes you say that?"

"The bodies were found in similar conditions in the same dumping ground. I have a bad feeling about this one." Hank sat back down.

"What can you tell me?"

"No, you tell me... any missing persons that you can think of?"

"The last missing persons case we worked on, the bodies were incinerated."

"I know. This is not related."

Jim thought for a moment. "Olivia Clayton."

"Clayton? You mean, like in Sam Clayton?"

"She was Sam's wife. Rumor has it she ran off with an artist from California. At least that's what Sam told everyone."

"When?"

"Quite a while ago. Maybe three years, I can't be exactly sure. I was with the Montana Highway Patrol at the time. McCoy told me about it."

"We should follow up on this aspect of the case before the FBI's reinforcements arrive."

"When will that happen?"

"Agent Harris decided to stick around and the district office in Kalispell referred the case to the FBI Evidence Response Team Unit. Harris said someone from their field office in Salt Lake City will be here on Monday."

Jim rubbed his forehead. "I knew you'd have to get the Feds involved."

"Possible multiple homicides on a federal reservation, I had no choice."

Placing his hat on the chair next to him, Jim ran his fingers through his long hair. "This place is going to get busy."

"You know," Hank said flatly, "when I took this job I wanted to ease myself into semi-retirement. I had no plans to get involved in a major investigation like last year and now it's happening again."

"Yeah, tell me about it."

"Jacob Walkabout called. He wants full autopsy reports on all three bodies."

"Yeah, I know."

"Do you have a problem with that?"

"Jacob and I already had a discussion."

Hank nodded. "Okay. Let me handle Walkabout. Peters is harassing me too and I've been able to keep the reporters satisfied by releasing a little information each day. That's kept them off my back and away from your office."

"I'm going to contact the sheriff departments in Lincoln, Sanders, Flathead and Lake Counties. I'll ask them if they have something like this going on in their jurisdictions or have seen anything suspicious."

"Good idea." Hank looked at his watch and got up from his chair. "Dammit, I've got an appointment at ten with the DA over at the courthouse. Can we finish this discussion on Monday?"

"Why not tonight, you're still coming over for dinner, right?"

"Of course but I never mix business with pleasure."

Jim stood up. "Then on Monday, can you open the morgue early? We need to talk about Clayton's wife. I also have more questions about the first body."

"How does six o'clock sound?"

"Fine with me."

They shook hands. Outside, Jim weaved his way through the gauntlet of reporters. Climbing into his SUV, he looked back at the State Crime Lab building. The reporters rushed the steps as Hank opened the front door. Jim hit the toggle switch for his emergency light bar, turned on his siren, and left rubber on the pavement.

The reporters ran from Hank and hurried to Jim's quickly departing SUV. Jim watched the small advancing crowd in his rear view mirror and saw Hank run to his car unimpeded. Jim laughed to himself as he drove away.

·8·

Jim stopped by the sheriff's office after meeting with Hank at the State Crime Lab. Rocky was working a full weekend shift and Jim wanted to update him on what he had just discussed with Hank. He got out of the SUV, walked up the ramp to the front door and brought Angel inside.

"Hey Angel, haven't seen you in a while," Martha said.

Angel barked in reply.

"Martha, is Rocky busy?" Jim then heard a voice from inside.

"I can be if you want me to."

That stroked a laugh from Jim. After the usual pleasantries, he filled Rocky in on the latest news. Rocky got up to leave but before he could, Jim called him back.

"The other day I spied on what appeared to be a white supremacist meeting at the Church of the Revelation. Can you spearhead this for me? Here are notes I took about what I saw. I can't get involved because my brother-in-law appears to be a member."

Rocky took the note pad from Jim. "Sure, what do you want me to do?"

"On Monday, contact Chief Peters and Captain Stevens and warn them about this. Work with Undersheriff Hyde, I want him to lead the investigation. Also contact Agent Harris and find out if he thinks it's a good idea to embed a surveillance operative."

"You got it."

"How about taking a ride with me to the washout? I'd like to find out if there's anything we missed."

Rocky nodded and sprang into action.

The low pressure system that had been causing havoc in the mountain states over the past few days continued its unpredictable movement. The drizzle was an irritation as Jim and Rocky climbed into the SUV with Angel in the backseat. Jim spied her wet nose tracks on the side window as he drove onto Main Street.

Taylor, a town of more than fifty-five thousand, just ten miles from the Idaho state line, had seen its share of natural calamities over the years. Bordered on one side by the Clark Fork River and on the other side by the foothills of the Cabinet Mountains, part of Taylor sat in a natural flood plain.

Jim hoped this rain would not swell the Clark Fork. The Little Bitterroot overflowing from the recent rains and the winter snow melt was one thing but a flood in a populated area would be catastrophic.

Jim's investigative eyes caught a few school age boys standing under the marquee of the Jubilee Theater. They waved when the SUV approached. Jim and Rocky returned their greeting while Angel barked excitedly at the boys.

From under a red baseball cap, a few strands of long blond hair managed to poke their way free as the boy yelled through his cupped hands, "Hey, Uncle Jim. How about a ride?"

"Josh!" Jim shouted as he slowed the SUV to a crawl. "By tomorrow morning, if the ballfield is dry, I'll meet you at the high school by eleven and hit some fly balls for you and your friends."

The boy's eyes lit up. "It's a deal. He turned to his friends and said, "Did you hear that! Tomorrow after church we're going to play baseball with the sheriff!"

Once past the theater, Jim noticed flashing lights in his rear view mirror. He slowed down. A black and white pulled up alongside. An officer that Jim didn't recognize sat in the passenger seat and waved for him to stop. The cruiser drove by, circled around, and parked facing Jim's SUV.

A police officer, his belt hidden from view by his potbelly, opened the driver's door. Using his raincoat to protect his balding head from the foul weather, he stepped onto the sidewalk and plodded up to the SUV's passenger door. "Buchanan, where are you going?" asked Taylor Police Chief John Peters.

"Up to the Little Bitterroot."

Angel growled when Chief Peters shined his flashlight into the backseat.

"Hey, keep that mutt away from me. She's already bit me twice."

Jim laughed. "Angel's never bit anyone she didn't hate."

"Very funny." Peters mocked. "I heard you found some bodies. Is that where you're going?"

"Yes, you want to follow us up there?"

"You know I can't. I got enough to keep me busy right here in town." Peters slid his fingers across the county insignia on the SUV driver's door. "Hell, I should have been the one going up there, not you."

"Listen Peters, the election is behind us. You'll get your chance to run again."

"Dammit Buchanan, you only won the election by nine votes. If it wasn't for your Indian voters, I would have won the election."

The passenger door of Peters' squad car opened and an officer with a blond, bushy mustache and dressed in full raingear stepped out.

Jim looked at him, then at Peters. "New officer?" he asked.

"That's my new deputy chief, Dave Anderson. He's from back east... was an MP in the Marines. Outstanding fella, been on the job two weeks. But never mind that, tell me about that body."

"Give Hank Kelly a call."

Deputy Chief Anderson chimed in. "Since the bodies are in Taylor we can handle it."

"The body was found on the Flathead Reservation," Jim insisted. "You have no jurisdiction. It's a county and FBI matter, not an issue for Taylor."

Peters put his hand on Anderson's arm. "Hold on, let me handle this. Buchanan, you got paperwork you can share with me?"

Jim responded, "I told you, give Hank Kelly a call."

"This conversation's going nowhere. I'll call Kelly and if I have any questions that he can't answer, I'll be calling on you." Peters and Anderson made their way back to the cruiser.

After they left, Jim pulled out his cellphone. He called Martha and put the phone on speaker.

"Dispatcher," the voice crackled from the other end.

"Martha, this is Jim. Did you get any inquiries from Chief Peters today?"

"No sir. Is anything wrong?" Silence permeated the vehicle. "Jim, you there?"

.   Pushing aside his concern, Jim answered. "Martha, everything's okay. If something comes up, call us."

"Okay, see you later."

Jim ended the call and then stared at Rocky.

"Everything all right, boss?" Rocky asked.

Jim tried to rub the weariness from his eyes. "For some reason Peters is agitated about the body. We may have a fox in the henhouse."

"What's that mean? I'm from Brooklyn. You know, paved roads, sidewalks."

Jim laughed. "My grandfather, Red Hawk once said, 'The Earth must breathe. It can't do that when you cut the trees and cover the ground.' "

"Now I'm even more confused," Rocky said.

Jim drove toward the location on the Little Bitterroot River where he had found the bodies. Startled flocks of yellow and gray meadowlarks and brown and white killdeers foraging alongside the road took flight as the SUV approached. Clutching the top of the steering wheel with one hand and pushing his ponytail aside, Jim massaged his neck with the other. Then he spotted Elijah sitting on the bank of the river.

Jim rolled down his window. "What are you doing here?"

Elijah turned to him. "A Flathead on reservation land should ask that of the police."

Jim and Rocky got out while Angel stuck her head through the open window and whimpered.

"Elijah, you're on the wrong side of that crime scene tape," Jim said.

When Jim was within arm's length of Elijah the Native man firmly grabbed Jim's arm. "The bodies were on our reservation. They belong to us."

"This county is my jurisdiction. If the bodies were tribal members we'll release them to you."

"The bodies must be treated with respect. Prayers need to be offered." Elijah stood at the guardrail overlooking the crime scene and began reciting the Hail Mary in Salishan. "Hoi chin-koiti-o Marie..."

Although Jim knew some words, he was not fluent in that native tongue.

"...Komi ezageil." Elijah finished his prayer. "I will go home now."

Before Elijah left, Jim said to him, "When you speak to your tribal council make them understand that a full investigation has to take place whether or not the bodies are Native. If they are Native they will be returned."

Elijah nodded and left.

Jim and Rocky inspected the crime scene. Careful not to disturb the area, Jim only wanted to put things into perspective.

"What do you think?" Rocky asked.

Jim pursed his lips and shook his head. "There's something wrong. Hank thinks it's a serial killer but I don't. There's a missing persons angle but I don't think that's the answer either."

"Revenge, crime of passion?" Rocky speculated.

"I don't think so. The killings seem too deliberate. Someone knew what they were doing and planned to conceal the murders. If it wasn't for the flooding the bodies would still be hidden in the riverbank."

Jim and Rocky turned their heads when they heard the squawk of the police radio. They rushed to the SUV.

"Can you get back to Taylor as soon as possible?" Martha asked.

"What's wrong?"

"Sam Clayton tried to rob Spot Liquors today. He threatened the owner and a stock boy with a knife but they pulled it away from him and then beat him up pretty bad."

"Where's Clayton now?"

"In Cedar County Hospital being treated for his wounds. Looks like they'll keep him overnight. Chief Peters wants him booked once they release him."

"He's been in jail seven times already this year." Jim thought for a second. "Martha, I'll be there to draw up paperwork for Clayton's AA meetings. Whether or not Clayton is prosecuted, if he skips those AA meetings we can nail him on a parole violation. Let Chief Peters know about that."

·9·

After returning to Taylor and dropping off Rocky at the sheriff's office, Jim completed the paperwork that would once and for all seal Sam Clayton's fate. After the rain ended, a small task awaited Jim before a Saturday dinner date with Kate, Hank, and his wife Mary. Jim arrived at Tracy's house and knocked on the door. Matt answered.

"You're bold enough to show your face around here. What do you want?"

"I'd like to speak with Josh."

"What about?"

"Sports."

"Is that it?"

"What's going on?" Josh peeked through the open door. "Hey, Uncle Jim!"

Jim asked Matt, "Can I show Josh where they plan to install the new lights for the football field?"

"Can I dad?" beamed Josh.

"I don't know..."

"Matt, I spoke to the high school football coach a few weeks ago. He's impressed by Josh's athletic ability in Little League. He wants Josh to try out for the football team a year from this fall when Josh is a sophomore. That is if you and Tracy agree."

"If we decide to let Josh play and he wants to, then... I'll let you know."

Josh interjected, "Can I go outside with Uncle Jim to see where the new lights will go?"

Tracy stepped up to the door. "Come on Matt, it won't hurt matters any."

Jim watched Matt stare at Tracy and Josh.

Then Matt relented. "All right." He whispered to Jim, "We need to talk."

"Call my office." Matt's nod telegraphed Jim that something was up. Jim turned to Josh and invited him to shadow him. "Let's go."

Josh followed Jim into the two-acre back yard. They passed a vegetable garden surrounded by small flowering trees and then traversed a landscaped walking path.

When they reached the end of the property, Jim said, "Look straight ahead." He knelt on one knee and pointed with his right hand. "They're going to excavate test pits this fall for the light towers. It'll be ready for the following year's football season."

"I'm graduating middle school this year."

"Then when you're a sophomore in high school, the year after next, the team will be playing under the lights."

Josh turned to face his uncle. "Maybe I'll make the team. Pa used to tell me how great you were in high school."

Jim breathed a heavy sigh. He recalled the hardships he endured to achieve success on the gridiron. He stood up and turned to Josh. "You stare at that field every day, you hear? Every time you look at that field, you see yourself running to the end zone." Jim watched Josh's smile crowd his face. Jim continued, "You're dodging tacklers, you're pumping your legs, the crowd's cheering, and no one... no one's going to stop you."

"I want to be just like you Uncle Jim. Maybe even a policeman someday."

"One step at a time Josh." Jim smiled and roughed up Josh's hair. "Let's go. Your mom and dad probably want you back inside."

When they returned to the front door, Matt said, "Go inside Josh."

Josh walked past his dad and into the house. "Ma... guess what!" he called.

Jim stood on the lawn facing Matt. "Now, what did you want to talk about?"

"Stay away from my family."

"Is that it?"

"Ain't that enough?"

"Are you sure there's nothing else you need to talk about?"

"I don't owe you a damn nothing."

"Look, I don't want any trouble."

"Then you shouldn't have come here in the first place."

"I had to speak with Josh."

"Are you treating my sister well?"

"Do you care?"

"Of course I do."

"Then why didn't you visit her after she came home from the hospital?"

"Get the hell off my property!"

Jim calmly tipped his hat and started to walk back to his SUV.

"Wait!"

Jim turned and spotted Tracy running toward him while Matt stared from a distance out of earshot. Tracy wiped her eyes. "We haven't seen you in church in a month of Sundays."

"I know."

"You and Kate want to come to church with me and Josh tomorrow? Matt won't be there, he has to work at the pharmacy."

"We can't."

"Why not?"

"Kate's still recovering from her ordeal. She's too weak to stand for an hour or more so she can't attend church."

"Then just you come. I heard you have a housekeeper looking after her. Can't she look after Kate so she doesn't have to be home alone?"

"I don't belong to your church. My family raised me Catholic."

"But you and Kate attended services at the Church of the Revelation in the past."

"I did that for Kate."

"Do you go to services at the Catholic church?"

"No."

"Don't you go to church at all?"

"After what happened to Kate and how Alma Rose healed her, I decided to return to the teachings of my mother. I'm trying to walk the Red Road."

"You need the Lord in your life."

"Kate almost died. My daughter saved her, not God."

Jim turned away and didn't look back. He climbed into his SUV and received a moist lick on his hand from Angel.

·10·

It was nearly 6 p.m. Jim had been preparing dinner for almost two hours when his cellphone rang. It was Hank. He was outside the front door and followed Jim's instructions not to ring the front doorbell. Kate had dozed off on the great room recliner under a pile of Native blankets and Jim didn't want her disturbed. He tiptoed across the great room floor toward the front door.

"And where do you think you're going?"

"Hank's at the door," Jim said.

"Get back in that kitchen." Kate laughed.

Jim smiled at her and then opened the front door. Hank and Mary stood there with gifts in their arms, a box of chocolates and a bouquet of fresh cut roses for Kate. Jim took the offerings and welcomed them into the house.

"Smells like chicken. Is that the recipe I shared?" Mary asked.

"It is," Jim said.

Kate struggled to get up but Hank and Mary convinced her to sit as they gathered around her in Jim's watchful presence.

"How are you?" Mary asked.

"I'm getting better."

"You look good."

A faint smile cracked Kate's face. "You're trying to be kind. I know I look awful."

"Kate, you just need more time. You'll get your strength back," Hank said.

"Uncle Henry, it's been four months already. I lost a lot of weight, I'm weak, I have headaches, I mostly can't sleep, but

51

when I do I have nightmares. I can't even remember some of the chords for the songs I've written." Kate began to cry.

Jim stepped past Hank and Mary. He knelt next to the recliner and cradled Kate in his arms. He kissed her forehead.

"You'll get better. Remember you have that trip to New York next month. I'll make sure you're healthy enough for that."

Kate's lips met Jim's and delivered a cold, dry kiss. Jim looked up at Hank and Mary.

"Why don't you guys get dinner ready and I'll stay with Kate," Mary suggested.

Hank and Jim stepped into the kitchen and put the final touches on the meal.

"Jim I want to ask…"

"Hank, I hope this isn't about work," Jim warned.

"It's about Alma Rose. How is she?"

"She's fine."

"Is she? I want to talk about what she did for Kate."

"She doesn't look well, does she?"

"You know, I'm a medical man and I'm not religious by any means but what your daughter did for Kate was miraculous. She basically brought her back from the dead. Can't she do anything for her now?"

"Hank, the tribe has rules that shamans must follow. Alma Rose didn't finish her apprenticeship. Shamans who fail to complete their initiations are not bestowed the privileges that come with the title."

"And that means what?"

"She's not allowed to practice without the tribal council's blessing. She didn't follow the rules but because she saved Kate's life she didn't lose her standing in the tribe. She has to finish her training to be fully recognized as a shaman."

"Would it be so wrong if she did something outside the tribes influence?"

"Hank, you went to medical school. Would you have treated someone if you hadn't yet graduated?"

"If it was life or death… dammit, I would!"

·11·

Jim woke up early Sunday morning. He threw on his hunter orange cap and matching windbreaker then fitted Angel with a reflective doggie vest. A mountain hike with her was first on his schedule, then breakfast and finally a pile of neglected paperwork at the sheriff's office. It was cold, damp and quiet at 5 a.m. but that's how Jim liked it. He needed the crisp morning air to help clear his mind, to sort out everything that had happened over the past two days.

Nearly three miles into his hike along a maintained notch on Government Mountain Jim noted the distinctive collective hissing of a startled flock of male spruce grouse flushed from their nests. He glanced behind and then heard the characteristic sharp crack above his head.

As soon as Jim dove to the ground, Angel huddled next to him whining in distress. He strained his neck and saw that the bullet tore a piece of bark from the cedar tree near him. Another shot rang out and hit a neighboring tree. Both marks were more than fifteen feet above the forest floor.

"Angel, listen to me. We're going home. Follow me."

Jim got up and doubled back on the trail with Angel running close behind. Another five successive shots followed, each well above his head and within Jim's first two-hundred foot scamper to safety. He got the message.

A long hot shower helped calm his nerves. Jim pulled on a 5.11 tan polo shirt and BDU pants, perfect for a weekend day at the office. He then went downstairs to feed Angel. Kate walked in on him in the kitchen.

"How was your hike?" Kate said preparing a cup of tea.

"It was okay."

"Shorter than usual… is anything wrong?"

"No." Jim poured a glass of orange juice.

"Is that all you're going to have? Where's the granola?"

"I'm… I'm not really hungry."

"What's wrong, dolly?"

"Nothing." Jim gulped down the OJ and then grabbed his Colt Python and gunbelt. As Jim headed for the door he heard Kate call to him.

"Where's my kiss?"

Jim stopped, turned around and planted a kiss on Kate's cheek. "I thought I heard a bear on my hike. Angel got skittish so please stay inside and lock the doors." He eyeballed Angel who had just finished her breakfast and was lapping up water from her dish. "Keep Angel close by."

Kate nodded and then Jim left without saying another word.

Except for the weekend dispatcher and a few deputies mired in paperwork, the building was quiet and empty. Jim made his way past the other employees and to his office. Unable to clear his thoughts of what happened this morning and the corpses at the Little Bitterroot, Jim's mind began to wander.

Then he shut the lights in his office, stood up, walked to his office door and closed it. The sunlight from the windows caught his attention and he shut the blinds one by one. In the darkened room he pulled a red, black and white blanket woven by his sister from the cabinet behind his desk, sat with folded legs on the floor and wrapped the blanket around his shoulders.

After a few quiet minutes, he descended into a deep meditation as images swept past his closed eyelids. Visions of violence that erupted more than one hundred years ago danced among the faces of heroic warriors, beautiful Native women and innocent children. After working up a generous sweat and feeling mentally and emotionally drained, he stood up and grabbed the telephone.

"Paul, I've got a hunch. There's something out there that we can't see unless we're above it. If you're not busy today I'd like to go there with you and Rocky. Good… see you in a half-hour."

Jim took a deep breath, uncapped a 12 oz. bottle of spring water and finished it off. He gathered everything he'd need, binoculars, headset, maps, and a blank flightplan.

He left his office and caught Deputy Rocco Salentino just as he was about to disappear behind a bank of file cabinets.

"Rock, are you busy?" Jim asked.

A folder slipped from Rocky's grasp and flopped onto the floor. "Just pulling permits for the Memorial Day Parade."

"You can finish that later. Something happened today."

"Like what?"

Jim whispered. "I was hiking and someone shot at me."

"Where?"

"On the mountains near my home."

"Did you see who it was?"

"No, they were about a hundred yards away."

"How do you know that?"

"Because it sounded like a .30-06 and if they were farther away the sound would not have been as loud."

"How many shots?"

"About a half-dozen or so."

"Jeeze, they could have killed you."

"They weren't trying to kill me."

"You mean they mistook you for a deer or elk?"

"I wore my hunting gear. No one could have mistaken me for game. They wanted to send a message."

"And what's that message?" Rocky asked.

Jim took a deep breath and responded to Rocky's quizzical look. "Stop the Little Bitterroot investigation."

"You have to report this incident."

"Rock, don't say a word about this to anyone, at least not just yet. I've got a hunch there's something hidden from us up at the Little Bitterroot. I'm flying a Cessna with Paul and I'd like you to tag along. Keep visuals balanced while I'm at the controls."

"To make sure I see what Paul sees?"

"Exactly."

The drive to Mackenzie Municipal Airport was uneventful except for the fact that Jim felt upbeat and he knew that Paul seemed perplexed. He assumed that Paul was unsure a flight over the crime scene would provide them with additional information. Jim knew better.

At the airport lobby desk, Jim rented a Cessna 150 and the additional equipment for Paul and Rocky. Once in the air, they headed toward State Highway 28 and the Little Bitterroot River.

"See anything unusual?" Jim asked.

He watched Paul cock his head and press his temple against the passenger window. "I can't see a damn thing. How high are we?"

Jim handed Paul his binoculars. "Use these. We should be over the crime scene now."

Jim felt a nudge from behind. "Can you bank the plane to the right?" Rocky asked.

Jim complied and heard Paul gasp. "There's something. I saw kids in the field... inside the crime scene perimeter. They scattered when you turned the plane."

"I saw them too Jim," Rocky said. "One was carrying a bag."

Jim shook his head. "They should know better than to trespass with crime scene tape still visible. Because it's reservation land I'll contact Police Chief Walkabout when we return."

Paul nodded, and then asked, "If you make another pass on the way back I'll check the other side of the river."

After Jim made the turn, Paul shouted, "I see a couple of coyotes pulling on something."

Jim took a look and barely made out what Paul witnessed. "I'll phone it in and have Undersheriff Hyde check it out. Elijah and I spotted a coyote scavenging the first corpse we found. This might be another body. Good job."

"I see something else." Rocky wiped the moisture from his breath off the side window. "There's a panel truck driving away from the area."

Jim cocked his head toward the backseat. "That's not unusual. There's a couple of farms in the area."

"The truck's not on Route 28. It's gathering up a dust storm on a dirt road."

Jim pulled the plane around and caught sight of the road. "That's the old logging road that connects with 228. They closed that to the road gangs years ago when they ran out of old growth and moved the operation west of here. When we get back to the office give Northwoods Logging a call. Ask for Stu Bauer and see if he knows who's using that road."

"We've got a crime scene trespass, individuals splitting the area, and now a truck racing away on a closed road. Jim, whatever happened down there is not over," Paul said.

"That's what I'm afraid of." Jim banked the plane and headed back to Taylor.

·12·

Jim's alarm clock blasted at five o'clock sharp, Monday morning. He slammed his hand on the snooze button, rolled onto his back and felt Kate's hand glide across his bare chest. Her eyes were closed and she didn't say a word. Jim knew she needed her rest and though his heart urged him to lie in bed with Kate, he had an important appointment with Hank.

Jim carefully slid her hand away and then popped out of bed. He showered, dressed, and took a quick swig of OJ. Pulling out of the garage, he greeted Jia Li upon her arrival.

"Jia Li, please keep an eye on Kate today. See that she eats, drinks enough water, and gets some sunshine."

"Oh Mista Jim, I take good care of Missa Kate. Do all that and more. I make her laugh today."

On the drive into Taylor, Jim noticed that the warm rays of the sun began to evaporate the pooled water littering Cedar County. Arriving at the State Crime Lab at six o'clock sharp, Jim went inside and worked his way to Hank's office. On the door was a scotch-taped, handwritten note that read, At the Morgue.

Jim walked down the hall, took the elevator to the first floor, and slipped into the old part of the building. He knocked on the morgue's door and when Hank answered he asked, "Got a cup of coffee for me?" He placed his Stetson on the hat rack and sat in a chair facing Hank's desk.

"You look better than Saturday and a hell of a lot better than Friday." Hank reached for a clean mug and filled it with black java. "I heard you took a flight over to the Little Bitterroot with Paul."

"Yeah. I had a hunch but it didn't pan out."

"What do you mean?"

"I asked Tom Hyde to check it out and all he found was the remains of a greater white-fronted goose that some coyotes were picking on."

"How did he know what type of bird it was?"

Jim laughed. "He's studying to be a veterinarian and the greater white-fronted goose has a patch of white feathers beneath the base of its bill. That's all that was left plus a few bones."

Hank shook his head. "Maybe he should have considered a medical examiner career path instead. We could use his help on this case."

Jim added, "We spotted some Native youth trespassing onto the crime scene."

"You have any idea what they were doing?"

"No. I called Police Chief Walkabout and he said he would check it out but they probably got home before he arrived. We also noticed a truck on a closed logging road. Rocky's going to look into that today."

"Didn't they use that road to reroute traffic when the roadway collapsed from that storm?"

"We only used it to get traffic to turn around and head back north on 28. As soon as the main road was passable we closed and blocked off the old logging road."

"Probably just some kids getting their kicks."

"Let's hope that's all it was," Jim said.

On the floor next to a desk sat an oversized box displaying a registered mail label.

"What's in the box?" Jim asked.

"I'm not sure. It wasn't there Saturday. Sometimes they put the mailroom on Sunday overtime if deliveries get behind. Leon worked yesterday. He must have signed for it."

Jim peeked at the label. "It's addressed to you from International Forensics. Aren't you going to open it?"

Hank laughed. "They always send me samples of their latest and greatest products. The department would go over budget if I ordered everything they send me. I open my mail at 10 a.m. like clockwork. That's when I have my second cup of coffee and one of Mary's baked goods. I'll wait for today's mail to be delivered and open everything at once."

"We need to talk," Jim said.

Hank set the mug in front of Jim. "How was church?"

"I see no value in listening to sinners' sermons."

Hank laughed. "If it wasn't for Mary, I wouldn't go either. From one agnostic to another, we need to get personal."

"About what?" Jim asked.

Hank opened the drawer to his desk and produced a shiny, metallic artifact. "Remember this?"

Jim took the object in his hands. "I remember, it's pure silver."

"Do you remember why you gave it to me?"

"Where's this going?" Jim frowned.

"You gave this to me when I moved to Montana. It came from the copper and silver mine near your home. You said no one ever knew that chunk of silver was there, in the mine, until it was brought to the surface. When it was brought up, it stopped being just a piece of rock and became what it truly is."

Jim fingered the lump of silver in his hand. "I learned those lessons from my mother and the rest of the elders from my tribe."

Hank continued, "You made me understand my own hidden faults and how to deal with them. I'm not angry at half the world anymore and I enjoy spending time with Mary much more than when I was the Chief Medical Examiner in New York City."

"That's great Hank but what does this have to do with me?"

"You have to bring your own rock to the surface, Jim. You have to confront things for what they really are. Your life is like this precious stone."

"What am I supposed to confront?"

"Good grief. Your wife almost died, your teenage daughter recently found out you're her father, and your sister is struggling after a liver transplant. Now, you're getting involved in another major investigation. Don't you think you deserve some time off to deal with your personal issues?"

"I'll deal with them in my own way."

Hank slowly shook his head. "Jim, I'm speaking as your wife's uncle not as a state employee. I think it would serve you best if you saw a therapist."

"A psychiatrist… no, that's out of the question."

"Therapy would do you good."

"I'm not going to a shrink!"

Hank took the silver back from Jim and placed it in his drawer. "I know a good therapist. She can help you come to terms with your issues. For godsakes, your family and friends deserve that."

Jim was silent for a few seconds. Then he asked, "If I see this… therapist, do you promise not to tell anyone?"

Hank reached into his shirt pocket and handed Jim a business card. "I promise."

Jim took the card and stared at it. It read <u>Teresa Merrick, LCSW</u>. He flapped the card against his left hand and said, "I'll call, but I can't promise anything."

Hank smiled. "Olivia Clayton and the black soil."

"What about them?"

"You tell me."

Jim breathed a deep sigh. "You want the truth?"

"Yes."

"Much of this is hearsay."

Hank smirked, "Now you sound like a big city lawyer."

A half-smile cracked Jim's stoic facade. "Some of this happened when I was a kid and the rest when I was in Kuwait and then with the Highway Patrol. Sam Clayton married Olivia when he got home from Vietnam in '74. They were each just twenty-year olds."

"And?"

"He was a war hero but he had nightmares. After the drinking and drugging started, he couldn't stay sober. They say he has post-traumatic stress disorder but they didn't call it that back then."

"What about Olivia?" Hank asked.

"Shortly after their marriage they began fighting. A few years later, she left him. Then Sam started getting into trouble. Nothing real serious, he was stealing to support his drinking and drug addiction."

"Go on."

"They were separated ten years... maybe more. They still saw each other. She'd come back from wherever she was for a few weeks at a time. I think she gave him money. She probably hated to see him living like a bum."

"So when and where did she disappear?"

"A few years ago they said she took off for good and headed to California. Rumor has it she lived in a commune with a bunch of bunny huggers. At least that's what Sam told everyone."

"Did you investigate it?"

Jim stood up and walked across the office. "I told you, I was with the Highway Patrol. It happened during McCoy's last year as sheriff."

"McCoy! Well now, that's a dead end."

Jim turned, faced Hank and defended his friend. "McCoy's a good man but he knows as little as I do."

"Good man? All I ever heard from county officials was how everyone had to fix whatever McCoy screwed up."

"That's not true."

Hank leaned forward on the edge of his chair. "Then tell me if this is true. Didn't anyone from Olivia Clayton's family check up on her?"

"She had no family. Her mom was a single parent, moved here from Canada and she died when Olivia was in her twenties."

"Where was Sam?"

"In jail."

"Any kids?"

"No, at least none that I know of."

"Tell me about Sam Clayton's record."

Jim gulped his coffee and thought hard. "Sam was finishing a 27-month sentence at the State Prison in Deer Lodge."

"For what?"

"Possession of marijuana."

Hank stood up. "That got him twenty-seven months?"

"That and an assault charge."

"He can't stay out of trouble, can he?"

"He attacked one of McCoy's deputies when they arrested him. Broke the deputy's arm in three places and forced an early retirement."

Hank walked over to a file cabinet and leaned his arm across it. "I heard he has no job. How's he getting by?"

"Not sure. He tried to rob Spot Liquors."

Hank chuckled. "I heard he got more than he bargained for."

"They released him from the hospital. Rocky has a warrant for his arrest. As far as how he's getting by, maybe he's stealing from the other bums on Warehouse Row," Jim suggested.

"These bums... could any one of them be involved in Olivia's disappearance or any of the murders?"

"I doubt it. They're pretty harmless."

"What about the people on the Flathead Reservation? Are any of them capable of murder?"

"I don't think so."

"Why not?"

"I know just about everyone on the reservation. Most are good people."

"What about the other towns or outside the county?"

"I've got Rocky checking with the police departments in Mallory, Spaulding, and Trout Hollow, the sheriffs in Lincoln, Flathead, Lake, and Sanders counties, plus the Highway Patrol."

"Harris from the FBI said he'd stop by to help. Let's look at that report on the black soil." Hank yanked out the top file draw and thumbed through the folders. He pulled one out, dropped it on his desk and settled in his chair. With his head down he muttered, "MT-CME Study 96-17. Soil composition consists of iron, magnesium, nitrogen, phosphorous, potassium and sulfur." He looked up at Jim. "Your dad was a farmer. Did his green thumb rub off on you and do you have any idea why this set of minerals is in the soil?"

Jim took a deep breath and leaned back in his chair. "I used to work the fields for him when I was in high school. I can tell you that iron and magnesium are essential for growing potatoes and he used to add cottonseed meal and bone meal to the soil. That'd create the nitrogen and potassium in that sample."

"So perhaps we're looking at a murder that occurred in a potato field?"

"Hank, do you know how many potato farms are in the area?"

"Tell me."

"Dozens."

Hank stood up. "Let's start with your dad's farm. I suggest that you stay out of it for obvious reasons."

"The county owns it. I'll contact Tom Hyde and have him run an investigation. He can send two of my deputies up there, take a few soil samples and check out the property."

A few minutes after 8 a.m. a knock at the door interrupted their conversation. Hank looked at his watch. "It's too early for Harris." He opened the door partway, and leaned against the doorframe.

"Captain Stevens, come in." Hank walked back to his desk.

Linda's uniform was crisp and clean. A seven-year veteran of the Taylor Police Department, she wore her blond hair short and professional. A sixth-degree karate black belt, her slim build, and sweet face belied her strength, focus, and mental discipline. She walked into the morgue as the handcuffs, secured to her waist, clanked against her nightstick. Nodding to Jim, she took off her hat and sauntered over to Hank's desk.

"How's Kate?" Linda asked.

Jim felt the inquisitiveness from her roving eyes. "We're managing."

"Good, maybe I'll stop by to visit her."

Hank, Jim, and Linda shared information on the missing bodies. Jim called Undersheriff Tom Hyde and assigned him the task to investigate his dad's farm. After more than an hour of reviewing evidence, there was another knock at the door.

Hank stuck his head from out of his office. "What now?"

Jim answered the door. Harris, neatly dressed in a gray suit, removed his sunglasses and held out his hand.

"Hello Sheriff Buchanan. As of yesterday, I'm permanently assigned to the FBI Evidence Response Team Unit. I'll be assisting with the Bitterroot Murders Investigation."

"I heard." Jim reached out and they shook hands. Harris' jacket lifted just enough for Jim to catch a glimpse of the snub nose revolver secured in its shoulder holster.

Paul placed his briefcase down and introduced himself to Linda.

"Hank, do you mind if I sit in on this?" Linda asked.

Hank replied, "If Jim and Agent Harris don't mind, I don't either."

Another lengthy conversation commenced. Each had their own version of what may have happened and who could be the victims. Then a few minutes before 10 a.m., Jim heard an audible click.

"Did you hear that?"

"Hear what?" Hank asked.

"It's coming from that package." Jim stood up and examined the box. Pristine shipping tape covered an older strip covering the label. It screamed tampering to Jim arousing his gut instincts. He yelled, "Get out of here! There's a bomb in this room."

Hank stuck the silver from his desk drawer into his pocket and grabbed folders from his file cabinets.

"What're you doing?" Jim asked.

"These are important!"

"Your life's important. Get the hell out of here." Jim grabbed Hank by the arm.

A few file folders slipped from Hank's grip. He reached for them but they escaped his grasp. "Out the back, it's quicker," Hank said.

Paul grabbed his briefcase and threw his arm around Hank. "Let's go!"

Jim noticed Linda frozen in place and called to her. "Come on." He pushed her toward the others as they hurried to the back door. They ran through the parking lot and Linda turned to look back. A loud bang, a concussive wave, and a snap of flames pierced the windows. The force of the blast blew the fireproof metal door off its hinges. Linda fell onto her back in the grassy area and Jim tumbled onto her. Pieces of wood, metal, insulation, and glass flew through the air. A splinter of wood bit into Jim's back.

"I can't breathe," stated Linda. "Get off me."

"I... can't... move," Jim replied in a labored voice.

·13·

Crouched along with Hank behind a few state vehicles for safety, Paul spotted Linda struggling to move under the weight of Jim's body. His instincts drove him to run toward his two fallen comrades. Protecting his nose and mouth with a handkerchief from the smoke and debris that clogged the air, he pulled Linda out from under Jim.

Once on her feet, Paul helped point her to safety. Then he stared down at Jim. A six-inch long by two-inch wide fragment of wood protruded from Jim's back. Embedded just below his right shoulder blade, blood spurted from the wound and saturated his shirt.

Hank ran to Jim's side and pressed against the wound to slow the bleeding as Jim grimaced from the pain. Paul watched Jim attempt to reach behind himself with his arms but he could only writhe in agony.

Paul pulled his cellphone from his jacket and called 911. He shouted into the phone, "Send an ambulance to the morgue... yes, I said the morgue! Officer down!"

The morgue, engulfed in a massive fire spewed a heavy dose of flames as Paul stared at the smoldering building. The flames continued to lick the sky as black smoke swirled in the wind. In the distance, the sound of sirens shattered the quiet laziness of the early morning.

"Hang in there, buddy." Paul offered words of comfort to Jim.

A smile grew on Jim's face. Despite the hectic atmosphere surrounding him, Paul managed to overhear Jim's conversation.

"Hank, McCoy never screwed up this bad, eh?"

·14·

Two fire trucks, sirens blaring roared through the town as residents stared in surprise at the uncommon spectacle. The vehicles, with red emergency lights flaunting their presence like a burning field of poppies, arrived at the morgue.

As the diesel engines idled, firefighters weighed down by their protective clothing, assembled their apparatus. They dispersed to fight the blaze and evacuated people from the adjacent State Crime Lab and the newer office buildings on the campus. With the morgue fully engulfed, the firefighters' intent was to prevent the blaze from spreading to the other buildings.

An ambulance swerved into the parking lot, its siren screaming for attention. With the vehicle still moving, an EMT jumped from the open passenger door, hit the ground running, and headed to where Jim lay.

"Where are you injured sheriff?" the EMT asked.

Jim moaned and motioned with his left arm toward his back.

Hank knelt down and explained to the EMT. "I think he's got a punctured lung."

The EMT spoke through his two-way radio, "I've got a patient here, chest trauma, possible life-threatening injuries. Code Blue, I repeat, I have a Code Blue. Call Air-Trauma. Have them fly a chopper to the helipad now."

"He pushed me out of the way... he saved my life," testified Linda as she tried to rub Jim's blood off her shirt sleeve. Her tear-filled eyes, laden with concern, commanded the attention of the EMT who proceeded to check Jim's injuries.

"Sheriff Buchanan, this is Chuck Egan. I'm the new EMT. We met a few weeks ago, remember?" Jim nodded. "We'll put you on a stretcher, move you to the emergency van, and meet the paramedics at the hospital. They'll evaluate your condition and then we'll load you onto the helicopter."

Jim nodded again and motioned to his mouth as he strained for a breath of air. He coughed, blood spurting from his lips.

"Even if you can, don't talk," shouted Chuck Egan.

Jim nodded a final time.

To ensure that Jim would not choke to death, Chuck established an open airway and suctioned blood from Jim's throat.

Hank asked Chuck, "Where are you taking him?"

"Taylor University Medical Center and Cedar County Hospital are both involved with a bus versus train, multiple injuries. We have thirteen criticals in both ERs. Our instructions are to request an air ambulance flight to Missoula Memorial for all future trauma patients."

"He might not make it," stated Hank.

"There will be a paramedic on board. We have to try sir."

A tear fell from Hank's eye as he looked upward and whispered a prayer. Linda stood up despite a firefighter's insistence to remain down until another ambulance arrived. Chuck and the van driver supported Jim's weight as they transferred him from the ground to the stretcher. Placing him on his side to prevent the wooden splinter from causing further internal damage, they wheeled him to the van and placed him inside.

Linda cringed when she saw Chuck continue to suction blood from Jim's mouth and then strap an oxygen mask to Jim's face. The EMT established an intravenous hook-up and then attempted to close the back doors of the van. A hand held one of the doors open.

"I'm going with him," Linda said.

Chuck shook his head. "You'll have to wait for another EMT to treat your injuries."

"I don't have any injuries that a Band-Aid couldn't fix. I ride with him or else."

Chuck paused, looked at Jim, then at Linda. He said, "Get in. You can fill us in on what happened."

Linda climbed in and sat across from Jim who was lying on the driver's side of the van. In solidarity with a fellow officer who had just saved her life, Linda reached out to hold Jim's hand.

Chuck closed the doors and slammed his open palm on the inside rear window of the cab. "Let's go, we're secure here."

The siren blasted loud and long as the county ambulance sped to the hospital and its waiting helipad.

·15·

The fire continued to rage. Part of the roof came crashing down triggering firefighters to run for cover. The small crowd that gathered responded in a collective exclamation of shock as police officers guarding the perimeter pushed the crowd farther back.

Paul took a deep breath and turned to Hank. "What does this do to the investigation?"

Hank pointed to what was left of the building. "My friend might die and you're asking about the investigation? Didn't Hoover teach you G-Men compassion?"

Harris raised his voice, "If it were me in that ambulance, the Bureau would already have another agent on their way up here to replace me. Nothing compromises the investigation."

Hank studied Harris' sharp eyes, which challenged him for a response. After a brief moment, Hank answered, "Hell, the bodies are all contaminated if there's even anything left of them. Most of my hard copy reports are gone too! The weekly computer file upload should have saved some of my data."

Harris reached for his cellphone and responded, "I'll call for a mobile forensic lab to process the evidence. It'll help us discover what happened."

"A mobile lab?"

"Yes. The department has portable refrigeration units. We use them for bodies, if what's in the morgue is still... whoa, hold on." Paul spoke into his cellphone, "Yeah, get me the division manager. Okay, I'll hold." He looked back at Hank and whispered, "Ever see those trailers at construction sites?"

"Sure."

"Same thing but they're refrigerated."

Hank buried his head in his hands and sighed, "Do what you have to do."

Paul stuck his finger in his right ear to block the numerous piercing sounds of the firefighting efforts. "Commander Parker, this is Agent Harris. We had an explosion here... the morgue. Yes, it smells like arson. We need a mobile forensic lab right away and one of those refrigerated units too. What... all right, if you fly it down I can get a truck transport arraigned. We'll coordinate a meeting at Taylor International Airport. I'll... what... yes. I've met with Henry Kelly... yes... and the sheriff too... what's that... yes, hold on." Paul placed his hand over the cellphone speaker and said to Hank, "My boss wants to speak with you."

Hank reached for the phone. "How do you put this on speaker? My damn ears can't hear in this racket that's going on." Paul pressed a button and gave the phone to Hank. "Hello?" Hank said.

"Doctor Kelly... I've heard a lot about you. This is FBI Director Karl Parker. I'm the assigned field commander on the Bitterroot Murders Investigation. B. Harlan Daniels at the National Crime Information Center told me about your assistance last year in cracking the international body parts ring."

"Sir, it wasn't me. Sheriff Buchanan broke it wide open," Hank replied.

"He mentioned that sheriff... Indian, right?"

"Yes."

"Is he there? Can I speak with him?"

"No, he's in critical condition from the explosion."

"I'm sorry to hear that. I pray he pulls through."

"We all do sir," Hank replied.

"Well, I just wanted to confirm to you personally that we'll be shipping a mobile forensic lab via Air Force transport and because your morgue has been destroyed, I'm also sending one of our mobile mortuary and autopsy system trailers."

"Thanks, that is very generous of you, sir."

"No problem, we're glad to assist."

Hank spotted Sam Clayton among the faces in the crowd that had gathered alongside the road.

"Commander Parker, I've got to go… something came up."

Hank handed the phone back to Paul. He turned to look where he had seen Sam Clayton but the only thing he saw was an empty spot in the gathering throng where Clayton's face had been.

·16·

L inda held Jim's hand as the emergency van careened into the parking lot and stopped in front of the Taylor University Medical Center's Emergency Entrance. Chuck opened the van's back doors and yelled to the health care workers waiting outside the hospital, "Let's go! We've got a Code Blue here!"

Linda jumped to the pavement as the van driver helped Chuck pull Jim's stretcher from the van. The nurses immediately transferred the intravenous hookup to a crash cart.

"Did you check his ABCs?" a nurse asked.

The EMT nodded. "I intubated his airway, got his breathing back to almost normal, and his circulation is still good."

They rushed Jim toward the waiting emergency air ambulance. While the paramedics secured him in the helicopter, Linda climbed on board and they lifted off.

Linda asked one of the paramedics, "How's he doing?"

The paramedic, a young Asian man with long black hair, square cut in the back, pointed to her bandaged right arm. "How are you doing?"

"It's only a scratch. Chuck took care of it on the ride over. What about Jim?"

The paramedic looked down at his patient. "We're a Code Blue. We have to stabilize him, then they'll take x-rays but he's going to need surgery."

"It's real bad, isn't it?" Linda asked.

After a pause his nod confirmed what Linda knew his silence implied.

After a forty-five minute flight, they touched down on the helipad of the six-story Missoula Memorial Hospital. The paramedics guided Jim's stretcher to the door. Linda remained by Jim's side, holding his hand. They rode the elevator down to the third floor and to the swinging doors of the operating rooms.

"Officer, you can't follow us in here," said one of the nurses to Linda. "Please sit in the waiting room."

Linda complied, and plopped herself and her emotions onto a green couch in the small waiting area. She stared at the emergency room door, barely curbing her urge to burst through to be by Jim's side as any fellow officer would have. They'd just kick her out, she thought, and it would do Jim no good.

She languished more than three hours waiting for news. An orderly handed her a clean, blue hospital shirt and pants. She changed in a restroom and stowed her bloodied police uniform in a shoulder bag along with her service revolver and holster. A nurse finally motioned for Linda to follow her. A ride in the elevator, a walk down the hall, then they were outside room number 363 in the intensive care ward.

Thick, striped hospital drapes hid Jim from Linda's view. A vinyl-cushioned chair next to the bed invited her weary body. She sat and continued her vigil until an older nurse emerged from behind the curtains. Her eyes settled on Linda. "He'll be sedated for a few hours. If you're hungry, the cafeteria is on the first floor… are you family?"

Linda hesitated and then shook her head. "I'm a fellow police officer and his friend."

Jim lay on the bed, unconscious, with a bandaged chest and intravenous tubing attached to his arm. Linda felt a nudge at her side. It was Rocky.

"How long have you been here… maybe you should go home?" he suggested.

"I'm okay. What are you doing here?"

Rocky plopped himself in a chair opposite from where Linda was sitting. "I jumped in the car the minute I heard."

"Oh, it was awful." Linda swung her chair next to Rocky. "But he saved my life."

Rocky put his hand on Linda's arm. "I contacted Kate. Jia Li is driving her here."

"Good, he'll need all the support he can get."

"What're we going to do without Jim? You should see the building. It's toast."

Linda wiped away her tears. "The hell with the morgue! If I find out who did this, I'll shove my gun down their throat."

A light rap on the door and the surgeon who had operated on Jim appeared in the room. "Are you relatives of the patient?"

Rocky stood up. "We're not blood. But we're close."

The doctor peered into a manila folder that contained numerous medical forms. He turned to Rocky. "I can't discuss specifics since you're not family but I can tell you that we almost lost him."

"Will he recover... when can he go home?" Linda asked.

"Let him rest," the doctor said. "They'll take good care of him here. He should be on his feet by the end of this week and ready to go home next week."

"Is there anything we can do?" Linda asked.

The doctor bypassed Rocky and Linda and stood next to the nurse. "Just let him rest for now. Will you excuse us? We need to check his vitals and draw blood."

"Of course, we'll step outside." Linda tugged on the sleeve of Rocky's uniform.

He backed toward the door. "Yeah, we'll be in the hall."

Linda watched the doctor and nurse draw the drapes as she and Rocky left. They shuttled past the nurse's station to the elevator. Once inside and alone together, Rocky said, "Agent Harris is downstairs."

The bell chimed and the door closed. Linda hit the button for the first floor. She grabbed Rocky by the arm. "Why didn't he come up to visit Jim?"

"He wants info from you on the fire and the bodies."

Linda let go of Rocky and leaned against the elevator wall. The bell chimed for the first floor.

"That bastard!"

"Wait a minute, what's the matter?" Rocky asked.

When the doors opened, Linda turned to face him. As she walked backwards, not breaking stride, she pushed her sunglasses up her nose, swiveled and rushed away.

"Hey," yelled Rocky.

Linda walked briskly, burst through the front doors of the hospital, and ran right into a sea of reporters. "I have no news! Let me pass!" With her shoulder bag bouncing about, Linda raced to the far corner of the parking lot to where Paul Harris was leaning against his car. She quickened her pace, occasionally glancing back to see Rocky trying to catch up. She watched him grapple with his Stetson as the wind endeavored to swipe it off his head.

"What's up, Harris!" Linda asked.

"Why the sour puss?"

Linda glared at him. "You're more concerned about a goddamn case than a fellow officer who almost died?"

"Come on," Harris said.

Linda clenched her fists. "Right about now nothing would please me more than decking you and I'd have no regrets about the consequences." After a few seconds, she thought better and cooled off. "You're in my territory now. If you want my help you better show us some respect."

Harris gazed at the sky for a split second. "All right... I'm sorry. I don't want to get off on the wrong foot. I'm sorry about what happened to Sheriff Buchanan. Don't worry, we'll find out who did this and we'll work together."

"That's the only way it can be," Linda said.

Rocky caught up to them. "What's going on here?"

Linda turned to him. "Everything's cool." She glanced back at Harris. "Right?"

"Right." Paul Harris reached into his car and pulled out a map. "I was looking at the area where Jim found the bodies. I'd like to get a look at the site and check for more evidence. Maybe it will tell us who's responsible for the explosion." He got into his car.

Linda pulled off her sunglasses. "Now?"

"We can. Are you coming with us?" Paul looked at Rocky.

"I'm in." Rocky took off his hat and glanced at the reporters who were only fifty feet away and closing fast. "Come on Linda, let's go now." He jumped into his car parked next to Paul's and spun the wheels before Linda was even settled in her seat.

After an hour of driving north on State Highway 200, they all stopped for lunch at a diner in the little town of Plains. Sitting in the back of the eatery, they discussed the facts of the case, the three bodies, Paul's list of missing people from other western states and Olivia Clayton.

"Any similarities with the OTC event?" Paul bit into a hamburger.

"OTC?" Linda glanced at Rocky for a hint.

Harris leaned back in his seat. "Organ Transplant Crimes from last year. That's how the Bureau refers to them."

Linda put her ginger ale down. "There were no bodies, after they took the organs, they incinerated the corpses." Linda stole a few French fries from Rocky's plate.

He pulled his dish away from Linda. "Hey, why didn't you order your own?"

Paul continued, "What about the doctor?"

Linda asked, "You mean the mayor?"

"Yeah, mayor... doctor... whatever?"

"He's in Helena, still awaiting trial."

"I know... did you get any info from him?"

Rocky interjected, "What does one case have to do with the other?"

Paul glanced at the other customers in the diner, leaned forward and whispered, "We have a major crime event in a county of one-hundred seven thousand people. It makes the national headlines and a year later, we begin finding bodies in the same county. Don't you think there's a connection?"

"No I don't," asserted Linda. She looked at Rocky. "Do you?"

Rocky shook his head. "Different MOs. Jim asked me to contact Stu Bauer over at Northwoods Logging. He said he knows nothing about anyone using that old logging road. It looks like we'll have to find that out for ourselves."

Paul sat back and said, "Look, I've seen a lot over the years and this could be related to last year's crimes. Someone you overlooked from the OTCs may have tried to destroy evidence today."

"Listen here," she asserted in a hushed voice. "I don't care what training you've had, or what you've witnessed, this case is going to require good, hard, field investigating. You don't get there by sitting in an office fitting things into a preconceived set of hypotheses."

Paul sat back in his seat. "Okay, okay. We'll take this from the ground up."

When they finished lunch, they drove north onto Route 28. They reached the spot where the highway crossed over the Little Bitterroot River and parked their cars on the shoulder just north of Jack Morton's repairs and before the bend in the road. Linda strapped on her gunbelt. They made their way down the river embankment. Torn, plastic yellow crime scene tape, stuck to small branches flapped in the afternoon breeze.

Linda asked, "What are we looking for?"

"Anything at all," Paul said.

Linda gazed across the river and saw something on the other side. "What's that?"

Among the tall grass near the riverbank, a coyote's hindquarters came into view as the animal struggled to drag something. Linda drew her service revolver, aimed, and fired one shot that sped above and past the coyote. A yelp and the coyote darted past the boulders beyond the riverbank and on into the buffalograss.

"That was a coyote, right?" Paul asked. "You missed."

Rocky smirked at Paul's assumption.

Linda stuck her gun back in its holster. "Missed my ass, it's not the coyote I'm interested in." She took off her boots and socks and waded across the Little Bitterroot. The river had receded from its flood stages and had now leveled out to a three-foot depth. Carefully avoiding the many small rocks in the riverbed, Linda climbed the bank and looked down at the grass. She covered her mouth and turned her head away.

"What is it?" Paul called out from across the river.

"There's a body in pieces." She hugged her stomach as if holding back her lunch.

Linda saw Paul pull out his cellphone and heard him shout. "Barry, remember that mobile forensic unit I requested from Parker this morning? Fly it here ASAP... I don't care. I need it today. There's another body."

·17·

It came out of nowhere... a thought, a vision, a memory perhaps. Jim was in a barn, a red barn. A machine dominated the center. It was gray and loud. Movement from below caused him to stare at the floor where he gazed at a quiet little chick with engaging eyes. When Jim picked it up he noticed its lower beak was against the chick's neck.

Jim gathered the tiny creature in his hands and held it close to his chest. He gently caressed the chick's neck just below its malformed lower beak. Within an instant the lower beak elevated into a normal state and the chick began to cheep. Jim set it free.

"I'm the foreman. What are you doing?" A man walked out of a dark corner of the barn.

"I was helping a living thing in need."

"That's what the machine is for."

Jim glanced at the contraption. A conveyor belt full of malformed chicks ran along the outside of the machine's wall and then dove inside. The clanging, rattling and banging from within the machine drove Jim to run to the other side. Where the conveyor belt exited was a mixed bag of broken bones, blood and feathers.

Jim glared at the foreman. "This machine isn't fixing them, it's killing them."

"Some get fixed, some don't. There's so many chicks what's a few dead ones?"

"All life is precious," Jim said.

The machine stopped and the foreman disappeared. From the left side of the barn a person wearing a black mask and a flowing black robe glided over to a throne and took a seat.

The person ogled Jim and pointed a bony spindly finger at him. "Listen carefully and answer my questions." After a pause the person continued, "I see the moon, what do you see?"

Jim responded, "A star."

"I feel the cold, what do you feel?"

"Warm blood running through my veins."

"I smell death, what do you smell?"

"Roses on my mother's casket."

"I believe in envy, misfortune and cruelty what do you believe in?"

"Love, kindness and charity."

"If you could visit with three people living or dead whom would you choose?"

"My wife, my daughter, and my mother."

Jim then watched the person remove the mask revealing a head of putrefied flesh.

"They are not here...I am the *ṁalyè es šeẏiłk*. End my killing on this earth. I am an old and tired woman. Help me seek my revenge against the man who abused and murdered me. His killing will not stop until I can return the wrath he visited upon me."

·18·

Jim awakened with a jolt and shuddered as he opened his eyes. The rays of the Montana morning sun pierced through the bedroom windows. He felt the familiar comfort of his Native blanket up against his chin. Wiping the cold sweat from his forehead he took a deep breath and sighed.

"It sound like Mista Jim have nightmare."

Jim turned his head as Jia Li walked in from the bathroom. "Yes, it was a bad dream."

"You sleep long while."

"What time is it?"

"Don't Mista Jim mean what day is it?" She laughed.

Jim stared at Jia Li. "Where's Kate?"

"Oh Missa Kate downstairs with guests."

"What guests?"

"They downstairs. If you get dressed, I call them up." Jia Li left the bedroom.

Jim threw the covers aside and attempted to get up but as he stepped onto the floor, he felt a stabbing sensation in his right side. "Damn." Reaching toward his back, he felt bandages and a gooey substance oozing from beneath the gauze. Sitting to let the pain subside, he sensed the aroma of freshly brewed coffee and what he thought was the scent of Kate's huckleberry pancakes.

A few minutes later, he heard footfalls on the stairs. Jim covered his pajama bottoms with the bedspread. He gazed at Kate peeking in the doorway and a smile enveloped his face.

"Kate, you look so much better than yesterday. It feels like every second is an hour. What time is it?"

Kate planted a kiss on Jim's lips. "Just past nine, your friends are downstairs."

Jim heard conversation but did not recognize the voices. "Who?"

"Linda and Rocky."

"Why was Jia Li in the bedroom, shouldn't she be taking care of you?"

"Doctor Donnelly gave me a new prescription last week and I feel much better."

"Last week? You were still sick yesterday!"

"Jim, you were in the hospital an entire week. I visited you every day. Alma Rose was by your side too until she left to stay with her mom."

He interrupted her, "What hospital?"

"Don't you remember anything?"

"I think I remember being hurt but I forgot what happened."

"The doctor wrote it down for me." Kate pulled a slip of paper from her pocket. "You had a pneumothorax with a pleural effusion. That's a collapsed lung with a build-up of fluid in your chest cavity. They extracted the object and were able to suction out the air and the fluid and stabilize you."

"I'm glad I don't remember all that."

"The doctor said another hour without surgery and the air in your chest cavity would have collapsed your other lung."

Jim sat there in a state of confusion. He realized how fortunate he had been to survive such a calamity but also how indebted he was not only to the medical professionals and to whomever delivered him to the hospital, but also to Kate whom he knew loved him dearly.

"What day is it?"

"It's Saturday, May twenty-fifth and your visitors want to see you."

"Send them in." Jim heard a knock and saw Rocky and Linda at the door as Kate left the bedroom.

"How are you doing?" Linda asked.

Jim thought for a moment. "I remember being in the morgue yesterday. What else am I supposed to remember?"

Rocky threw down a file folder titled <u>Autopsy Report</u>. "You were at the morgue a week ago last Monday, the day of the explosion."

"What explosion?"

"Do you remember meeting Agent Harris at the morgue?" Linda asked.

"No."

"Man, you must be on some heavy duty drugs." Rocky pointed to the folder. "That file is on the fourth victim."

"Fourth?"

"Yeah. The morgue was destroyed but two bodies in the crypt weren't damaged."

"Destroyed... what happened?"

Rocky continued, "Someone planted a bomb at the morgue. You were impaled from a piece of the doorframe. How do you feel?"

"Except for a dull pain when I try to take a deep breath, I'm okay. Where are the bodies now?"

Linda replied, "Harris requested a mobile forensic lab and a refrigeration unit. We put three bodies in it plus the one that Elijah found. That one's a little overcooked." Linda's cellphone rang. She looked down and said, "Dammit... it's Peters. He makes my life a living hell. I wish he'd retire now!" She walked to the door. "I'll be outside." Turning back, she pointed at the bedridden sheriff. "Rocky, fill him in on the photos."

"What photos?" Jim asked.

Rocky walked up to Jim as Linda exited the room. "The high school photography club was taking pictures by the railroad bridge on 228 the day of the explosion. The teacher developed them and saw something on the prints."

"Go on."

"She shows them to the principal who gets his magnifying glass and thinks he sees a body being pulled alongside the railroad tracks. They show them to Hank and we go out there a few days later."

"What did you find?"

"No body, except that Paul finds footprints and evidence that something was dragged along the old logging road. And then we found tire tracks along the road."

"And then what?"

"Then nothing... the trail goes cold."

"Maybe it's that phantom truck we saw from the air. Did you take impressions?"

"Harris did."

"Can we see him today?"

"The doc said you have to rest up all this week."

Discouraged, Jim sighed. "What's new at the office?"

"Harris is working on the case and Tom's helping him. Keeping those reporters away is a full time job for me." Rocky leaned in. "And I didn't tell anyone about the shots."

"What shots?"

"You told me someone shot at you while you were hiking."

"I remember the shots. I told you?"

"Yes, you told me to keep it quiet."

"I'm not hanging around my house. I'm going to the office. Maybe work will jog my memory."

"Hold on. I did what you asked."

"About what?"

"The white supremacist group meeting at the church."

"I remember that too."

"I told Chief Peters and Linda. They're keeping their eyes open. Undersheriff Hyde is conducting an investigation but I asked Harris about embedding a surveillance operative but he said it's premature."

"Why?"

"He said it's a waste of resources at this time. If any crimes are committed or people's rights threatened then the FBI can get involved."

"Great... just great. Do they want us to wait until someone gets hurt before they do something?" Jim shook Rocky's hand. "Thanks for your help. At least I knew I could trust you."

Jim sent Rocky into the hallway while he pulled off the bandages. He examined his wounds using a handheld looking glass and the bathroom mirror. The gooey mess seemed to be an antiseptic but the stitches were clean and neat, not swollen or red.

He showered and Kate applied new bandages and helped him dress. Jim gingerly walked downstairs to meet up with Linda and Rocky. They had breakfast together and when they were finished, Kate planted a kiss on Jim's cheek. Jim noticed Linda and Rocky watching. Even Jia Li sneaked a peek.

"Hey guys, can I have a minute alone with Kate?"

After Linda, Rocky, and Jia Li stepped outside, Kate asked, "What's up?"

"Kate, it's not safe for you to be here. After what we went through with you just a few months ago, I don't want to put your life in danger again."

Kate laughed. "It seems like you're the one who needs protection. I'm not in danger."

"Kate, I didn't tell you but someone shot at me while I was hiking with Angel. I want you to go to New York like you planned and stay with your cousin Karin until I can get some answers about what's going on."

Kate stared at Jim, smiled, and then broke out into a laugh. "You're kidding, right?"

Jim stood silent and watched the smile evaporate from Kate's face.

"I'm not kidding. Tomorrow I'll have Rocky drive you to the airport. Get a flight to Billings, pick up Alma Rose and I want the two of you to take the next flight to New York."

"But I need to help you get well again."

"Kate, I'll be all right. Don't argue."

Speechless, Kate frowned but then agreed. "I'll call Karin and Alma Rose."

Jim left and told Rocky about Kate's flight. Jim's injuries had kept him away from the case and he knew that he needed time to heal. The investigation of the unknown bodies however, could not wait.

Jim convinced them to meet him at the sheriff's office. When they arrived they not only discussed the case but Rocky told Jim that the FBI and ATF completed their investigation into the morgue fire and demolition of the old structure had begun. The State of Montana pledged to accelerate the erection of the new state-of-the-art facility before the end of the current year at the construction site on the State Crime Lab campus.

Close to an hour later while the three were sitting in the conference room, Martha's voice crackled over the intercom. "Jim, we have a situation. Come to the dispatcher's desk."

When they reached Martha's desk, Jim asked, "What happened to protocol?"

"I don't have time for that. They found a couple of boys in a field near the Little Bitterroot. They're in bad shape. They may have been drinking, can you go?"

Jim glanced at his friends and then replied, "Martha, can you provide us with directions?"

"Remember where you found that body a few weeks ago, across the river, two-hundred yards upstream?" Martha asked.

Jim nodded. "Anyone there now?"

"Elijah Sizemore called it in a few minutes ago. I just dispatched the EMTs."

"We're on it," Jim said.

Linda hopped into the front passenger seat of Rocky's patrol car while Jim eased into the back. At speeds close to one hundred miles per hour, with wailing sirens and flashing lights, they rushed to the sparse landscape near Lonepine.

·19·

The EMTs had just arrived and parked off the road in the field of buffalograss. Rocky drove his car up to the emergency van and Linda jumped out before he could set his brake. She ran across the field through the curly green leaves of the ankle-high grass. Rocky exited his patrol car with Jim running behind with a limp, holding his side. His injury from the explosion sent stabbing pains up his ribcage with each step he took.

When Jim arrived he looked down. Two boys wearing jeans and flannel shirts lay in the buffalograss, their faces a gray shade of blue. They were Native with long black hair. One was on his back and the other lying sideways across the other. "What happened?" he shouted to the EMTs.

Chuck Egan and the other EMT repositioned the boys so they could begin CPR. As he cleared vomit from one boy's open mouth, he responded, "It looks like alcohol poisoning." He pointed to the open bottles next to the two boys. "A fisherman found them."

Throwing back his ponytail, Jim noticed one capped whiskey bottle on its side containing a few remaining ounces of the firewater and another one nearby, empty of its intoxicating brew. Next to them was an open pint of vodka, also on its side with a saturated spot on the ground where the contents had poured out.

"Where's Elijah?" demanded Jim.

Chuck pointed to the south where Elijah, knelt with his face to the sun reciting Indian prayers in his native tongue.

"He won't speak with us," Chuck said. "Maybe he'll talk to you?"

"I'll try," Jim said as he limped toward Elijah.

The wind blew over the buffalograss as Jim stood behind Elijah and waited for him to complete his prayers. When he finished and stood up, Jim noticed the tracks of Elijah's tears running from his reddened eyes and down the side of his face.

"One is my cousin's boy. The other is his friend from my wife's clan." Elijah continued, "They're only twelve and thirteen."

"What can I do?"

"This is sacred land. The white man killed my people on this ground and now they've done it again." The sadness in Elijah's eyes seemed to punctuate his response. "Kill the man who gave them the liquor," screamed Elijah.

He tried to step past Jim but the sheriff took hold of his arm. "What do you know about this? There's something you're not telling me."

Elijah pulled his arm away. "Jim, to these boys the world is like a dark machine. They were stuck on a conveyor belt with no way off and heading to their demise."

It was as if Jim was reliving his nightmare. As he stood frozen from Elijah's choice of words, the Native holy man climbed into the emergency van. The EMTs closed the doors and the truck drove through the buffalograss toward Route 28. Jim watched Elijah stare at him through the back windows of the van. While the dust from the retreating rescue van swirled in the air, Jim felt like he had all the pieces to the puzzle but his hands were tied behind his back.

He stoically walked over to Linda and Rocky. "Rock, let's collect the evidence." Jim turned to Linda. "You have plenty of work in town I don't expect you to stay."

"I want to help anyway I can," she replied. She pointed to Jim's side. "You're bleeding."

Jim looked down. Blood from his wound had saturated his shirt. "I'll patch it up when I get home."

Jim, Rocky, and Linda scoured the area over the next two hours. They used gloves and bags that Rocky kept in his car. They collected anything that seemed related to two underage kids obtaining liquor. When they finished, they sat in the car and Jim called Community Hospital in the town of Mallory.

"Yes, this is Sheriff Buchanan of Cedar County. You should have received two Indian boys this morning, possible alcohol poisoning. Can you tell me their status?" Jim pulled the phone away from his mouth. "A doctor is going to give me an update."

Jim put the phone on speaker. After a few minutes, they heard, "Sheriff Buchanan, this is Doctor Livingston."

"Hi doctor, what happened to the boys?"

"It appears they were drinking for quite some time. They may have begun last night. They both exhibited signs of hypothermia."

"How are they?"

There was silence and then the doctor replied, "Both their families are here with us. One boy was dead on arrival. He was unconscious because of the alcohol intoxication. He choked on his vomit and died by asphyxiation. The other is in intensive care. He had a series of seizures. We suspect he may have brain damage. He's on life support."

A tear ran down Jim's face. "Can I help?"

"Find out how they got the alcohol."

"I will."

Linda hung her head and Rocky slowly paced the ground, kicking the dust and muttering to himself. As they drove back toward Route 28, Jim collected his thoughts. Two young boys, alcohol poisoned on the reservation, close to the discoveries of four headless corpses. Could this be just an unusual coincidence?

He thought about his dream, the machine, the conveyor belt, the foreman's disposable comment about the chicks and the appearance of the *ṁalyè es šeýiɫk*. Then the recollection of Alma Rose's premonition flooded his brain. *You ran into a field of buffalograss. You were bleeding.*

·20·

Roy Lewis sat at his cluttered desk covered with sticky notes provided by his producer. On the wall hung a multicolored glass decal with the radio station's call letters, KCHM. Wearing a blue golf shirt and khaki dungaree shorts with side pockets he reviewed his daily program schedule.

Monday mornings were always an opportunity for Roy to set the tone for the rest of the week and he was on his A-game. Grabbing an uncapped bottle of spring water, he slid away the headset that partially covered his shaven head and took a swig.

He pushed a button on the panel in front of him, cleared his throat and asked, "Doozy, why isn't Buchanan on my schedule?"

Through his console speakers he heard the response from his producer, Doug Zimmer. "That sheriff is still recuperating at home."

"What did he say when you invited him on my show?"

"I couldn't get through to him. The office takes a message and then I never hear back from them. Want me to try again?"

"I'll go with the script for today's show. Too bad though. I would have pressed him about those bodies."

"You make the show lively, Roy."

"Have to. That's how we make our money. My audience doesn't like good news. I have to keep them jumpy."

Later, when the clock approached 9 a.m. Roy Lewis tensed his arms and legs, took deep breaths and then pounded his fists on the desk. He was ready.

"Good morning, this is KCHM's conservative voice of reason, Roy Lewis bringing you news and commentary of vital importance to those of you willing to listen to the truth. Today is our one-year anniversary on the air and I trust I've made an important impact in your lives."

With that introduction, Lewis began taking pot shots at the media, the government, and what he called the liberal nutflakes. After close to an hour of his diatribe, intended to incite and agitate his audience he took several calls.

"Hello, Scott from Mallory. How are you today?"

"I'm good Roy... no, I take that back. I'm pissed off. Can I say that on the air?"

"You just did. We don't censor within reason here on the Roy Lewis Show. Just say what's on your mind."

"Thanks Roy. I want to make a comment on those bodies they've been finding."

A smile broadened across Roy's face. "Go ahead."

"I think the government's been killing agitators like me and you and burying them. We're only trying to get out the truth and they can't take it."

"You're right about the truth but I can't say that the government is behind the killings. They control too much of our lives as it is but I don't think they'd go that far."

"Roy, I know how far they go. If they ever come onto my land I'd give them some Montana hospitality along with a ticket to their Maker."

Roy Lewis chuckled. "Now, now Scott, threats like that will only give them a reason to come after you."

"I ain't afraid of them. We need to take back our country."

"You mean through voting, demonstrations and civil disobedience, right?"

"No I mean through insurrection and forced exile. And if they don't cooperate we go the whole nine yards."

"Scott, here at KCHM we don't advocate violence. You do know that, right?"

"I know. Leave it in my hands and a few thousand like-minded individuals. We'll get this situation corrected."

"Well Scott, I see I have more callers so I have to move on. Have a nice day and keep the fight in the crosshairs."

Roy ended that call and took another, then another and another. Although many of the callers either invoked the notion of a government conspiracy, a conservative bias toward liberals or disgust at minorities, each presented a different slant on the subjects. One commonality was the anger in the voices of the callers and the extreme solutions offered for the perceived problems.

Roy had his audience stroked and provoked and that's how he and his sponsors liked it.

During a commercial break, Doug Zimmer notified him of visitors in the studio. "Three Taylor residents are here and would like an on-air audience."

"Who are they and what's their beef?"

"The town's fire marshal, attorney and a local real estate owner... they want to introduce a new organization formed to combat the liberal loonies."

Roy laughed. "Send them in. Let them have their say."

Cy Taylor, Harold Porter and Jeb Peck cruised into the recording studio and were granted seats at Roy's desk. Doug Zimmer ran the post-commercial countdown and then pointed to Roy when it reached zero.

"Roy Lewis back once again. Today we have visitors in the studio. Gentlemen, would you like to introduce yourselves?"

Cy spoke first. "My name is Cy Taylor and I'm the spokesman for this group. My great-great grandfather, Elbridge Taylor, explorer, surveyor, fur trader and well-known mountain-man who founded the first settlement in this area and for whom this city is named after, envisioned a land where people could live in peace and harmony without the threat of losing that security from outside influences."

"What outside influences are you talking about?" Roy asked.

"I'm talking about the dangers we face every day from people who don't share our values. They move into houses and apartments then trash them right in front of our eyes. They live off state aid then have babies out of wedlock. They bring drugs, prostitution, and crime into our neighborhoods. Then they want to marry our daughters. No outsider is going to mess with my family's gene pool."

"Well Cy, don't you believe that law enforcement will protect us from all of that?"

"They're not doing the job they were paid to do. Look at the killings going on in Cedar County. Rumor has it there's Indian voodoo involved. I mean these heathens actually believe in stuff like that, play god-awful music and dance around wearing weird costumes. I'm convinced they're the ones responsible for the murders and we got to stop it now before the killing spreads off the reservation and affects decent folk like us."

"I think you're right that these killings have the locals stumped. That's why they brought in the Feds." Roy harrumphed. "Good luck with that one."

"Luck... it's just plain luck that bodies haven't turned up in Taylor but I'm sure they will. My ancestors fought for the rights we take for granted and I'll be damned if these animals are going to strip them from me and my family."

Harold Porter and Jeb Peck nodded in agreement.

Roy took a deep breath and quickly blew it out. "Well Cy, that's a mouthful. I'm sure that our government be it local, state, or federal will do its best to prevent anyone from harming its own citizens."

"I would disagree. Look at our sheriff. He's not one of us. Long hair, half-white… he's a disgrace to the office. You expect us to trust our sheriff to protect us from people who look just like him and even worse?"

"I'm still waiting to have him on my show. I think he's dodging me because he can't defend his policies, actions or shortcomings. He's been a failure ever since he took office."

"Police Chief Peters is a good and decent man and should be our county sheriff. He lost the last election by only nine freaking votes. Those people on the reservation bandied up together and voted for one of their kind just to piss us off."

"There's always next year's election. You can vote him out then."

"We can't wait for that, Roy. That's why we created G.O.D., the Guardians of Doctrine. We aim to take back our town and make it a safe place where innocent people like us can live and feel protected."

"How do you plan to do that?"

"Rallies, protests, fundraisers… we even formed a militia."

"How can interested people learn about G.O.D.?"

"We meet every Wednesday night at eight at the Church of the Revelation right here in town. We welcome all as long as they share our values."

"There you have it folks. At least one group is trying to bring back the American values our forefathers and heroes fought for and that we all take for granted. You heard it here first on the Roy Lewis Show."

·21·

It was now 10 a.m. on May 27, Jim's first day back sitting at his desk and staring at his cluttered inbox. Angel stretched out on her dog bed in the corner of his office. Even though it was Memorial Day and against his doctor's advice to report to work this soon, it was completely necessary as far as Jim was concerned. Besides, yesterday Rocky drove Kate to the airport for her trip to New York City so there was no one at home to keep him company.

The interior walls of Jim's office were pine-darkened and their waist-high windows stretched to the ceiling. A pedestal fan stood silent in the corner and two cushioned, maple armchairs faced his mahogany desk. A rotary phone sat next to his inbox and wooden file cabinets lined the back office wall.

Paperwork seemed to be the focus of the Cedar County Sheriff's Department. The Taylor Police Department handled the real work, the interesting and exciting work. The police officers patrolled the streets of Taylor, responding to drug dealing and drug use, fights, break-ins, and car mishaps. They turned the offenders over to the county sheriff's office for incarceration and rehabilitation leaving the sheriff's staff with the less important and boring duties of responding to calls of rabid animal sightings and coyote attacks. But what had transpired over the past few weeks threatened to toss the usual protocols out the window.

After ending a phone call from Hank, Jim heard Martha buzz in a visitor. Through the glass windows of his private office, Jim watched Paul Harris walk up to his door carrying a briefcase.

Dan McCoy held the security door open as he lingered in conversation with Martha.

Jim waved his hand and bellowed through the open office door, "Just because you used to be sheriff, doesn't mean you can socialize with my help during working hours." Jim held his side as the pain shot through his ribs.

Dan waved to Undersheriff Tom Hyde behind the front desk. Then he walked past Paul and entered Jim's office. Martha left the dispatch center and walked inside to get a cup of coffee.

Dan glanced at Martha and spoke in a hearty laugh. "See Jim, I'm just being friendly so she'll offer me her pasty dish covered in her famous gravy."

Jim said, "Three years number one at the state fair."

Martha blushed. "Danny Boy, I always knew your appetite came first."

Dan winked. "Come on darling, now didn't I treat you good all those years?"

Martha looked at Jim, then back at Dan. "Not nearly as good as Jimmy Boy treats me now."

Jim responded, "Good answer."

Dan pointed his index finger at Martha and laughed. "Get back to work, darling." He walked toward Jim with his arms open. "Haven't seen you in what... almost a month?" He continued to laugh.

Jim remained seated behind his desk and thrust out his open palm to block Dan's approach. "Don't, I'm still recovering from surgery."

Dan backed away. "Oh, I heard about that. Some folks said you almost died."

"I was there," Paul said leaning against Jim's office doorframe. "It was touch and go."

"So... how are you on this fine Memorial Day?" Dan's voice was overly jovial to mask the seriousness that hung in the air.

"I'm doing okay but I miss Kate. She left for New York with Alma Rose yesterday."

Dan nodded. "Good idea. New places, new faces, it'll help her recovery but how about you?"

Jim leaned back in his chair. "I'm still on antibiotics and painkillers. Rocky has to give me and Angel a ride back and forth to work but it's good to return to the office. I see you're still driving that old fifty-five Buick Century they let you keep as a retirement gift."

"You betcha. I'm driving it in today's parade. I spent many a night when it was blacker than the inside of a cow sleeping in that goddamn tank. Hey, why aren't you outside waiting for the parade to begin?"

Jim tried unsuccessfully to stifle a smile. "It seems so long since I've been away from the office. I just needed the feel of sitting behind my desk again."

"The parade starts at eleven." Dan looked at his wristwatch. "You got thirty minutes to change your mind."

"Not me... I'm in love with my job."

"Jimmy, this place has bad memories for me. That's why I moved to Whitefish. Now, I get to sleep late every morning and sit at Campy's Bar every evening watching the dancing girls. Every weekend my girlfriend comes over too... I got it made." A smile emerged from the corner of his mouth.

"You've got a girlfriend?" Jim asked.

"Yeah. She's a Flathead." Dan winked.

Jim raised his eyebrows. "A Flathead?"

"Her dad's Flathead and her mom's Mexican. She's a mixed-blood, just like you."

"She lives on the reservation?"

Dan raised his voice. "Yeah, so what... can't a white man date a Flathead?"

"That's not my point. Aren't you a little old to be dating?" laughed Jim.

Dan looked into Jim's eyes. "What's age got to do with it? Damn, I'm gonna live my life the way I want and if I die having fun, then I die having fun."

Jim cautioned, "Be careful what you wish for. The way things are going any one of us could end up flat on our backs in the morgue." Jim stared at Paul. "Now that I've had time to recollect, you seem awfully familiar."

Paul smiled. "We were rookies the same year in the NFL. I played wide receiver for the Rams."

"I remember now."

Harris laughed. "You leveled the hell out of me in the NFC Championship game."

"That seems like such a long time ago. But let's not waste the government's time." Jim gestured for Dan and Paul to sit.

Dan took off his faded gray Stetson, revealing a wide bald spot surrounded on three sides by curly wisps of white hair. "Listen you two. People been jawing about that wacko show on KCHM."

"You mean Roy Lewis?" Jim asked.

"Yeah, that hateful nutjob. I caught part of his show this morning and he had Cy Taylor on. Him and a couple three other loonies started a group that I think is gonna cause trouble."

"You mean the Guardians of Doctrine?" Jim asked.

"Yeah, you know about that?"

Jim leaned forward in his seat. "I'm keeping an eye on them. We can't do anything because they haven't broken any laws."

"Well, I think their dangerous," Dan said.

"I agree."

"They trashed you on the air."

"What did they say?"

"They called you half-white and a disgrace."

Jim laughed. "Half of that is true and the rest is just their opinion."

"I don't like it, Jim. Twenty years ago I would have thrown them in jail and charged them with something that corresponds to their evil treachery."

"Dan, it's not twenty years ago."

Paul spoke up. "Even though we can't provide any enforcement, I can still contact my superiors and look into each member's background."

Jim cast a stern stare at Paul. "We don't want the Feds involved in our town's goings-on any more than they have to. Let us handle this at the local level. Right now it's just a bunch of disgruntled townsfolk spewing their frustration. We've got more important matters to deal with."

"You're talking about the bodies, right?" Dan asked.

Jim placed his arms on his desk. "Yeah, the bodies. We don't know where they came from and we don't know how many more there are."

Paul said, "My men and an ATF agent are investigating the explosion. It's arson all right."

"Any leads?"

"No, the place was damaged pretty bad. All we found were remnants of RDX."

"I remember RDX from when I was in 'Nam," Dan said.

"It's also used as a major component of plastic explosives," Paul added.

"Well, I hope you're cross-referencing your military look-up lists with purchases and criminals arrested for bomb making," Jim noted.

"It's covered. We should come up with a suspect list in a few days," Paul replied.

Jim turned his attention to Dan. "Did Paul explain that I need your help?"

Dan put his hat on Jim's desk. "Yeah... why do you want an old fart like me running around goddamn Cedar County for? Ain't thirty years enough?"

"A few minutes ago you were complaining that I thought you were too old to date... I want your help," Jim insisted.

Dan took a deep breath, and exhaled slowly. "Why, to do the talkin' to reporters?"

Jim laughed. "I did get a call today from KTAY. They want to interview me. Even apologized for what a reporter said to me a few weeks ago."

"And what was that all about?"

Rocky knocked on the office door. Jim motioned with his arm to invite him in. Rocky said, "I don't mean to be interrupting but we just got a call from the hospital that the other boy just passed away."

Jim pounded his fist on his desk. "Dammit!"

Dan shook his head. "What a shame. Young kids like that."

"Boss, would you like me to do something for the families?" Rocky asked.

"Good idea Rock. Ask Tom if the budget has some extra money for a donation. Let's supplement it with a collection," suggested Jim.

Rocky nodded. Then Martha buzzed another visitor into the office. It was John Peters dragging a handcuffed, incoherent Sam Clayton past the heavy security door. They were followed by Jack Morton. He deposited the prisoner at the foot of Tom Hyde's front desk.

"Got your favorite resident here," Peters stated.

Jim, Dan, Paul, and Rocky watched the scene unfold from inside Jim's office.

"What's it this time?" Tom stood up.

Peters tried to keep Sam steady on his feet. "Drunk and disorderly… he broke a couple of vehicle windshields at Jack's business. Give him a day or two to sober up. Jack's pressing charges. He said it'll keep Sam out of further trouble."

Tom replied, "You got that right. I'll keep an eye on him."

Dan asked Jim, "Clayton's still up to his old tricks?"

Jim got up and walked out of his office. "Hold on Peters. I was on the phone with Hank this morning and he told me he saw Sam outside the morgue right after the explosion. I want to know how he got out of the hospital after that liquor store robbery attempt and why he wasn't sent to jail once they released him. Anyway, now he's in violation of his probation."

Jack's eyes lit up like fire. "Wait a goddamn minute. Can't he just sit in your jail 'till he's sober so he stays out of trouble?"

Sam Clayton doubled over and began to throw up.

"Hell, just put him in the jail for now. I'll call his probation officer," yelled Jim who clutched his ribs in pain.

Rocky, Dan, and Paul ran to assist Sam.

"If you keep him in there any longer than he has to then I ain't pressing charges," Jack said.

"Forget it Jack. I'll make sure he gets a ticket straight to the state prison in Deer Lodge," Jim replied.

Jack took a step toward Jim but Tom got in-between them.

"Jim, I can handle this, I've taken care of Sam before. I'll put him in a cell and I'll take full responsibility," Tom said.

"Yeah, Tom can handle this," Peters replied.

"No... we're going by the book. No more free passes for Sam," Jim emphasized.

"Hey, you got anything to settle him down?" Peters asked. "He's got a loud mouth when he's drunk like this."

"I got something I can give him," Tom said.

"Where did you find him?" Jim asked Jack.

"I ain't his goddamn babysitter and I sure as hell ain't your suckup," Jack said. "I ain't gotta tell you nothin'."

Sam fell and continued to puke on the floor. He pushed himself up into a seated position and wiped his mouth across his sleeve. Sam's glazed eyes slowly looked around. He muttered, "Charlie's a'comin'. Get yer asses behind that ridge."

"What the hell's he babbling about?" Peters asked.

"The guy's having' a flashback from Vietnam," Dan said.

Jim relented. "Aw hell, clean him up and then throw him in cell four. Jack, I hold you responsible if you don't press charges and he gets into more trouble."

"You can't pull that shit on me. I know my rights."

"Jack, help us with him," Tom pleaded.

Tom and Peters lifted Sam under his arms while Jack and Dan grabbed his legs. They carried him into the cellblock.

When they were out of earshot, Rocky asked, "Think he'll be all right?"

Jim stood outside his office. "Hell, I've seen him drunk worse than this before. He'll be okay but Jack is pissing me off. If he pulls more crap like this in my office he'll be in a world of hurt."

A couple of deputies were distracted from their duties and Martha removed her headset at Jim's comment.

Rocky walked up to Jim, placed a hand on his shoulder and whispered, "Man, cool down."

Jim's focus returned. "You're right. I'm under a lot of stress. This is just too much."

·22·

Jim asked one of the deputies to disinfect the front office where Sam had vomited and douse the air with a can of Lysol. He noticed that the men were still occupied with getting Sam situated and gestured to Rocky to meet him in his office. There they discussed the issues at hand.

"Jim, you need to take some time off. You came back too soon from your injury plus someone took a shot at you, remember?"

"I remember."

"No wonder you're on edge. Plus the fact that we have a major homicide investigation going on here. I can't even imagine how difficult it must be for you to cope with Kate's recovery."

"I might take Hank's advice."

"What's that?"

"He wants me to go to counseling."

"That's not a bad idea."

"Isn't it a sign of weakness?"

"Listen buddy, when my marriage fell apart I spent two years in counseling. It saved my sanity."

Jim slowly nodded. "You're right. I should go, at least for Kate's sake."

Dan McCoy barged into Jim's office. "Where were we?"

"Can you assist with the investigation?" Jim asked.

Dan leaned back in his chair, "What are you paying?"

"Ten dollars an hour."

"Don't jerk me around. I can earn that tending bar at Campy's, plus tips... and then I get to see the strippers for free every night."

"What strippers?" Rocky asked.

"How about fifteen... plus expenses," suggested Jim.

Dan rubbed his chin. "Let me think about that."

"What strippers?" repeated Rocky.

Paul returned to Jim's office using a paper towel to wipe his hands.

"Sam all squared away?" Jim asked.

Paul dropped the paper towel in Jim's wastebasket. "Looks to be... Tom and Jack are staying with him a bit to make sure he doesn't choke on his vomit if he falls asleep."

Jim turned to Rocky. "Can you excuse us? I want to talk with Dan and Paul in private."

Rocky pointed to Dan. "I'll catch up with you later on those strippers."

Dan laughed. "No problem, city slicker."

Rocky closed the door behind him.

After the men settled down, Jim said to Dan, "This is hard for me to say."

Dan grew serious. "You're worried about Kate?"

Jim nodded. "Yeah, Kate."

"Aw hell, Jim. This thing will consume you." Dan let out a huge sigh and leaned back in his chair. "You're a glutton for punishment." Dan pointed at Paul. "You listen up here. This man's life ain't a pleasure to relive but you gotta know a little bit of his past."

"Go ahead. It'll stop me from thinking it's all a bad dream," pleaded Jim.

Dan began, "Jim's wife Kate was kidnapped and almost died."

"You're referring to the body parts ring?" Paul asked.

Dan leaned back in his chair. "Yeah."

"I followed that case. At the time I was working on a diplomat's murder in the Bahamas," Paul said.

"Then you know? Hell, the whole country was following that case on CNN. Jim, you'll have to testify," reminded Dan.

"Yeah, I'm not looking forward to that."

Dan put his hand on Paul's shoulder. "Since you know the basics, let's not put Jim through any more agony than he's already been through. Let's talk about this case." He leaned forward. "Jim, is there anything else we should know?"

Jim hesitated and then said, "There is one thing that's odd."

"What's that?" Dan asked.

"I found a few grains of black soil on the corpse. They remind me of that rich farmstead soil north of here."

"Why is that significant," Paul asked.

Jim replied, "You wouldn't see that soil where the bodies were found. There's nothing but light colored sand there."

Paul cocked his head. "You think the bodies were killed elsewhere and dumped there?"

"Maybe," interjected Dan. "Or maybe that soil came from somewhere else and got transferred to the body."

"Dan, sounds like you accepted my offer."

Dan waved his finger at Jim. "Hey, I ain't said yes. I'm still thinking it over."

Jim glanced at the briefcase that Paul positioned on his lap and heard him flick open the latches.

"I've got something to show you." Paul grabbed a pair of latex gloves from his pocket, reached into the briefcase, pulled out an evidence envelope and extracted a cloth wrapping. He placed it on Jim's desk. "Take a look at this."

They heard the front door open as Paul unfolded the cloth, uncovering an artifact. Jim rubbed his forehead. "This isn't good."

"Why?" Paul asked.

Jim whispered, "It's an arrowhead with a hole in the center. It looks too old. Jacob will be all over us. He'll shut down the investigation."

Paul snatched the arrowhead off Jim's desk, rewrapped it, stuck it back in the envelope and buried it in his briefcase. He pulled off his gloves, jammed them in his pocket and set the briefcase down on the floor next to his chair. He spoke softly, "I found it on the banks of the Little Bitterroot. We'll do testing on it. You can thank the rains for uncovering it and a coyote for digging it up."

Jim's phone rang. "Yes Martha... oh... send him in." Jim stared at Dan and Paul with caution in his eyes. "It's Jacob Walkabout," he whispered.

A knock, a door hinge squeak, and then Jacob Walkabout poked his head inside. "Mind if I join you?" Jacob asked. He remarked to Dan, "What brings you here old man?"

"I'm helping with the case. What's it to you?"

"Don't show your wrinkly face on the Rez again." Jacob sneered at Dan.

"Hey, they'll be no talk like that in my office," Jim said.

Jacob pointed at Dan. "This man's got no business seeing Esmeralda Hightower. She's got a teenage son to care for, she don't need to be caring for an old man too."

Dan stood up and raised his voice. "I'll see whoever I damn please!"

Jim got up from his chair. "I said they'll be none of that in my office."

Jim spied Jacob looking around for somewhere to spit tobacco juice.

"This chaw's about ready to spurt," Jacob said.

"Here." Jim removed the wastebasket from under his desk and placed it in front of Jacob.

Jacob leaned over, held his braided hair back, and spat a brown, streaky fluid into the basket. "Jim, I got the autopsy report from Kelly." Jacob stared at Paul. "But the FBI won't release the bodies to my tribe. I can't be responsible for the *ṁalyè es šeýiłk.*"

"The what?" Paul asked.

Jacob glanced at Jim. "Tell him all about it. That's why the storm hit there, why more bodies turned up, and why two boys from the tribe died. I warn you, there will be more death and destruction unless the bodies are returned to us and purified."

Paul turned to Jim. "What is this all about?"

"Don't worry, we'll fill you in," Dan said.

Jacob again spat into the basket. "Jim, I want to know what else you found."

"See Deputy Rocky Salentino outside. He'll fill you in on what we know."

Jacob's piercing eyes stared at Dan. He spat again into the wastebasket, and then walked out.

"Dan, stay in the building until Jacob leaves the property."

"What the hell for?"

"I don't want any trouble."

"What am I gonna do inside here?" Dan asked.

Jim suggested, "Find out where Sam got the liquor."

Dan shook his head. "That'll be like talking to the damn wall."

Jim turned to Harris. "Paul, let's take a ride to the railroad bridge. I want to see what's going on up there."

Paul grabbed his briefcase. "Sure, let's go."

The two got into Paul's car and headed toward U.S. Highway 228. Jim brought Paul up to speed regarding the legend that Jacob spoke about.

Paul had to stop for a herd of bighorn sheep that partially blocked the road. He glanced at Jim. "Interesting story that legend but what I really want to know is why you retired from the NFL."

Jim stretched his arms. "It's a long story."

"I've got time. Was it for the salary you're making now?" Paul said sarcastically.

Jim stared into space and responded truthfully, "It was three years of playing, the injuries and... missing my wife."

"Did they void your contract?"

"When I was drafted, I signed a three-year deal. I fulfilled my contract and then told them I was retiring. They even let me keep my signing bonus."

"I heard that was worth over a million. Hell, I only got a hundred grand each for my two seasons. Were they pissed when you left?"

"My line coach, Joe Jackson, still calls me once a year in the spring hoping I'll change my mind."

The sheep finally climbed onto the shoulder allowing Paul to drive past. "You're closing fast on that window of opportunity. Think you'll ever go back?"

Jim stared at the sagebrush along the highway. "I'm not getting any younger. I don't think I'd go back."

Paul changed the subject. "Do you really like it out here?"

"I was born and raised on the Crow Reservation until I was sixteen. I was riding bareback over the *Baahpuuo Isawaxaawuua* before I ever learned to drive a car."

"What's that mean?" Paul asked.

"The Hitting Rock Mountains. White people call them the Pryor Mountains. My tribe believes the Little People live there."

"What little people?"

"Little People with spiritual powers."

"I'm finding there's a lot to learn about your people. Tell me why you left the reservation."

Jim turned to Paul and warned, "Don't ever ask me that again."

"Sorry." Paul stared at the pavement.

They reached the spot alongside the road where the high school photography club had taken the pictures. Paul parked the car while Jim got out and looked toward the bridge through his binoculars.

"See anything," Paul asked.

"Nope. Here you take a look." Jim handed the binoculars to Paul and then crossed the road, over the guardrail and down the embankment.

Harris put the glasses down and yelled, "Hey, what are you doing? Hold on." Paul rushed to where Jim had climbed the guardrail and looked for him in the brush. Jim had walked nearly twenty yards as the agent desperately tried to catch up. "I thought you were supposed to be recuperating from surgery?"

"I'm fine," Jim said. He continued through the brush toward an old logging road that scooted under the bridge.

When they reached the spot where Rocky had said Paul found the footprints, Harris grabbed Jim's arm.

"Right here. This is where I found the tracks," Paul said.

They investigated the area and looked for additional evidence to prove that someone had been there. After more than twenty minutes without having found anything, Jim walked up the graded hill to the tracks. He called to Paul, "Get up here."

The FBI agent, out of breath from the run up the hill, looked toward where Jim was pointing. Lying on the railroad ballast was a small bleached object no longer than an inch or two. Paul reached into the pocket of his suit jacket and pulled out another pair of gloves, tweezers, and a plastic bag. With the tweezers in his gloved hand, he picked up the object and placed it into the plastic bag.

"What do you think," Jim asked.

"Looks like a small piece of bone with some skin and hair attached. If it's human we can test for a DNA match with the other bodies."

"This is not good."

Paul said, "I don't like the feel of this either. My experience tells me this isn't your typical serial killer. This investigation is going to keep spinning its wheels until we get more resources up here. I'll call in a profiler and have the Salt Lake City Field Office set up a temporary headquarters."

Jim stared at the sunny skies with its wispy clouds, spread from horizon to horizon. With fists clenched he said, "Don't do this to my ancestor's land, she doesn't deserve it."

Paul wiped the perspiration from his brow. "I know how you feel, but we have to conduct a thorough investigation."

Jim stared at Paul. "I wasn't speaking to you or about the investigation."

"Then who were you speaking to... and what were you speaking about?" Jim turned away but Paul put his hand on Jim's shoulder. "Look, so far this has only caught the county and state news but once we bring the regional guys up here, it'll get national attention. The wire services that follow our VCMO crime unit will be on this like flies on butter."

"VCMO?"

"Violent Crimes and Major Offenders Task Force," Paul replied. Without a word, Jim stared at the blue sky. Paul tapped him on the shoulder. "Come on; let's search for footprints and tire tracks."

·23·

A few days later, on an early sunny morning, a two-door Red Jeep Cherokee slowed to a stop on the eastbound shoulder of U.S. Highway 228. A sandy-haired young man dressed in khaki shorts with multiple pockets on each leg picked up his duffle bag and ran to the vehicle's open passenger door. An olive safari shirt and straw hat completed his outfit.

"Where are you heading?" asked the driver, a middle-aged man dressed in jeans and a flannel shirt. His bronzed skin and craggy features betrayed the outdoor lifestyle and the manual labor that had taken a toll on his body. He wore a braided ponytail. Red, white, yellow, and black beads fashioned in the form of a necklace peeked from under his unbuttoned shirt.

"My name's Steve Clancy. I'm meeting a county engineer near Lakeside up by Flathead Lake. He's with the Solid Waste Authority."

"Pleased to meet you, my name's Willie Otaktay. Where's your elephant gun?" Willie asked with a smile after staring at Steve's outfit.

"Pardon me?" Steve replied.

Willie laughed. "You look like you're hunting for big game. Where're you from?"

The boy pointed to the tattoo on his forearm. "Can't you tell, Ohio State Buckeyes."

Willie laughed again. "I knew you weren't from around these parts."

"You can tell?"

"Let me give you a piece of advice. Go to the nearest Salvation Army Store and buy a pair of worn jeans and a flannel

117

shirt." Willie pointed to Steve's head. "And get rid of that hat. Where's your car?" Willie asked.

Steve took off his hat. "I don't have one. I just started this job with the National Conservation Alliance. Until I get settled in Montana, I'm staying at a motel in Sullivan. I'm an environmental scientist."

"Come on in. I can take you as far as Big Stump. You'll have to hitch a ride from someone else the rest of the way."

"That's fine with me." Steve threw his bag in the back and climbed into the Jeep. As he sat in the passenger seat, he grabbed his side.

"You all right?" Willie asked.

Steve shrugged. "It's an old football injury. I'll be fine."

Willie and Steve remained silent as the Jeep headed east toward the western arm of Flathead Lake. Finally, Willie turned to the youngster and said, "You should be careful hitchhiking around the Rez."

Steve noticed the pearl handle hunting knife in the brown leather scabbard that hung from the dash. "Why?"

"There's a serial killer on the loose. At last count, they've found about four or five carved up bodies. You best watch yourself."

Steve gulped. "Is it women that they're killing?"

Willie laughed. "Now, how the hell would I know? I did hear a rumor that they didn't find enough body parts to tell if they were men or women."

Steve shuddered. "What man would do that?"

"My people say it's an evil spirit but don't believe that shit."

Steve looked out the window, and then turned to Willie. "You're Native American?"

Willie nodded. "Otaktay is Sioux for *Kills Many.*"

Steve shuddered again.

"Do you live on the reservation?"

"Have all my life except for the time I spent in prison."

"How is it there?"

"Prison sucks."

"No, not prison... the reservation."

Willie slowly turned his head and faced Steve. "It sucks too. My father died when I was nine and my mother died when I was eleven. My seven brothers and me went to live with my aunt and her boyfriend. My two younger sisters got adopted by white people when I was thirteen and I haven't seen or heard from them since."

"I'm sorry."

Willie's attention returned to the road. "I don't need pity from white people."

"I'm not trying to pity…"

"Shut up!" shouted Willie, and then went on as calmly as could be. "One of my brothers hung himself when I was fifteen and when I was nineteen two others got arrested for murder. Another one's in prison for selling drugs and another left. We haven't heard from him in seventeen years. My oldest brother, the normal one of the bunch, has diabetes and heart disease. That's who I'm going to visit today in Horace."

"I'm sorry. You've really had your share of bad luck."

"Bad luck? You don't know what bad luck is." Willie slammed on the brakes and steered the Jeep to a halt on the shoulder. He stared at Steve while the boy reached for the door handle. Willie grabbed the boy by the arm. "Bad luck was seeing my dad come home drunk and beat my mom right in front of my eyes and then watch him blow his own head off with a shotgun. Bad luck was knocking on my cousin's door in January to share our government-issue cheese and then finding his family frozen to death because they had no electricity or the money to heat their trailer."

Willie released his grip on the boy's arm and then the boy asked, "I'm sorry, what can I do to help?"

"You want to help? Tell your friends what I just told you. There are some people who don't know this exists, more who don't believe it exists, and the rest just don't give a damn."

Steve said, "My best friend's dad is a United States Senator from Ohio. I'll write to him about what you said and mail it today." Steve asked, "If he wants to speak with someone out here, can they contact you?"

"Keep me out of it."

"Why?"

"Don't ask."

"Isn't there someone that he can contact if he has questions?"

"*Issaxchí-Káata.*"

"Who?"

"Little Hawk... Jim Buchanan. He's the sheriff of Cedar County." Willie turned to Steve. "Think you can remember that name?"

"Little Hawk... Sheriff Jim Buchanan. I can. How do you know him?"

Willie laughed. "The last time I got in trouble he was the highway patrolman who arrested me. That's when I turned my life around. If it wasn't for Little Hawk I'd be back in prison."

Steve opened the door a crack. "Thanks for the ride. You can let me off here."

"Hey, I said I was going to drop you off in Big Stump. We ain't there yet."

"I think I'll find another ride."

"Look, I'm sorry if I laid too much on you all at once. I've had a bad day, got three construction job rejections already. You don't have to worry, I'm not going to hurt you."

Steve closed the door. "Okay, but just as far as Big Stump, right?"

"Right... just as far as Big Stump."

Willie drove the Jeep back onto the road.

Steve asked, "Why did they send you to prison?"

"Which time?"

"I dunno... the first?"

Willie winked at Steve. "Manslaughter."

·24·

It was the end of the workweek. Inside the sheriff's office, Jim sat at his desk reviewing the autopsy report on the body Linda found. He heard a car drive up. Pushing aside the blinds, he watched Rocky climb out of a brand new SUV. Jim hurriedly went outside.

"Ain't she a beauty!" Rocky patted the shiny new, black Ford Expedition as if it were a puppy. "I picked her up this morning, spent an hour washing and waxing it."

Jim beamed a smile. "It's huge. How did you get everything done so quickly?"

Rocky smiled. "Last week Mayor Evans appropriated the money that was voted on at the last town meeting and had a check cut. Tony at the dealership had this on the lot. He sent it to get decaled when I gave him the word it was okayed. He got a good deal on some used equipment from the highway patrol."

Jim's eyes drifted from the grill to the side panels and then to the enormous wheels. He locked in on the Cedar County insignia on the driver's door. "I'm speechless. It's perfect."

Rocky opened the passenger door. "Look, I even got you a new shotgun setup in the front, just like your old car. I even got you a new Bowie knife in a special attachment on the dash. Tony installed them just like I told him."

While Jim and Rocky admired the new car, a Taylor black and white drove into the parking lot. Captain Linda Stevens, Police Chief John Peters, and Deputy Police Chief Dave Anderson stepped out of the vehicle.

"Hey, new SUV?" Linda asked.

Jim smiled. "Yeah… doesn't it look great?"

"Yeah it does. Good for you," she said.

Peters walked up to the car. "So, got yourself a brand new car to replace the one that got all burnt up?"

"What now Peters?" Jim asked.

"Nothing, just looking at your fancy new car," Peters replied as he circumnavigated the outside of the vehicle. He bent over to inspect its every line and feature.

"What do you want?" an impatient Jim asked.

"Nothing about the car, but the investigation… that's what I'd like to talk about." He motioned to Deputy Chief Anderson. "Dave, there ain't even one dent on this monstrosity."

Deputy Chief Anderson laughed.

"Of course not, it's brand new. I haven't even driven it yet," Jim testified. "Don't you have any town business to attend to?"

"Only when I get some details on the investigation," Peters insisted. "I have a right to know what's going on." He looked back at Anderson and smiled.

"You want information, check with Hank Kelly. I haven't completed my report."

"Kelly is stonewalling. Even on the body that Captain Stevens found."

Jim walked up to Peters. "Find out anything about that white supremacist group at the church?"

"I passed it on to Deputy Chief Anderson."

Jim turned and glanced at Anderson who was out of earshot of the conversation. "What did he find out?"

"Nothing yet but he's working on it. We do know that group is planning to hold a rally in front of the town hall today. We're going there to make sure it doesn't get out of hand."

Peters turned toward his car, one hand on the door handle. "Buchanan, we need to work together on the bodies. Aren't you coming?" Peters barked out at Linda who walked up to him.

"Go on without me. I'll see if I can get the info you want on the body I found and then catch up with you later."

"Good, you do that!" Peters and Anderson climbed into the squad car and drove away.

Linda turned to Jim. "Chief hasn't been himself lately."

"That election loss is consuming him."

Linda stared at Jim long and hard. "It ain't all about the election. Ever since he brought Anderson on the job he's been acting different. Anderson suggests something, Peters does it. Anderson criticizes protocol and Peters makes changes. I'm worried if I say or do the wrong thing I'm going to lose my job. I can't afford for that to happen. Every month that apartment costs me a week's paycheck."

"Linda, maybe you need a roommate to share the costs?" suggested Rocky.

"I'm not rooming with you," she said and walked toward the sheriff's office.

Rocky shouted to her, "Hey, I wasn't talking about me." He turned to Jim. "I wasn't talking about me."

Jim laughed and said to Rocky, "Can you take care of the office? I need to speak with Linda." Rocky agreed and Jim walked toward Linda, calling out, "Hold on, Linda." Jim caught up to her. "We need to discuss what's going on here in private... away from the offices. Can we meet sometime after work?"

"Where?"

"My house a week from Saturday. Kate is in New York with Alma Rose. It didn't feel safe for her to be here after what she went through. I hired a housekeeper. She'll cook us dinner. Then we can talk in private."

"Okay... what time?"

"About six, is that good? Do you have any other plans?"

"Plans? No, I don't have any plans."

"Good. Then keep that date open. It'll be nice to talk and keep it confidential."

Jim heard the sound of a car pull into the parking lot. Paul Harris stepped out as Jim glanced inside to see Hank in the passenger seat.

"Hank and I were wondering if you wanted to take a ride up to that railroad bridge and look for more evidence?" Paul asked.

"I'll do that. Maybe Linda wants to come too?" Jim suggested.

"Yeah, sure I'll go," Linda replied.

Paul slid into the driver's seat while Jim and Linda climbed in the back. Hank nodded to them and they exchanged pleasantries. After a short drive along U.S. Highway 228 they arrived at the location where Jim and Paul had stopped the day before. Paul grabbed a forensic kit from his trunk and they hiked down the embankment, trampled through the brush, and then onto the old logging road. They examined the area for tire tracks but only found the ones previously identified by Paul and marked with crime scene flags. The warm morning sun took its toll as they finally reached the railroad bridge.

Hank gazed at the elevated grade. "You expect me to walk up that?"

Jim laughed. "I can carry you."

"No one is going to carry me." Hank trudged up the hill as Paul, Jim, and Linda followed.

Reaching the track bed Paul gazed at the landscape. "You really get a good feel for the wide-open spaces up here."

Jim pulled off his Stetson with his right hand and rubbed his left forearm across the sweat on his brow, "The last time I was here I felt the spirit of someone protecting us. I can't say that today."

Paul mocked him. "Another Native American legend?"

Jim placed his hat back on his head and looked at the FBI agent. "Believe what you want, just be careful."

Linda tried to change the subject. "Look at that big sky."

Hank scanned up and down the railroad tracks. "The hell with the scenery. Let's do our job and get out of here. I've got plans this weekend."

The morning breeze increased in intensity. The group of four turned their heads to avoid the wind-swept dust particles swirling in the air. Each had taken gloves, evidence bags, and tweezers from Paul's car. They split up in pairs and all agreed to meet back at the bridge in one hour. Paul and Linda waved to Hank and Jim as they parted.

Paul and Linda hiked down the tracks, past the bend and out of sight to the west about a half-mile from the bridge. Jim instructed them to work their way back while Hank and he searched the area closest to the bridge. The two men scoured the area without finding any new evidence.

Hank sat on one of the rails. "I'm too old for this."

"I wish old age was my only problem. I'm falling apart," confessed Jim who sat on the graded track bed.

"I'm good at dissecting. How about giving me a shot at putting you back together." Hank laughed.

"Just work on rebuilding your office."

Linda and Paul, continuing their search for evidence farther down the tracks, just reappeared from around the bend and were about three-hundred yards from where Hank and Jim waited.

"Look at them," Hank sighed as he pointed to the younger pair. "They have the energy we used to have." Hank watched Linda walk on the railroad ties between the tracks and Paul followed along the left side of the graded track bed. "What was that?" Hank asked.

Jim frowned. "What was what?"

"That!"

Jim stood up, walked over to Hank, and placed his hand on the rail. "That?"

"So now you feel it. What is it… an earthquake?"

"No."

"Then what?' asked Hank.

Jim squinted up and down the tracks and then his gaze centered on a glare from the direction of Taylor. It grew brighter and the vibrations intensified.

"What do you see?" Hank turned toward the direction of Jim's stare.

Jim scrutinized Linda's oblivious behavior. He yelled to her, "Get off the tracks!" Jim stared but saw no response from her. Jim pushed Hank away from the tracks, cupped his hands, and yelled as loud as he could, "Linda, get off the tracks!"

Jim ran toward Linda. The distance between them reminded him of the length of three football fields but this opponent was more formidable than any Jim had ever faced on the gridiron.

Jim noticed Linda watching him run to her and that is when the sound of two SD-40-2 locomotives, over one hundred ninety tons each with a more than fifty-car freight train in tow, rounded the bend. Traveling at twenty miles per hour, Jim knew a full emergency stop would still have the engines blow right by them.

The train's horn blared loud and long and its wheels squealed on the iron rails as its braked approach narrowed the distance between it and Linda.

She turned to pivot off the tracks but her foot became lodged in-between one of the rails and a railroad tie. She tried to pull off her boot but as she struggled, her foot lodged deeper. Linda screamed for help against the wailing of the train horn.

Paul ran up to her and struggled to free her boot. As the heat of the train's engine engulfed them, Paul pulled again and freed Linda's boot.

She took one last look when the train was only a few feet away and then Paul pulled her off the tracks. They tumbled down the embankment, through the sagebrush, and fell head over heels down the hill as the train rumbled by.

·25·

Jim jumped out of the way as the train breezed by finally screeching to a lumbering halt. The noise from its air brakes scattered the little critters that had been hiding in the brush.

Jim peered under the train's wheel trucks for Paul and Linda. His view was blocked and his attention diverted by the sound of the train's sliding cab window.

"Goddamn fools," shouted a voice from within the cab of the second locomotive. The loud hum of the idling diesel engines filled the otherwise quiet morning air. A man with a full gray beard poked his head from the window and threw an apple at Jim. "Don't you know to stay off the tracks when you see a train a throttlin' eight?"

Jim stood his ground as the fruit hit the gravel roadbed twenty feet in front of him. "Sparky, I don't have time for this," Jim shouted. He crouched and ran under one of the train's boxcars across to the other side. Jim lost his footing on the steep grade and he rolled with the fall.

He finally came to rest halfway down the embankment and felt the scratches along his arms from the tumble. He saw two motionless bodies farther away. "Linda!" he called and ran to her.

When Linda moved her legs she yelled and grabbed her knee.

"Anything broken?" Jim asked.

"I hope it's just a sprain from the fall. Check on Paul. He hasn't moved."

Jim braced Linda's arm over his shoulder and they walked toward Paul. He was face down at the bottom of the embankment, his intact forensic kit just a few yards away.

"Are you all right?" Jim asked.

Paul slowly lifted himself off the ground. "My head's killing me."

"You saved Linda's life."

Linda deadpanned, "You guys are going to kill yourselves trying to save me."

Jim smiled but then changed his mood abruptly when he spotted an embedded bottom half of a broken liquor bottle with its attached label intact in the ground next to Paul. He pulled an evidence bag from Paul's kit and pulled on a pair of forensic gloves. Jim firmly grabbed the item and dropped it into the bag. He felt Linda and Paul's intent gaze.

"We should investigate this entire area," Jim said.

Paul set small yellow flags from his forensic kit at every spot where they found possible evidence. After nearly ten minutes, the powerful blast of the locomotive's air horn ended their forensic exploration.

"Let's discuss our options up there." Linda pointed toward the tracks.

They collected the individual evidence bags and packed them in a large heavy duty plastic bag. Jim glanced back and observed an extensive field of yellow flags. The group then limped up the hill toward the train's locomotive.

The signalman from the caboose joined Hank who had been speaking with Sparky and his apprentice outside the cab. Hank gestured to Jim. "They have a first aid kit."

Sparky opened the door to the cab revealing its small but efficient working quarters. "We got bandages here." Exposed to most everything on the job, the railroad engineer was well equipped. He gave Linda an ace bandage and she wrapped it around her knee over her uniform pants.

Hank pointed to the plastic bag that Paul carried. "Looks like you collected evidence, good work." He grabbed a bag of ice from Sparky and handed it to Paul who was rubbing the side of his head. "You probably suffered a slight concussion. This will hold you over until you see a doctor."

"Thanks for the help." Paul placed the ice pack to his head.

"Seeing that y'all could have died, you owe me an explanation." Sparky barked.

Paul replied, "I'm with the FBI and we're investigating a series of homicides."

"Not a one's been killed on these tracks in more'n ten years," Sparky stated. "What'cha lookin' fer?"

"Do you have the train schedules for this track."

"Call Mike Mezerock at the Missoula office. He has that information. All I'll tell ya is what you can see wit yer own eyes. There's morning freight every other day. That's what this is, and there's a return freight in the afternoon on the following day."

"Where do you start and what time do you leave?" Paul asked.

"Like I said, call Mezerock."

"Can we look in your cars?"

"You got a warrant?" Sparky asked.

"No but I can get one easy enough."

Sparky pointed his index finger at Paul. "Then you do that. This is company property. I ain't authorized ta let anyone search it, much less some government suit."

"Hold on Sparky," Jim said. "Have you seen anything unusual around this bridge?"

Sparky stroked his white beard. "Around this bridge, not on railroad property? Yeah, I seen somethin', most every time in the afternoon shadows."

"What did you see?" Paul asked.

Sparky stared at Jim. "I'll answer your questions but not from this guy."

Jim took over the conversation. "Please tell me what you saw."

"Ya see, there's this old truck. Sometimes it's there, sometimes it's not. You can't see it from the tracks. Ya gotta be up high, like in this here cab."

"What color is the truck?"

"Rusty old thang. Blue, green, it was hard to say where the color ended and the rust began." Sparky stroked his beard and boasted, "Used to wager with my men whether the truck would be there or not."

"That's an old logging road down there, right?" Hank asked.

Sparky waved his arm. "Yeah but they don't use it no more. Loggers have better ways to get in n'out. We don't even haul that much timber no more, damn truckers took that over."

"So where is this vehicle parked?" Jim asked.

"North of the bridge, this side of the loggin' road."

"Can you show us where it is?" Hank asked.

"If it's there you'll find it. Gotta go."

"Thanks," Jim said.

Sparky nodded and the four civil servants stood by the side of the tracks as Sparky revved up the diesel engines. The boxcars lurched as the wheels struggled to gain traction against the rails. It was like tires on ice as the train began its slow arduous task to build up speed. Jim and the others waited to cross the tracks while the boxcars rolled by.

Paul tore off a bandage from his arm. "I hate it when people don't cooperate."

"Sparky?" Jim laughed. "Today was one of his better days. People around here don't like the Federal Government. Try greeting them with a handshake and you're liable to find yourself staring at the business end of a shotgun."

Linda suggested, "Let's look for that truck and see if there's more broken bottles like we found up here."

As they trudged down the embankment, Jim showed Hank the bone fragment they had found. Jim also worried about him. Hank was older and perhaps this was too much for him.

Reaching the bottom, they encountered the old logging road, a dirt path that contained ruts, gullies and sprouted weeds. Used decades ago when the timber industry was booming and relied on the railroad to move lumber, it had since fallen into disrepair.

"I don't see a truck," Hank said as he sat on a rock to rest.

"Based on what Sparky said, we probably can't see it from the road," Jim said. "Paul, let's take a walk."

Paul and Jim left the group and walked a few hundred yards from the bridge. They noticed a new set of tire tracks and followed them for a few hundred feet along the side of the road until they disappeared. In the belly of a little gully, where there was barely room for a vehicle, they saw the dull, rust-pocked grill of a truck half-covered with loose brush.

Paul pointed. "We found it."

They drew their guns and cautiously approached the vehicle. The truck appeared to be either a green or blue panel truck but the paint was so faded and along with the rust, it resembled a multi-colored tapestry, just like Sparky described.

Jim remembered the panel truck as the type that farmers used to haul produce to the market. Covered with scratches and dents, it emitted an odor of decay reminiscent of spoiled eggs.

"What do you make of it?" Paul guardedly kept his voice low.

Jim assessed the truck. "It has no plates. As far as I'm concerned, it's an abandoned vehicle."

Donning the latex gloves he kept in his pocket, Jim tried to open the passenger door but a large dent effectively welded the door to the frame. They walked to the back of the panel truck where Jim stood guard with his revolver. Paul reached for the door handle but the leaves and branches that covered the door limited his progress.

"I can't get to it," Paul said.

Jim holstered his revolver. "Let me try."

Paul stood back and raised his pistol. Jim reached past the shrubs and grabbed the door handle. After a few tugs, it opened. Jim quickly buried his nose in his armpit to block the smell of decay. He peered inside. He noticed that the truck was empty except for a rusted red cooler behind the passenger seat and three empty wooden crates in the middle of the truck with the labels, Canadian Whisky, Scotch Whisky, and Kentucky Bourbon.

"Paul, see these crates? We should check to see if any of the bottle fragments we found match what was once in these crates."

"It may link the illegal liquor sales on the reservation with this truck and the railroad."

"It's our best guess right now." Jim crept up to the cooler. "We need to get this cooler to Hank right away."

Paul asked, "Why, what do you see?"

"Check the bottom right corner of the cooler."

"The maggots?" Paul asked.

Jim slipped on a new pair of gloves. "It's what's attracting those maggots that I'm concerned about." He focused on a stain dominating the floor of the panel truck next to the cooler. "It looks like blood. Can you take a sample?"

Paul scraped some of the dried blood and secured it in an evidence container. "Got it."

Jim opened the cooler and looked inside. He turned his face away as a horde of flies escaped into the air.

"Look at this," Jim said.

Inside the cooler, Jim pointed to a crusty clump of dried blood upon which sat a disembodied head missing its eyes, ears and lower jaw.

·26·

Hank called in a helicopter from the State's Medical Examiner's Office and at Jim's request had Rocky travel with them. Upon arrival, a forensic team snapped pictures of the area around the panel truck and then secured the cooler. They then transported the evidence back to Taylor. Hank drove Paul and Linda to the hospital in Paul's car. It was close to two o'clock in the afternoon when Jim and Rocky watched the 1977 blue GMC wrecker carefully maneuver onto the old logging road.

Jim stood up and greeted the truck driver. "Jack, about time you arrived."

Jack exited the truck with a cigar between his yellow-stained teeth and handed Jim a clipboard full of paperwork. "Don't complain Jim, this is your lucky day."

Jim signed his name and placed the pen on the clipboard. "Haul it to the garage in back of the sheriff's office."

Then Jack grinned. "No problem, but it'll cost you extra."

"Why?"

"Hell, this is off-road! My truck's alignment could get ruined from driving on this crap."

"You never towed off-road before?" Rocky asked.

Jack gave Rocky a sneer. "I have but I always tow with my lucky piece. Now it's missing."

Jim handed the paperwork back to Jack. "Lucky charm or not, my office has to pay for your overpriced tow."

"It's not overpriced. Tell you what, buy me a case of brown ale and we're square."

"Buy your own booze."

133

"Hey sheriff, you don't have to be a hardass."

Rocky took a step toward Jack. "Don't talk to my boss that way.　About time you learned some respect."

Jim held Rocky back. "Jack, just do the job you were called out for and give us a ride to town."

Jack hitched his winch to the underside of the panel truck and reclaimed the mountain of evidence from the brush. Jim and Rocky climbed onto the passenger side of the bench seat in Jack's truck. It was an uncomfortable threesome in the front made worse by the Roy Lewis Show on the radio.

"You like that crap?" Jim pointed at the dashboard speaker while his arm hung out the passenger window.

Jack spoke through a space between his cigar and cheek. "Only truth that's on the air and Roy says it like it is."

"I'm sure a lot of people would disagree," Rocky said.

Jack smiled. "Non-believers are trouble makers."

"Trouble is the game that radio show is playing," Jim said.

"Com'on sheriff. Roy's just spicing up the airwaves. What'cha got back there?" Jack asked as he puffed on his cigar, put the tow truck in gear and headed toward U.S. Highway 228.

"I can't tell you."

"You can tell me. I won't repeat it to a soul."

Jim removed his Stetson. "You know I can't discuss an ongoing investigation."

Jack blew smoke out the driver's window. "You mean the investigation the news reporters been hounding you about?"

"Yeah."

"Any suspects?"

Jim stared at the empty landscape that whizzed by. "Let's end this conversation right now."

Jack tossed his cigar from the truck. "Fine."

Jim turned away and stared at the road, which became a salient blur of light brown to his tired eyes. They reached the sheriff's office and pulled into the back lot. Jack maneuvered his tow truck to one of the garage bays and unloaded the panel truck.

"Anything else you need me for?"

"No," Jim said flatly.

"Hey, don't be pissed at me," Jack said with a sly smile. He tipped his cap and drove away.

·27·

When Jim returned to the sheriff's office he didn't waste time. He requested a ride from Rocky and they drove to the medical examiner's office. Julie Franklin from KTAY was already waiting in the parking lot along with newspaper reporters from the Taylor Bulletin and the Cedar County Ledger along with a bevy of TV camera operators.

Jim rushed to the building's entrance with Rocky running interference. When they reached Hank's office they were met outside the door by Paul Harris. "Paul, how are you and what did you find out?" Jim asked.

"I'm fine. Hank confirmed the head inside the cooler was male. We also found a small pile of black soil. Hank is holding the bottles for later examination. He wanted to work on the soil and the head before any possible DNA evidence further degraded."

Jim gestured toward the office. "Can we go inside and speak with Hank?"

"Let's do it." Paul turned the doorknob.

They met Hank and sat inside his office.

"What can you tell us?" Jim asked.

Hank got up from his desk and faced Jim. "We have a positive ID with the truck's black soil and the black soil from the Little Bitterroot River bodies. The head was in pretty bad shape. It wasn't so much that it was partially decomposed, it was grossly mutilated. As you may know there were a few missing parts."

"We assumed someone was in a hurry to either cut it into pieces or render it unrecognizable. We may have recovered it just in time," Jim suggested.

"I have a better guess," Hank said.

"What's that?"

"I've seen this repeated so many times in New York. It's a classic mob hit."

"In Montana… please explain?"

Hank continued, "When the mafia conducts a remote hit they need confirmation they got the right guy. So they cut off identifiable body parts and return them to whoever ordered the contract. My guess is the guy's ears, eyes and perhaps his lower jaw or even his teeth had discernable features, tattoos, piercings, gold fillings, or surgical implants that would identify the intended target."

"Why not just take a picture?" Jim asked.

"Photos can be faked. There's nothing like holding the real thing in your hands to prove they snuffed the right guy. Plus they can abuse those body parts any way they wish to insult the victim after death or show them to next of kin as a future threat or intimidation."

"Do we know whose head it was?" Rocky asked.

Hank continued, "Besides the blood and the teeth in the upper jaw there are a few strands of hair with the roots intact. We're checking them for hair color and we'll run a full DNA test on everything found in the cooler. That may take a while but we're sure that we can make a positive ID through dental records."

"Who contacted the media?" Rocky asked.

"I have no idea." Paul shrugged his shoulders.

"Someone is releasing information and I want to know who it is," Jim said.

Hank sat back down. "No one from my department."

"Maybe someone from the media saw the copter land?" Paul suggested.

"Rocky, can you look into this?" Jim asked.

"Will do."

"Good. Let's stay ahead of this. It's not just the fact that we've got bodies popping up all over the county but now someone is leaking info to the media. That will only complicate the investigation," Jim warned.

Hank said, "There's a guy from the Bureau I used to collaborate with when I investigated mob hits. I think he can help. I asked Paul to contact him."

·28·

The following Wednesday afternoon, after a bite to eat with Undersheriff Tom Hyde at Lucy's Luncheonette, Jim returned to the sheriff's office. Still unable to drive on his own, he thanked Tom for the ride and then waved to him as he drove away. Jim spied Dan McCoy sitting on the wooden bench outside the building.

"I heard you and Tom were at Lucy's. Where's he going?"

"He's said he had to study for a summer school test." Jim removed his Stetson and ran his fingers through his hair. "What are you up to?"

Dan suggested to Jim, "Let's talk in private."

They went inside and walked past the dispatcher's office. Jim waved to Martha and then ran his card through the card reader. Dan took a seat in front of Jim's desk, and leaned forward. "What's going on with that panel truck?"

"We completed a preliminary investigation. Harris brought the evidence to the FBI mobile lab. We found a head in the panel truck. Two full-time technicians are working on it."

Dan pointed his thumb toward the window. "The town's talking, Feds running around, harassing people, sticking their noses where they don't belong."

"The FBI is going to run a multiple murder investigation the way they want whether we like it or not. But you know Dan, this isn't the Taylor we grew up in. Something's not right. I don't know, I just don't know."

"What do you mean?"

"The people are different. They're not the same people you cared about when you were sheriff."

137

"Jim, you and I are the same. We haven't changed. If it takes the two of us to set things right, you can count on me. Now tell me like it is."

"We're keeping the truck impounded until we have an ID. Harris has his people doing a thorough look-through this week. He called in a profiler. The attorney general is providing him an office in the State Crime Lab building. Hank also called in an old FBI friend he said can help."

"This is getting way too deep for us," Dan said.

"That's not all. We found black soil in the cooler. That old clunker reminds me of the panel truck my dad drove when..."

"When you were a young kid dating Kate in the Taylor we grew up in?"

Time suddenly seemed to stand still for Jim. He heard Dan's words as a glaze seemed to envelop his eyes. He realized he had a private life as well and that Kate made him whole.

Dan continued to speak. "You're getting too involved, like when Kate got kidnapped. Take some time off."

"I'll think about it. So what've you been up to?" Jim asked, directing the focus away from him.

Dan stretched in his chair. "I've been busy. From the forensics the FBI did, the explosive charge in the morgue fire was confirmed as RDX."

A volley of words flew from Jim's mouth. "Great, now all we need is to find out who has access to that stuff."

"I can do one better."

"What's that?" Jim asked.

"Sam Clayton."

"Why Sam?"

"You may not know this but Clayton was a demolition expert in 'Nam. He blew up bridges, ammo dumps, buildings..."

"I knew he was in Vietnam but do you think he could have done this?"

"With his background and the flashbacks he gets, anything could set him off. He may have thought he was blowing up a machinegun battery."

"How's that possible?"

"Hell, the smell of diesel, the sound of an engine backfire, even silence. Shoot, he was just an eighteen-year old kid dropped into the middle of hell in '72. Damn, he even spent time as a POW in the North before some Army Rangers freed him."

"So you think he did this?"

"Let's just say that we need to ask him some questions."

"He's still sitting in my jail. Let's go talk to him."

Jim and Dan walked into the cellblock. Behind the maze of gated bars in cell number four, Sam snored on his bunk.

"Sam! Wake up!" shouted Jim.

Sam rolled onto his side, pulled the blanket over his shoulders, and faced the wall.

Dan banged his foot on the bars. "Sam, get the hell up."

Sam covered his head with a pillow. "Leave me alone!"

Jim opened the cell door, cuffed and dragged Sam outside, and brought him into the interrogation room and threw him down at a table. Jim and Dan sat across from him.

"Do you know anything about the explosion at the morgue?" Jim asked.

"No."

"A military explosive was used. If you had anything to do with this, you need to come clean. It'll hurt you in the long run if you're keeping anything from us."

"How in the hell would I get my hands on that shit?"

Jim warned, "Sam, you're looking at hard time in a federal prison. The fire is now part of an FBI investigation and the Feds don't know you from Adam. They won't be so easy on you like we are in Taylor."

Dan hollered, "You want to get your meals through a bean chute for the rest of your life?"

Sam sat upright. "You got a Marlboro or a Camel?"

Dan pulled a pack of cigarettes from his shirt pocket and handed one to Sam. He then grabbed his matches and lit the cigarette. Sam took a deep drag on an unfiltered Camel.

"You gonna talk now?" Dan asked.

"I'm innocent. I don't know nothin'."

Jim stood up and leaned over the table. "Sam, we'll charge you with attempted murder unless you tell us who else was involved. Are they worth it?"

Sam took a drag, exhaled and pulled off an Irish Waterfall. "I ain't going to the big house again." He glanced at the floor, then looked up and stared at Jim. "I want a lawyer."

"I'll get you one."

After Sam finished his smoke, Jim led him back to his cell, uncuffed him and then locked the cell door. Jim and Dan walked to Jim's office.

Dan sat down. "I think he did it. Why didn't you ask him about the murders?"

Jim replied, "I doubt he's a murderer. Blowing up the morgue is one thing but a federal conviction for multiple murders is a sure death sentence. I want to keep our options open and find out what he knows. Maybe he's responsible for the fire and maybe he's committed the murders. If that's not the case, he may at least lead us to the killer."

Dan said, "I see what you mean. It might be he didn't do anything. He could just be afraid of the Feds. He blames the government for everything that happened to him in 'Nam." Dan put his hand on Jim's shoulder. "Now, let's go take a good look at that panel truck together."

It was a sunny Saturday on June 8th. Jim returned home after a testy day at the office. Still waiting for information on the mutilated head from the panel truck, Jim's patience was wearing thin. There in the kitchen, Jia Li stood at the center island with a knife in her hand surrounded by a variety of vegetables.

"I say, Mista Jim! You late. Five-thirty! Soon Missa Stevens be here. Mista Kelly came while you out."

"Hank's here?"

"He upstairs in office looking at little men."

"Those are trophies, Jia Li."

"Look like little men to me."

Jim's weariness momentarily abated and he cracked a smile. Then he changed the subject. "Everything smells great."

She held the carbon steel wok up to Jim's nose and offered it to him. "Mandarin chicken stir fry. You have before?" she asked.

"No but you're a great cook," Jim said.

"Work as little girl chef in *Kě'ài de long*."

"English, please?"

Jia Li giggled. "Mista Jim you no understand my English anyway." She giggled again. "Word mean Lovely Dragon. It nice place in China. I show you sometime… you and Missa Kate come be my guest at home… I show where I work before I move here."

Jim patted her on the head just as he would have if Jia Li were his own daughter. He headed to his upstairs office and spied Hank reading the fine print on his Outland Trophy. "Got that in '83," Jim said.

"It doesn't look like that Joe Theisman award. You know where that player is sticking his arm out."

"It's not the Heisman Award it's the Outland Trophy... and it's called a stiff arm."

"Well, whatever they are, what's this one all about? I don't follow sports all that much."

"It's given every year to the best lineman in college football."

"Really, you're that good?"

"I was. That was a long time ago."

"What, thirteen years is long? Wait until you hit my age. Collecting a social security check is sobering."

"Hey do me a favor, go downstairs and wait for Linda to show up, I'm going to take a quick shower."

"You didn't tell me that she was coming."

"Surprise."

"Why?"

"I didn't want the two of you exchanging info about the case before we met tonight."

"Makes sense."

After his shower, Jim dressed and then rushed down the stairs. When he slipped back into the kitchen it was five minutes to six and the doorbell rang. Jim ran to get it.

Jim smiled. "Hi Linda, Hank's here. We'll have dinner and then talk about the case."

"Hank... great, I hope he has something to tell us."

Jim turned and walked back inside. Linda grabbed her hidden cane just outside the front door and limped forward. Jim noticed and asked, "I forgot... how's your knee?"

Linda grimaced. "It's a bad sprain. The doctor said I'll be fine in another four to six days. I have to ice it and keep off it."

"I'm glad it's only a sprain."

"No, I'm glad for what you did on the tracks... and at the morgue. I owe you a couple for watching my back."

"I know you'd do the same for me or for any other fellow officer."

Hank entered the foyer. "Linda, how are you?"

She hobbled along. "I'm not done yet, so don't write me off."

They entered the kitchen. Jim introduced Linda to Jia Li.

"So nice to meet you." Jia Li reached to shake hands but Linda took a step forward and her knee buckled. "Missa Linda, you hurt bad?"

Hank interjected, "She's got a sprained knee. Linda, make sure you keep that leg elevated tonight. I'll get some ice."

The four shared a cordial dinner.

Linda said, "Jia Li, thank you for a lovely meal. It was truly delicious."

"I'm glad you enjoy," Jia Li said graciously. "Oh," she said suddenly. "I almost forget!" She raced into the kitchen and took something from her bag. She brought a small green box back to the dining room table. "Mista Jim, this for you and your people at work." Jia Li handed the box to Jim. It was an unopened container of Chinese melon seed tea.

"Thank you, I'll bring it to the office."

Jia Li smiled and Linda nodded her approval. When they had finished dessert, Jia Li cleared the table.

Jim stood up. "I'm going to grab what we need to speak about from my upstairs office." When Jim returned he sat in an armchair.

"Hank, can you tell us anything else about the evidence we found in the cooler and around the railroad tracks? It's been more than a week now."

Hank stood up and strolled about the room assuming the type of posture and mannerisms as if he were presenting a lecture. "The soil composition was quick and easy and as you know we confirmed a match with the soil found on the bodies. We submitted a DNA request for analysis of evidentiary material from the head and provided the proper chain of custody forms. The FBI has now given priority to this case since it appears that organized crime may be involved but we still have to be patient and allow the process to work its natural course. DNA testing takes time and it's not like we can leapfrog ahead of every single other case in the pipeline. The backlog is four weeks. We did find a few hair roots and they will proceed with that and the remaining teeth for their DNA analysis as well. Once we have a DNA profile it will be easy to run the results against the FBI's database of known criminals."

"Any word on the bottle fragments we found by the railroad tracks?" Jim asked.

"We found fingerprint matches between some of the bottle fragments, the metal parts of the crates in the panel truck, and on the door handles and dashboard. They plan to run them through the database on Monday."

"It's good news that things are moving forward," Linda said.

Jim pointed out, "The soil confirmation seems to tie the bodies we found with the panel truck and possibly the liquor on the reservation."

Hank said, "Seems like. Now we just need to associate some names and faces with those prints."

"Hank, tell us about the panel truck. Did Harris share any evidence he found at the scene?" Linda asked.

Hank reached down and pulled a folder from his briefcase. "Paul conducted a full crime scene investigation. He's good."

"What did he find?"

"There was no other evidence in the truck that would ID who it belonged to; no marker, no registration. The VIN number was filed off both the dash and engine block. I remember a test I heard about in New York where they perform a chemical analysis on the VIN number area to reveal the filed down numbers. I ordered a kit." Hank got up and handed Linda his folder.

She thumbed through the papers. "Harris did a great job."

Hank restarted the conversation. "That black soil in the truck, it might be the same as what was found on the bodies. The lab is doing a DNA analysis on the bodies recovered so far, even the ones damaged in the morgue fire. They're also dusting the truck for more fingerprints."

"Where is that panel truck now?" Linda asked.

"In the county garage behind the sheriff's office," Jim said.

Hank continued, "They also found that the tire tracks from near the railroad bridge match the tires from the truck. That means that panel truck was driven recently."

Jim got up from his seat. "I guess we're making progress. Dan and I spoke to Sam Clayton. I think he's involved."

Linda piped up. "Clayton?"

Jim nodded. "Yeah, Clayton."

"I think you're barking up the wrong tree."

Jim stood up and gave Linda a queried expression. "Clayton was a demolition expert in the Army and they found RDX explosive residue at the morgue."

"He may be an arsonist but he's no murderer," Linda said.

"I know that but he also asked for a lawyer when we asked detailed questions."

"Jim, can you blame him?"

"There's something else I need to tell you both."

"What is it?" Hank asked.

"My dad used to have a truck just like the one we found on the old logging road."

Linda shook her head. "I don't know where you're going with this."

Jim took a deep breath. "If this truck was my dad's and the soil came from our farm, people are going to think I had something to do with this."

"I don't know who would," Hank said.

Linda laughed. "I think people are smarter than that."

"This town's changed. It's different here now."

"What do you mean?" Hank asked.

Jim shook his head. "This isn't the town I grew up in."

"I'll agree with you on that," Linda said.

"I spied on a white supremacist meeting in the basement at the old church on West Street. You think that's a group of smart people?" Jim asked.

"Now I have to laugh," Hank said. "Aren't prejudice and stupidity synonymous... maybe it's in response to the bodies being found?"

"I don't know. Matt Nelson is involved with the group."

"Nelson? He's got no record," Linda said.

"I know but I also don't want to hear that one day he took out his family and then blew his brains out. Linda, do me a favor and keep an eye on him?" Jim pleaded.

"Sure. That'll be easy. He works at the pharmacy across the street from the police station."

"Don't speak a word of this to anyone, especially his wife," Jim said.

"Will do. Does he still hold a grudge against you?" Linda asked Jim.

"The last time I saw him he told me to get the hell off his property."

·30·

Jim took a personal day on Monday to iron out some issues. First, he needed to call Kate in New York. Worried about how she would react to the news that more bodies have been found, Jim braced himself. The fact that he intended to tell her about the panel truck and the planned visit with a therapist gave him pause.

"Kate, how's New York... that's great. Listen, something's happened. Things are getting complicated. The investigation has expanded... no, it's okay, just a bit convoluted... how convoluted? More bodies have turned up and we found evidence in a panel truck that may have belonged to my dad... whoa, hold on. Just know that Hank and Linda are helping me. Look, I scheduled a visit with a therapist so that we can iron out some lingering issues... no, don't worry I've got everything under control." After nearly a half-hour conversation centered on his coming visits with the therapist, Jim ended the call with a, "Love you too."

Jim then telephoned Teresa Merrick, LCSW. She had a cancellation on her schedule so Jim booked an appointment for 2:30 p.m. that same day.

The clouds began to gather when Jim arrived in his white Ford pickup truck at a modest two-story gray building two blocks from the Taylor University Medical Center. Wearing khakis and a polo shirt, he waited in the truck for nearly fifteen minutes, then got out, stuck his hands in his pockets, put his head down and walked into the building five minutes early.

After the customary introductions, Teresa began the session. Jim spewed out his guts and told her everything. He began with his life on the Rez; his Crow mother Jenny Nightstar,

147

his Scottish dad's resentment that his son was a Mixed-blood Native, and his adolescent romance with fellow clan member Shoshanna Pepper that resulted in the birth of his daughter, Alma Rose Two Elk.

He then came clean about Kate and her health issues, the baby they lost earlier this year and the stressors related to his job. After more than an hour of therapy the session was almost over.

"You told me that Kate had a near-death experience."

"Yes... no, she really died. My daughter, Alma Rose is a shaman. She helped Kate navigate the path back from the other side."

"So you almost lost her."

Jim hung his head. "Yes, almost."

"I know why you are overly protective of your wife."

Jim felt his anger boil over. "I want her to be safe."

"Jim, it's one thing to worry about your wife's safety or to have your department place her in protective custody. You still haven't come to terms with losing your stillborn child but it's an act of desperation for you to demand that Kate travel to New York."

Jim repeated, "I just want her to be safe."

"By having her escape the situation, you are confirming that fear is ruling your spirit. Instead, you want to live your lives from a position of strength. That way you can confront the issues and empower yourself."

"How do I do that?"

"By being the kind and loving husband you are, realize that Kate is your partner and let her make decisions for herself."

"How will that keep her safe?"

"It will allow her to look after herself. If you are doing it for her it actually makes her more vulnerable."

"I worry that Kate won't be able to care for herself. The person or persons responsible for the murders may want to get to me through her."

"You said that Kate grew up in Montana."

"Yes she did. Right here in Taylor."

"Can she shoot?"

"She was actually a member of the high school gun club."

"Does she have access to weapons for protection?"

"She owns a Beretta pistol and the same Remington 700 bolt-action that she used in high school."

"Has she kept up her skill level?"

"We used to go shooting a lot when we were first married. She has a better eye than me." A wry smile escaped from Jim's otherwise solemn face.

"Then what are you afraid of?"

"We haven't gone as much since I started in law enforcement."

"Why is that?"

Jim thought for a moment amid a wave of epiphany. "I guess I want to protect her myself."

"You can't protect her all the time. She's her own best protector."

"Trusting Kate to protect herself is going to resolve my problems?"

"I didn't say that."

"Then what?"

"Based upon what you told me, the real reason why you want to protect Kate is that you couldn't protect your own mother from your hateful father. You also couldn't protect Shoshanna when she became pregnant with Alma Rose. You also couldn't protect the son you and Kate lost earlier this year. Finally, you couldn't protect Alma Rose because the tribe's council took her away from you and forbade anyone to tell her that you were her father."

"That changed earlier this year."

"For sixteen years you lived a lie?"

"You could say that."

"You couldn't even save yourself from yourself."

The convulsing slowly began deep within Jim's abdomen, and then erupted into a fit of trembling. He wept openly and ran his wrists across his eyes. Teresa handed him a tissue.

"I'm sorry." Jim took the tissue, wiped his eyes and then blew his nose. "I want to change my life."

Teresa handed Jim a book about a natural diet. "Take this… change happens not only when we modify our brain but also what we put into our body. Food affects our mood, confidence, and thought processes."

Jim took the book from her. "I will read this, thank-you."

"I believe it would be helpful for us to meet weekly."

"For how many weeks?"

"Until we can resolve the issues from your childhood. That would go a long way toward helping you recover your emotional well-being." Teresa pulled out her appointment calendar.

"But how long… a month, a year… five years?" Jim asked.

"As long as it takes."

·31·

It was a rainy Wednesday morning. Hank sat at Jim's desk in the empty sheriff's office sipping the coffee he had just brewed. Out of curiosity he first looked for Jia Li's melon seed tea by the coffee station but then realized that Jim hadn't been to the office since that Saturday dinner at his house. Hank knew what he really needed was a strong cup of coffee to kick start his morning.

He stepped up to the dispatcher's office. "Martha, it's a quarter after eight! Are you sure he's coming in today?"

"I'm sure," Martha replied. "It's his first day driving since the accident plus he was out Monday and Tuesday. He said he had issues to deal with. Give him a few more minutes."

Not a minute later Hank heard the outside door to the sheriff's office open. He stared at the bulletproof glass and noticed Jim standing in the doorway, his yellow raincoat dripped rainwater onto the tiled floor. After Jim removed his coat, Martha buzzed him in.

"Hey, you made it," Hank said, cradling his coffee cup.

Jim stood silent for a few seconds then walked past Hank. He hung his raingear on the coat rack behind his desk. His Stetson, lined with a waterproof cover took its customary place on top of the rack.

"So, you're not talking," Hank said matter-of-factly. "What the hell is bugging you now?"

"Nothing's bugging me," Jim said in a sharp tone. "Let me get a cup of coffee."

When he returned, Hank kept up the fusillade. "You sound pretty irritable to me, like you're on edge. Is there something on your mind?"

Jim placed the cup down on the table behind his desk. "It's private. I can handle it."

Hank laughed. "I know... you're missing Kate."

Jim raised his voice. "I said I can handle it, let's move on."

"Okay, okay." Hank smiled. "UPS finally delivered the VIN kit, and I got the DNA results on the bodies." Hank noticed that Jim's eyes widened.

"You did?" Jim asked.

Hank stood up and paced inside Jim's office. "Four bodies... one female, three male."

"Give me the autopsy summary."

Hank sat down. "The female is young, between twenty and thirty. Two of the men range in age from forty to seventy. The other is in his twenties. All appear to be Native."

"What about the head from the panel truck?" Jim asked.

"Doesn't match up with any of the bodies we found but its male too. We're still checking dental records but so far no luck."

"Any IDs?"

Hank sipped his coffee and then said, "We found Sam Clayton's fingerprints on the bottles, the crates and the panel truck. It looks like he's involved."

"He's sitting in my jail. I'll talk to him later. What about the testing on the bodies?"

"We haven't identified them yet. We think we know who the young woman is. I'm waiting for some info from Paul." Hank put his cup down and stared at Jim. "Can you get me names, dental records, and DNA samples from family members for anyone missing from the Flathead Reservation?"

Jim nodded. "I'll get them for you. I'm sure Jacob will cooperate."

Hank continued, "Paul checked with the railroad."

"Any leads?"

"The FBI spoke with every conductor that traveled on the route near the old logging road. They didn't see anything. Paul wanted to check every boxcar that came through Taylor. Some went to Chicago and other points out east. The ones that headed west ended up in Portland, Oregon. Anyway, there'd be hundreds of them to track down and with all the loading and unloading of cargo, any evidence in those box cars has long been destroyed." Hank leaned forward. "Because the bodies are Native, I think the media lost interest in the story." Hank noticed Jim sigh heavily.

"So you have the VIN kit?" Jim asked.

"I've got it right there in my briefcase."

"The truck's still in the garage. Just let me know when."

"Let's do it now."

"I'll grab some tools and we'll head out back."

Hank stood up and reached for his raincoat. "Do you mind if Jack Morton joins us? He called my office a few times. Wanted to know when we'd do the testing. Said he'd like to watch us work on the panel truck and he may be able to help us if we have any questions." Hank noticed Jim wince.

"Now he's an expert?" Jim asked.

"He claims he actually saw the highway patrol apply the test on a vehicle in Logan County last year."

"You give him a call... I won't," Jim said as he grabbed his coat.

Hank phoned Jack and invited him over. Then Jim drove Hank to the back garage in his SUV. Jim parked in front of a bay door. The men ran through the steady rain and accessed the garage through a side entrance.

They closed the door and removed their raincoats. The panel truck, a presumed silent partner to the hellish deeds that transpired in the Bitterroot Valley, sat parked next to a workbench and under a suspended florescent light fixture. The federal investigators removed much of the stench of decay as well as the surface evidence found inside the vehicle.

"Did you start it up?" Hank asked.

"We hotwired it. It runs great even though the body's shot to hell."

They examined the vehicle for at least half an hour. The rain pelted the garage bay door. Then they heard the sound of a truck. Jim opened the garage side door and let Jack inside.

"Glad you remembered me," Jack said. "It ain't often I get to see real police work." He smiled and pulled off his raincoat.

"No problem, maybe you can help us," Hank replied.

Jim lifted the hood of the vehicle and shined a utility light over the engine block where the VIN number had been. Hank opened the kit and began the chemical etching process. He cleaned the area and then applied the special fluid.

"Hank, how does this work again?" Jim asked.

"The fluid reveals the structural deviations of the characters. The original stamping process hardens the surface area and any latent characters that were defaced will show through."

"What will they think of next?" Jack asked.

"We're trying to stay ahead of the criminals," Hank replied.

"Is that all there is to the test? Just a few squirts, then we sit and wait for the results?" Jim folded his arms.

Hank smiled. "Pretty much."

The three men sat and waited for the chemicals to react.

"Who do you think committed the murders?" Jack asked.

Jim turned to Jack. "We already went through this before. Even if I knew, I can't talk about an ongoing investigation."

Jack pleaded, "Aw, come on now. Tell me what you know."

Before Jim could respond, a car pulled into the back parking lot. The driver slammed on the brakes and slid to a stop on the wet gravel. Through the garage door windows Jim noticed Elijah open the driver's door and run to the garage. Jim again opened the door.

An out-of-breath Elijah huffed, "Little Hawk... the woman in the office said you were here... I have to speak with you!"

"What's the matter?" Jim asked.

Elijah bent at the waist, resting his hands on his knees. "I can't believe it... I found another body!"

Hank noticed Jack stare at Elijah, then at Jim and then slowly back up.

When Jack was more than an arm's length away from Jim, he said, "I know you guys are going to spring into action so I'll let you do what you have to do."

Hank watched Jack leave and for a few seconds thought his abrupt retreat seemed unusual. The tow truck backed up quickly and then left even faster. The tires spun on the wet gravel as the tow truck sped out the back lot.

"What was that all about?" Hank asked.

Jim took off his Stetson and rested it on the panel truck's fender. "I'm not altogether sure."

Elijah took a deep breath and sat in a chair next to a workbench. He first ran his hand across his sweaty forehead and then on the back of his neck. "I was fishing again," his voice hurried. "I thought the rain would make them bite today."

"Just take it slow," Jim said as he handed Elijah a towel.

Elijah wiped his face. "I decided not to fish the Little Bitterroot anymore so I drove to the end of Route 354 hoping to catch some brookies."

"What's at the end of Route 354?" Hank asked.

"The Flathead River," Jim replied. "It's a dirt road in the middle of nowhere."

"Is that on the reservation?"

Elijah answered, "Yes. I set up on the riverbank and put on my wading boots. That's when I saw it."

"What did you see?" Jim asked.

"It looked like a freshly dug grave. I couldn't see it from the road."

"So what did you do?" Hank asked.

"I remembered what Little Hawk told me so I came here."

"How do you know it's a grave?" Hank asked.

Elijah's body trembled as he said, "I found this." He removed a plastic bag from his pocket and handed it to Jim.

Jim opened the bag, pulled out a wrapped cloth and unraveled it. All three men stared at a small piece of flesh that still clung to a fragment of bone.

Jim asked, "Hank, what do you make of this?"

Hank examined it. "Take us to where you found it."

"When did you want to go?" Elijah replied.

"Now," Hank said.

"What about the chemicals from the VIN kit?" Jim asked.

Hank wiped his hands on a rag from the workbench. "It'll be all right. If you lock up the garage, we'll check it later and make an assessment."

Jim pulled his cellphone from his pocket and contacted his undersheriff. "Tom, come out back and secure the garage area. Then park my car out front. I'm leaving with Hank and Elijah to investigate a possible crime scene. Elijah said he found a body by the Flathead River. No, I'm not kidding about the body. Put a tail on Jack Morton for me. He's acting real edgy. Yeah, good idea. Lance is itching to do some real police work. It'll give him some experience. Tell him to keep his distance." Jim hung up and turned to Hank. "I'm also going to call Linda and ask her to keep an eye on Jack."

Hank nodded and asked Elijah to drive them to the FBI's temporary forensic facility. When the three of them arrived at the makeshift morgue, Hank discussed with Leon about preparing the cargo van for a body extraction. Once in the van, Hank, Leon and Jim followed Elijah's car through the town of Ronan and onto Route 211.

They drove by the open prairie of the Bitterroot Valley bordered by the Mission Mountains on the east and the Salish Mountains to the west.

Hank noticed Jim leaning his arm on the passenger door. "I admire this landscape," Hank said.

"Thousands of years ago, these hills held the backed-up waters of the Clark Fork River," Jim said.

Hank stared at the tall mountains, their uppermost peaks still capped by snow. He laughed. "You're kidding, right?"

Leon, who sat between Hank and Jim on the bench seat piped in, "He's not. These hills above us became the shores of the Great Glacial Lake and…"

Jim interrupted, "When the ancient lake burst through its ice dam, the Indian Legend of the Great Flood was born. If there's one thing that I know, it's the land where my ancestors lived."

Leon added, "What secrets do these mountains hold?"

Elijah turned onto Route 354, a gravel road. After five miles, they turned onto a drivable trail, which led them to a fishing spot on the Flathead River. A half-hour walk took them to the location where Elijah had said he found the body.

Hank and Leon set up their equipment and performed the task of extricating the body. Not long afterward, with the body in the van, they prepared to leave. Hank was packing his forensic tools when Jim walked up to him.

"Any opinions?" Jim asked.

Hank took a deep breath and sat on the back bumper of the van. "Head, hands and feet are missing like the others but it's obvious this is a young male victim. I hope he speaks to us like the other bodies couldn't."

"The smell isn't as bad as the others," Jim replied as he sat beside Hank.

"He may only have been buried a week at most. I might be able to extract the stomach contents. That could tell us where and possibly how he was killed."

"I'll have to call Jacob Walkabout."

"The victim's not a Native American," cautioned Hank.

"How can you tell?" Jim asked.

"He's fair-skinned."

Jim shook his head. "No, I saw the body."

"The blood that settled and coagulated in his muscles makes him look darker."

Jim leaned over and held his head in his hands. "I was hoping this was Native too. Someone has to be targeting Natives."

Hank gazed upward toward the sky and shook his head. "In all my years, I've come across dozens of young investigators like you. They look for a convenient explanation that fits the evidence." Hank stood up and pointed with his index finger for emphasis. "Sometimes the answer is right under your nose and it'll even defy every single shred of evidence."

Taking in a deep breath, Jim met Hank's gaze. "I know you're right."

"Call Paul Harris. He needs to know about this. This body has a gaping wound in his chest and most of his internal organs are missing. This looks like a cult killing," Hank said.

"You mean a religious cult?"

"Religious, Satanic... call it what you will."

Later that afternoon, when Jim got back to the sheriff's office he caught up with Rocky.

"Rock, go to the cellblock and bring Sam into the interrogation room. We've got questions for him to answer. They confirmed that his prints were on the panel truck, the liquor bottles and the crates."

"Can't."

"What do you mean, can't?"

This morning Jack Morton got a lawyer for Sam and they delivered a court order to release him on bail since he wasn't charged with any major offense."

"When did this happen?"

"Jack posted it while you were meeting with Hank. Jack then said he'd stop by to see you in the garage and talk about it."

Jim thought for a moment and then issued his marching orders. "Round up Bill and Pete. I don't care what they're doing. I want each of you to search the town inside out for Clayton and bring him in. If you can't find Clayton haul in Jack Morton for questioning. Get going."

By the end of the workday Sam Clayton was nowhere to be found. Rocky brought in Jack Morton but tagging along was his lawyer who advised him to refuse to cooperate. Jim threatened to arrest Jack but the lawyer called Jim's bluff.

Facing an uphill battle with the court order to release Sam Clayton, Jim had no valid reason to suspect Jack acted in violation of any law and let him go. Jim was able to get the judge to revoke Sam's bail but the judge refused to forfeit the bail bond due to the court being unaware of Sam's pending arrest. Jim's only alternative was to issue a BOLO for Sam Clayton and develop a personal aura of suspicion regarding Jack's motives.

·32·

The next morning, Jim was up early. Through the windows of his bedroom, he noticed the dim, overcast skies shrouding the Clark Fork River Valley. After yesterday's drenching rain, a cloudy day was a blessing. A shower, denim jeans, a black, short sleeve tee shirt, a pair of old, dusty cowboy boots, and a Montana Grizzlies ball cap and he was ready to leave.

Jim spotted the green box of Chinese Melon Seed tea that Jia Li had given him. He picked it up and headed for the door. "Come on Angel, let's go for a ride."

He climbed into his SUV and noticed that something was missing from his dash. "Where's my Bowie knife?" Jim said to himself. Not wanting to drive the SUV until he located his knife which could be in reach of a prisoner if it were in the backseat, he got out of the SUV and instead piled into his white Ford pickup truck.

Maneuvering through the streets of Taylor, Jim slowed down for the children. The small crowd of young boys and girls waiting for the school bus ran to greet their county sheriff. Josh Nelson waved as the sheriff tooted the horn of his truck.

Josh yelled, "I've been picturing myself running on that football field Uncle Jim."

"Keep it up Josh," Jim replied. He waved goodbye to the children and his truck disappeared around the corner headed for the sheriff's office.

He told Angel to stay, reached to grab the box of tea and walked into the office. He approached the dispatch desk. "Martha, I'll be gone all day. Has anyone seen my Bowie…"

Martha interrupted, "I like your hat… GO GRIZ!"

"I'm in no mood for joking. I have business in the field."

"First things first. Hank Kelly is waiting for you and that hat ain't going to change HIS bad mood."

Jim nodded and then asked, "Martha, please put this near the coffee station." He handed her the box of tea.

"Isn't this interesting? I never saw tea like that before. Where did you get it?"

"Jia Li gave it to me. It's from China."

Martha cradled the box in her hands. "Everyone will want to taste this treasure."

Jim slid his cardkey in the reader, opened the door, and noticed Hank inside his office with a manila folder in his hands.

"What's up?"

"I shouldn't reward you with this for screwing up on Clayton but here's my report on that boy's autopsy and the results for the VIN number test."

"Tell me the news in one sentence."

"The boy's been dead about a week and the panel truck once belonged to your dad."

Jim closed the door behind him and sat at his desk. He picked up the folder and flipped through the pages. "You're sure about the truck?"

"VIN number is a perfect match."

"But my dad got rid of it when I was a kid. Must have been about twenty years ago."

Hank pointed to a name on a page of the report. "The last person it was registered to was a Richard Reynolds of Billings, now deceased."

"Where's his body?" Jim asked looking up.

Hank waved his index finger. "I know what you're thinking... and no, he's not one of the bodies. He died of cancer about seven years ago and his family had his body cremated. They gave the panel truck to a relative and he reported it stolen a few years later."

"Tell me about the boy."

"He looks to be between twenty and thirty, fair complexion. That's all we know."

"So he really isn't Native."

"No, he's not."

"Is there anything else I should know about the body?"

"He had skin carved off his forearm in addition to the missing head, hands, and feet. We think he may have had a tattoo. Whoever killed him, made damn sure he wouldn't be identified. They say dead men tell no tales."

"But do their spirits?" Jim asked.

Hank sat down. "That legend again? Paul Harris is pretty upset about Sam Clayton's disappearance but he seems interested in the new discoveries. Remember that arrowhead he found on the reservation? The FBI did a thorough check on it and it's an authentic Native American arrowhead. But get this... it's not from around here."

"What do you mean?" Jim asked.

"It's from the southwest. They verified its composition. The stone is unique to Arizona and the way it was carved is similar to Apache arrowheads."

"How did it end up near the bodies on the Flathead Reservation?"

Hank leaned forward in his chair. "That's what we have to find out. That hole in the center... we found microscopic shards of leather. Someone may have used it as an ornament. Maybe they hung it from their neck."

Jim placed the folder down on his desk. "We have work to do." Jim noticed Hank surveying his outfit.

"Y-o-u have work to do, I did my part. Where are you going... fishing for Clayton?" Hank asked.

"You could say that."

"Where?"

"I'll tell you when I get back."

Jim waved goodbye to Hank. As he walked past the dispatcher's desk he said to Martha, "I'll be gone for most of the day."

She placed her headset down. "Where will you be if someone calls?"

"Have them contact me on my cellphone."

Jim walked up to his truck. Angel stuck her head over the rolled-down passenger window. Jim opened the driver's door. "Come on girl, in the back." He reached into his pocket and handed her a few dog biscuits. Angel quickly devoured them and then jumped onto the truck's mini-bench seat where Jim secured her dog harness. He climbed into the driver's seat and started the engine.

Jim stopped at Lucy's for a bite to eat. He moseyed over to the far end of the lunch counter next to the back window and settled onto his favorite stool. Its red vinyl seat, worn in the middle and patched with gray duct tape marked by curled and frayed ends revealed how long it had been in disrepair.

Lucy, a large woman with auburn hair pinned back in a mass of bobby pins walked over to him. She wore her traditional blue and yellow apron and dropped a menu on the counter.

"How's Kate doing?"

"Better but it looks to be a slow recovery."

"Give her my best. Now, what'll ya have?"

"I'm going light today... how about a bowl of granola and a glass of orange juice?"

"Jimmy Boy are you going Sierra Club on me? Where's the bacon and eggs, home fries and coffee you usually order when you stroll in here with Mr. McCoy?"

"I'm trying to eat healthier."

"A big strong guy like you needs a heftier breakfast."

"Lucy, you're looking at the new me."

"There weren't nothing wrong with the old one."

"I'm a mess and I need a big fix in my life."

Lucy leaned on the counter. "What's bugging you?"

"This town seems to have lost its way."

"Do you mean that guy on the radio or that group that meets at the church?"

"Both."

Lucy looked down the counter toward the front door and across the room at the tables where patrons were engrossed in conversation. She whispered, "Be careful whenever you deal with Jack Morton... he's a loose cannon."

"Why do you say that?"

"He seems to be acting funny lately. And I seen him meeting in here with guys from that church group, that new officer Chief Peters hired and then some fellas I never saw before."

"Like who?"

"I dunno… one was an Indian fella, another was some kid dressed in this godawful outfit. He looked like he was from back east. Anyway, I heard the kid say he wanted to meet with you and then Jack tells him to keep it down."

"Never met the kid, what happened next?"

"All I know is that Jack paid the bill and they left like they was best buddies and I ain't never seen that kid again."

"I don't recall Jack ever springing for someone's meal."

"See what I mean?"

"It's not a crime to all of a sudden become a generous person. Did Jack call him by name?"

"I do remember the name Steve. Then he had this funny tattoo on his arm."

"Tattoo?" Jim asked.

"Yeah, the kid said something about the bodies you been finding and meeting with a guy named Willie."

"Willie Otaktay?"

"Yeah, that's the name."

"Willie's had a rough go of it but he's following the Red Road now."

"Just seems odd that this kid shows up out of the blue, starts yammerin' about Willie and the bodies, wants to meet you but didn't and then never shows his face in this town again."

"I'll have to ask Jack about it when I see him."

"Just be careful Jimmy Boy. A lot of people in this town… the good people, we depend on you."

"I will. Are you gonna get me that granola?"

Lucy pulled her arms off the counter. "How about a coffee instead of the OJ to keep it honest… whadda say?"

Jim smiled. "Black, no sugar."

"That's more like it. Be right up."

Jim's thoughts centered on Hank's message about the latest body. "He looks to be between twenty and thirty…He had skin carved off his arm…We think he may have had a tattoo. Whoever killed him, made damn sure he wouldn't be identified."

·33·

Jim left Lucy's, drove along U.S. 228 for a few hours and then cutoff onto an old country road that split the distance between the Cabinet and Salish Mountains. The land was flat and a natural valley of the Little Bitterroot River carved by the glaciers and deepened by the growth of the young mountains.

He approached a weathered sign that hung by the road and marked a dirt driveway. The left half of the sign was missing but on the right side were two rows of letters:

HANAN
RM

They were the last remnants of the original sign, BUCHANAN FARM.

Jim pulled off the road and drove up the long driveway. He passed an old barn that leaned slightly eastward. A silo with a large hole in its side and three or four rotting chicken coops in various stages of disarray stood next to the barn.

Finally, a farmhouse that had long since felt its last touch of human care came into view. It was not as he had remembered. The farm used to be a busy place that he once called home. Jim parked near the front porch, unharnessed Angel and took in the full view of the property.

He thought, how long has it been... five years? No, that's when dad died, the farm closed down before that. Yeah, that's right. It was nine years ago, just after I left the NFL.

Jim still recalled the words his white father spoke to him the day he arrived on his farm. "I don't want to hear one damn heathen word from your mouth again, or I'll cut your tongue out."

Jim did speak the *Apsáalooke* language as a young boy on the reservation but years long gone have a way of diluting one's culture.

Kraaasssh!

Startled by a loud bang and the sound of footsteps, Jim instinctively drew his revolver, and ran toward the sound. Angel jumped through the truck's open passenger window and with a burst of speed, flew past Jim toward the rear of the building. At the sound of a scream, followed by Angel's barks, Jim cocked the hammer of his Colt Python.

Boxed in by Angel were three young boys against a corner wall of the back porch, just a few feet from their bicycles. Two boys, one tall and one short, wore shoulder length hair while the other sported a red bandana across his forehead that kept his wavy black hair in place. Attired in jeans and tee shirts, they cowered as Angel stood her ground and snarled, her muzzle wrinkled with anger above her gleaming teeth.

"Heel!" commanded Jim. Angel whimpered, ran to Jim's left side and sat. "What are you boys up to?" Jim asked.

"We didn't do anything," the oldest boy said.

"You're on private property."

"No sir. This is abandoned property," said one of the boys.

"Who told you that?" Jim asked.

"Jack Morton," said the boy who promptly received an elbow in his ribs from the boy standing next to him.

Jim commanded the boys to sit on the steps and holstered his revolver. "What do you boys have to do with Jack Morton?" No one answered. Jim noticed the shortest boy looked familiar. "Abraham Sizemore... is that you?"

"Yes sir," the boy said, hiding something behind his back.

"What do you have there?"

"Nothing."

"You want me to let the dog loose? She's liable to tear each of you apart. We won't know if there were two, three, or four of you."

The three boys replied in unison, "No sir."

"Then show me what you have in your hands." Abraham placed a half-empty bottle of wine on the porch steps. "Where did you get that?" Again, no one answered. Jim raised his voice. "Where did you get that!"

Abraham relented. "It's in the house... there's more there... all kinds of different stuff. We got it from Jack Morton. Sheriff Buchanan, please don't tell my father."

Jim pulled a notepad from his back pocket. "I want names and ages."

The boy with the wavy hair replied, "I ain't telling nobody nothing."

Abraham looked at his friend and then at Jim. "Abraham Sizemore, thirteen, my dad's name is Elijah and my mom's name is Singing Bird."

The tallest boy, obviously frightened in the presence of Sheriff Buchanan, blurted, "Aaron Walkabout, thirteen, my father's name is Jacob Walkabout, and my mom is Sharon Bear Cloud. They don't live together anymore."

"I know your dad. The son of a tribal police chief should know better." Jim turned to the boy with the wavy hair. "What's your name son?"

He remained silent.

"I asked you... what's your name!"

The boy pulled a jackknife from inside his pants pocket, opened it, and pointed it at Jim. "First you're going to kill us and then bury us, just like you did to the others."

Angel growled but Jim reached down and held her back. He instructed sternly, "Put the knife down."

The boy stiffened his arm and blinked a half-dozen times as a few tears rolled down his cheeks. Jim approached and sidestepped the blade. The knife-wielding adolescent moved ever so slightly and the blade grazed Jim's left arm just above his elbow. It cut into the flesh and sliced a deep two inch gash. Blood flowed freely as Jim flinched, grabbed the boy by his arm and twisted it backwards. The teenager screamed and dropped his knife.

"Please sir, don't kill me... I didn't mean to hurt you. I was afraid."

Jim held the boy's arm, pushed him facedown onto the ground, and placed his knee on the boy's back.

"Tell me your name, age, and your parents' names."

Beneath the vice-like grip of Jim's leg, the boy sighed. "My name is Eagle Spirit."

"Your baptized name!"

"Antonio Hightower."

Suddenly Jim remembered Alma Rose's premonition of the letter A three times and the three boys whose names began with the letter A. The thought about her warning that after the fourth A, something terrible would happen. But where was the fourth A, was it Angel?

Jim asked, "How old are you!"

"Fifteen."

"And your father's name?"

"I have no father. My mother is Esmeralda Hightower."

Jim removed his knee from Antonio's back. "Is Dan McCoy your mother's boyfriend?"

Antonio pulled himself up onto his hands and knees and spat on the ground. "I curse that white man."

Jim picked up the pocketknife, closed its blade, and then lifted Antonio onto his feet. He dropped the knife in his back pocket and looked at the boy.

"You'll have to ask for that knife from the white man you hate so much." Jim grabbed his left elbow and felt the warm moistness of his own blood. He pulled a handkerchief from his pocket and wrapped it around his arm. He tied it and pulled it taunt with his teeth.

Jim said, "I want to know where the rest of that liquor is."

He drew his revolver and followed Abraham, Aaron, and Antonio into the basement. Stacked against the far wall were ten cardboard cases each containing twelve bottles of wine. Beneath the window were four wooden cases of Kentucky bourbon, five more of Scotch whisky along the wall and two cases of Canadian whisky in a bin next to the hatchway door. Alongside the staircase to the first floor were six cases of Russian vodka stacked two high. Piled on top of them was a case of brown ale. Jim remembered Jack's request, *a case of brown ale*.

Jim surveyed the area and noticed the black soil on the crates, on the stairs, and on the floor. Jim lifted his left foot and looked at the sole of his shoe. A few grains of the black soil had stuck to his boot.

When he turned around, he saw impressions of his footsteps in that black soil that was everywhere. Jim stared at the boys for a long moment and then reached into one of the cases and pulled out a bottle of wine.

"Jack Morton told you about these?" Jim asked. No one answered. "I'll ask just one more time."

"Are you gonna arrest us?" Aaron asked.

"I'll do something far worse. I'll tell your mothers what you're up to."

Abraham spoke up, "Yes sir. He gave us keys to this house and said we could have one bottle every week if we kept an eye on these crates for him and kept it a secret. He said if you ever found out you would kill us just like you killed all those other people."

"Give me those keys now."

Abraham handed the keys to Jim.

Antonio said to Jim, "You can't do this. We have rights."

"Those two boys who drank themselves to death a few weeks ago had rights too. Did they get the liquor from here?" Simultaneously, two boys replied yes and one said no. "Who's telling the truth?" Jim asked.

Abraham looked at his friends and then replied, "They were helping too. But we're not like them. They stole the liquor. They thought if they drank it, they would see visions of warriors in the buffalograss."

Jim shook his head. "Stupid legends. What does Morton do with this liquor?"

"He sells it to the tribe," shouted Antonio.

"Did you boys see anyone else with Jack Morton?" They each stared at Jim but remained silent. "If you boys cooperate, I won't tell anyone you were here not even your mothers. Now, was Jack Morton alone?"

Aaron spoke up. "There was one white man and sometimes another white man."

"Did you ever see them before?"

"No."

"If I showed you pictures would you remember them?"

"I would," Abraham replied.

"I would too," Aaron stated.

"What about you?" Jim asked Antonio.

"Why should I tell you?"

"Because it's the right thing to do."

Antonio looked at his two friends and then at Jim. "Okay, I'll help you."

Jim removed his hat and wiped his brow with his forearm. "This was my dad's farm. I still have a key to a secure storage bin in the barn. It's eleven o'clock now, by noon, I want every single one of these crates moved to that storage area. Then I want you to ride your bikes back to the reservation and never come back here again. I don't want you to tell anyone what happened here today. If you do, I'll have a talk with your parents."

"Are you going to keep the booze for yourself?" Antonio asked.

"I'm holding it as evidence."

"Evidence for what?" Abraham asked. "Didn't you arrest that other white man? Did he tell you to come here?"

"What are you saying, son?"

Abraham gave a sideways glance to his friends then looked at Jim. "That white man you call Clayton, he was here with Jack Morton almost every time."

"Was he one of the white men you were talking about? Who was the other one?" Jim asked.

"I don't know the other man," Abraham said. "He had a mustache."

Aaron said, "I saw a fourth man that I never saw before."

"I'll stop by the reservation this week. Show you some mug shots. Maybe you'll spot someone else you know," Jim said.

"You're not mad at us for drinking?" Abraham asked.

Jim hesitated, then explained, "When I was about your age I did a very foolish thing and I've had to live with my mistake ever since. It wasn't drinking but it was something that hurt a lot of people and changed some lives forever. No, I don't blame you... just don't do anything stupid like this again."

170

Each boy responded, "Yes sir."

The boys carried the cases from the farmhouse to the barn and into the storage bin. When they finished, Jim covered the cases with a tarp and then locked the storage bin. He ordered the boys to return to the Flathead Reservation and they scooted away on their bicycles.

Jim and Angel got into the truck and Jim placed Antonio's knife on the console between the seats. A series of thoughts raced through his mind. I need to speak with Jack Morton, give him one chance to confess. Clayton's involved too.

He drove the truck onto the road and headed back to Taylor. He picked up his radio and tried to contact Martha but there was only static. Jim reached for his cellphone. He wanted to call Martha and then Linda but saw the NO SERVICE message on the screen. He glanced at Angel on the back seat. "I bet you could tell me where I left my Bowie knife."

·34·

Taylor Police Chief John Peters sat alone at his office desk establishing an outline for Friday's daily roll call and personnel inspection and beginning the monotonous task of completing the work schedule for the following month.

A knock on the door and then Linda walked into his office. "Chief, you busy?"

"Not now." Peters grinned. "I'm buried in paperwork and I didn't want to be disturbed but now that you're here, you can close that damn door."

Following an awkward half-smile, Linda complied with his request and took off her hat. "I thought I'd check in on Jack at the body shop. He's been acting a bit strange lately."

Peters sat back in his chair. "How strange?"

"Like he's hiding something… know anything about it?"

"No but Anderson's been working with him on our fleet repairs. Maybe he knows something?"

"Where's Anderson?" she asked.

"He's inventorying weapons in the basement tactical gear lockers. You can ask him about Jack."

"I'll do that. Are the officers still setting up the review stand for the 4th of July Parade?"

"Yep, it's going to be a dandy this year."

"Anything else going on right now?" Linda asked.

Peters thought for a moment. "Yeah, there was an attempted break-in on Boulder Road. Can you check it out?"

"Sure, what happened?"

"Old man Walsh found the deadbolt on his front door tampered with."

Linda nodded. "The poor guy lives alone. I'll speak with Anderson first then I'll check it out. I should be back by three."

She turned to leave but Peters called to her. "Linda I'm cooking for a few friends this weekend, want to join my wife and me?"

"No thanks boss."

"Other plans?"

Linda hesitated, and then said, "I'm on a social fast."

"A what?"

"Never mind."

"If you reconsider, drop over. We'd love to have you."

"I'll see. I can't promise." She turned and headed for the exit as Peters got up from his chair.

As she walked to the main elevator, past the desks of the police station staff, Peters spied her every move from his office windows. He took a deep breath and exhaled slowly. He muttered to himself as he walked back to his desk, "Why is it so much easier for my wife to make friends?"

·35·

Linda took the elevator down to the basement. When the door opened, she felt the musty smell of decades-old paper seep through her nostrils. There in the bowels of the police station she found Deputy Chief Anderson along with one of the patrol officers inventorying the stored weapons in the gun vault.

"Hey Anderson, I heard you're working with Jack Morton on some vehicles."

Deputy Chief Anderson looked up from his paperwork as Officer Conant continued to inventory the weapons in the vault. "Yeah, what's up?"

"I heard that he's been acting strange lately and was wondering if you knew anything about it."

"Where'd you hear that?"

"That's not important. Did you notice anything unusual?"

"Why do you need to know?"

The heavy basement air continued to engulf Linda. "All I want is an answer."

Anderson chuckled. "Well, as the deputy police chief to a l-o-w-l-y captain, I have no answer to give you."

Linda knew the conversation was going nowhere and she had to look in on old man Walsh before it got any later. "If you see or hear anything suspicious you let me or Chief Peters know right away."

Anderson turned his back to her and barked, "Yep," without glancing up from his paperwork.

Linda left the basement, headed to her squad car and drove off for Boulder Road.

·36·

Once Deputy Chief Anderson and Officer Conant completed the weapons inventory in the basement, Conant headed to the high school for class dismissal security. Anderson decided to check in on Jack Morton. He snooped around the body shop and noticed that Jack was alone in his office. He opened the door.

"What the hell is going on?"

Jack looked up at him. "What do you mean?"

"You're drawing suspicion."

"From who?"

"That asshole lady cop."

"Stevens? She knows not a damn thing."

"Not as far as I'm concerned. And if I'm worried you should be too."

"Relax." Jack smiled. "I have something to show you." He pulled an object, wrapped in newspaper, from under his desk. "Look what I got here." He unfolded the object, holding it in his gloved hands.

"A Bowie knife? Why the hell do you want to show me a goddamn Bowie knife?"

"Oh, this ain't just any Bowie knife. Its Buchanan's Bowie knife," grinned Jack.

Anderson backed up and sat in a chair at one of the old desks. "What are you doing with the sheriff's knife?

"The other day, right after I sprung Clayton I was at the sheriff's garage watching them use this solution on the panel truck's engine block. On my way out, I passed the sheriff's brand new SUV. I looked through the open window and saw this here knife attached to the dash next to the jockeybox. I used a clean neckerchief to open the car door, took the Bowie knife, then got back in my truck. No one saw me... it was a piece of cake." Jack laughed. "I got a plan. This knife's got the sheriff's fingerprints all over it."

"So what."

"I'm going to stick it in one of the bodies we just buried."

Anderson shook his head. "You're not going back to where we buried the bodies. Do you know how long it took us to find a new spot to bury them? It's bad enough they found the ones we buried near the Little Bitterroot. You start acting suspicious and you'll lead Buchanan, Kelly and that FBI agent right to the new graves and then to us."

Jack sat on the desk. "They already found the body of that environmentalist we buried by the Flathead River."

"We're fucked." Anderson shook his head.

"Take it easy, no one's gonna find out anything. I'll explain."

"This ought to be rich." Anderson pulled his chair up close to the desk.

Jack grabbed one of the old wooden office chairs lying around, sat in it backwards and faced Anderson. "They brought in that old wreck we used to transport the booze from that mobster's train to the farm along that old logging road. Anyway, I was tired of keeping that piece of junk running."

"That's it?"

"No, here comes the plan. Tonight, we take a ride out to the Flathead River where we buried the bodies. They ain't gonna find all of them that we buried, so we dig one of them up, sink this here knife into its back and rebury it with the knife sticking out of the ground. When they look for more bodies, they find Jim's knife and he gets arrested. Ain't that what we planned?"

"When the hell did you grow brain cells to make up plans?"

Jack laughed. "Yeah, I'm good, ain't I?"

"No, shit for brains. That won't work."

"Why ain't it gonna work? With Buchanan gone you throw all the construction jobs my way throughout the entire county, and that gives me cover to use my own trucks to smuggle in a lot more booze. That way you get to sell even more of it to the Indians on the reservation."

Anderson stood up. "Your plan won't work, dumbass. They have forensics. They can tell if a body was stabbed before or after death, they can tell how long the body's been in the ground. No one will believe Buchanan did it."

Jack leaned across the desk and repeatedly poked his finger onto Anderson's chest. "Bullshit! Smuggling booze was one thing but I ain't making the kind of money you promised when you asked me to help you bury the bodies. And then you had me bring that kid who was nosing around, looking for Buchanan up near the Flathead River for a meeting. I had to hear his screams while the boss finished him off. I want a bigger piece of the pie."

Anderson fixed his shirt where Jack's finger pointing had rumpled it and wiped sweat from his forehead. Then he pulled out a pair of forensic gloves from his pocket and made sure to put them on just out of sight of Jack's eyes. "I got my own business to worry about and what you want to do ain't worth the risk."

Jack slammed his fist on the desk. "Who's risk? I'm doing all the horseshit work here and you and your Guardians of Doctrine buddies that meet at the church are making out like bandits."

"Hey, they're not all involved in this. Don't go shooting off your goddamn mouth at tonight's meeting… you tell anyone you're going?" Anderson asked.

"No… who the hell would I tell anyway?"

"Good!"

Anderson grabbed the Bowie knife off Jack's desk with his gloved hands and swung his arm forward, thrusting the fourteen-inch blade up to its hilt into Jack's gut, and then let go of the handle.

Jack Morton's eyes bulged out of their sockets. He stood up, staggered backwards a few steps, and let out a groan that seemed to erupt from deep inside his throat. Grimacing, Jack's face reddened and saliva dribbled from his lips when he tried to mouth some words. He looked down, and grabbed the handle of the knife.

Anderson grasped the knife with both hands, blanketing Jack's ice-cold fingers. Anderson pulled the razor-sharp blade of the knife upwards and across Jack's midsection.

Jack moaned and doubled over as blood gushed from the mortal wound and sprayed across the concrete floor. Jack slapped his hand across the gaping cut on his midsection as pink and grey matter bathed in the redness of his own blood oozed through his crimson colored fingers.

Jack fell backwards in a state of free fall onto the arm of his chair. He toppled onto the floor behind the desk, his chair crashing onto him. Jack clutched the knife handle and feebly gathered the warm, bloody intestines that had spread across the floor with his other hand. Anderson pulled off his drenched gloves inside out and tossed them in the wastebasket.

Jack lay on the floor breathing heavily. With each successive gasp of air, his bloody mouth spoke each word slower and slower, "You... son... of... a... bitch."

Turning to leave, Anderson shut the lights and uttered the last human words Jack Morton would ever hear, "Change of plans, asshole."

·37·

Sheriff Jim Buchanan shut off his truck's engine in the parking lot of the Taylor Police Station. It was two-thirty in the afternoon. He reached for his radio and then hesitated. He grabbed his cellphone instead.

"Martha, this is Jim... I'm outside the police station. I'm going to grab Chief Peters and Linda to give me a hand. Send Rocky over. No, the radio is fine. I'm on my cellphone because I don't want this broadcast across the radio airwaves. I have business with Jack Morton. It could get real ugly. I'm going to rattle his cage. Check on that BOLO for Sam Clayton and get back to me."

Jim said goodbye, placed his phone down, and walked inside the station. He ran his cardkey through the reader. He spied Jenny Farrell, the Public Information Coordinator, thumbing through a file cabinet. Jim glanced at Peters' empty office, and then asked Jenny, "Have you seen Chief Peters?"

"He took a call a couple three minutes ago and then left."

"Do you know where Captain Stevens is?"

"No, she left a while back. I'm not sure when either of them will return."

Jim nodded. "Okay, I'm going to head over to Jack Morton's. If Chief Peters or Captain Stevens get back send them there and tell them it's important."

Jenny Farrell nodded and Jim left.

Jim reached Jack Morton's body shop and construction business. With his right hand on the grip of his revolver, he knocked on the door. "Morton... you inside?"

Jim turned the doorknob and entered the building. Cloaked in a darkened pall, except for a sliver of natural light that pierced the opening between two blackout drapes, the room slipped a chill through Jim's bones.

He felt along the wall for a light switch and then noticed a wide dark spot on the floor. He knelt down to touch the stain. It was wet with a foul odor. Jim reached the light switch, flicked it on and noticed the trail of blood that emerged from behind a desk. There on the floor was the body.

"Jack!" Jim knelt down and felt for a pulse. He noticed the sizeable wound on Jack's abdomen and a familiar knife handle protruding from his stomach. Jim stood up and stepped backwards. He wiped the cold sweat from the side of his face as the creak of the door caused him to wheel around.

"Jim?" Captain Linda Stevens asked.

"Stay where you are."

"I spoke with Jenny. What are you doing here?"

Jim noticed her glance at his bandaged elbow, now soaked in blood. Red stains darkened his knees, hands and one side of his face where he had wiped his sweat.

"Linda, stay there."

She walked toward the desk. "My God... what happened?"

Jim took a deep breath. "I found him like that."

"Why is your arm bloody?" Linda asked.

"I had trouble earlier today."

"With Jack?"

"No, not with Jack... I mean, yes it probably has to do with Jack but he wasn't there."

Linda drew her service revolver and pointed it at Jim. "Drop your gunbelt, now!" she yelled.

Jim unbuckled his gunbelt and placed it on the cement floor. He raised his arms above his head. "Linda, I didn't do this."

Linda reached for the microphone near her uniform's shoulder board. She contacted the dispatcher at the sheriff's office. "Martha, have the morgue send their van to Jack Morton's body shop. We have a deceased male here. Do you know if Jack Morton was expecting any visitors? What did you say... rattle his cage?" Linda stared at Jim and cocked the hammer of her gun. "Martha, call up the Rapid Response Team. Have them secure the perimeter of Jack Morton's business and cordon off a six-block area." Linda gestured to Jim to sit in one of the office chairs. "I don't know what happened here between the two of you but you'll have time to explain."

Jim took a seat. "Nothing happened between us."

"Just sit tight until backup gets here." Linda said with a slight quiver in her voice.

"I don't suppose you'd let me put my arms down."

"Keep them up."

"Want to uncock that hammer so you don't shoot an innocent man just because he might sneeze?"

Letting go of the gun with one hand, she wiped a sweaty palm on her pant leg. Then gripping the gun, she wiped her other palm dry. "Shut up and keep your hands up."

They remained in a stalemate for close to three minutes before Deputy Chief Anderson, dressed in civvies and Officers Michael Wilson and Jonathan Tillman entered the building.

"Linda, I left work right after the weapons inventory and went home. I was driving by on my way to visit a friend when I heard the police call." Anderson took off his ballcap and ran his fingers through his short blond hair.

Linda motioned with her head. "Look behind the desk."

Anderson did as she suggested. "Son-of-a-bitch. Did he do this?"

Linda kept her eyes trained on Jim. "He says he didn't."

"I didn't kill him," argued Jim as he stood up.

Deputy Chief Anderson walked up to Jim. "Bull! That looks like your Bowie knife. It looks like we caught you before you could carve up poor Jack Morton."

"What's that supposed to mean?" Jim asked.

"Before you could bury him like you did the others."

"Dave, shut your mouth," ordered Linda.

Jim shouted, "I didn't kill Jack."

Anderson yelled, "All I know is we got a dead man over there and a bloody sheriff over here. We caught you red-handed."

"I said, shut up Dave," hollered Linda. "Cuff him for me." She tossed Anderson a pair of handcuffs from her belt.

"I want a lawyer," declared Jim.

Anderson bound Jim's hands behind his back. "You have the right to remain silent and refuse to answer questions. Do you understand?" Jim remained silent. "I said, do you understand!"

"Yes."

"Anything you say may be used against you in a court of law. Do you understand... do you understand?"

"Anderson, back off!" Linda shouted.

"I'll process this arrest," Anderson barked. "I'm senior officer here."

Linda said firmly, "Follow protocol, Anderson. I'm the arresting officer. I was first on the scene and you're off duty."

Anderson pointed at Linda. "You better make sure that you know what you're doing." He hurried past her and went outside.

Linda turned to Jim. "Sit back down."

Jim complied and Linda resumed the Miranda Warning.

"Knowing and understanding your rights as explained to you, are you willing to answer my questions without an attorney present?"

Jim looked into her eyes. "I know this doesn't look good but I showed up a few minutes before you. If you were here first, I'd be asking you the same questions."

Linda didn't say a word.

"Can I ask you one favor?"

"What is it?"

"Angel is in my truck. Can you have someone get her out and bring her home so she doesn't see me leave in handcuffs? Also call Jia Li and ask her to take care of Angel for me."

Linda nodded and delegated the tasks to one of her fellow officers. After a half-hour, the medical examiner's van pulled up to the body shop. Hank Kelly and Leon stepped out and ran into the building. Hank shook his head when he saw Jim handcuffed.

"What the hell did you do now?" Hank asked.

"Nothing but everyone's already convicted me."

Hank shot Linda a nervous glance then opened his evidence kit. Snapping on a pair of latex gloves and slipping plastic booties over his shoes, he began to review the crime scene.

Rocky arrived and stopped in his tracks when he saw Jim. "Boss, what's going on? I heard the calls over the radio."

Jim opened his mouth but Linda interrupted, "Rocky, please process Jim on suspicion of murder."

"Murder... whose murder?"

With her gun still aimed at Jim, she said, "Jack Morton is dead and Jim was standing next to the body when I arrived."

Rocky saw the knife that protruded from Jack's belly. "*Mala Madre Di Dio! Santo Christ!*" He looked at Jim and then at Linda.

Jim sighed. "Yeah, it's my knife. I don't know how it got here. It's been missing for at least a day, maybe two."

"Oh man, this can't be." Rocky turned to Linda. "Jim couldn't have done this."

"They'll be time to investigate that. Right now, we need to process him."

"You want me to lock up my own boss in his own jail?"

"It's the county's jail."

"Rock, it'll be all right. We'll get this straightened out. Let's go," Jim said.

Linda and Rocky left the building each with a grip on one of Jim's handcuffed arms. A few residents stopped on the street to gawk at the procession.

A news truck with a KTAY logo on its side panel drove up and parked next to Rocky's patrol car. Reporter Julie Franklin jumped from the media vehicle with an EV RE-50 microphone in her right hand. A cameraman exited the back of the truck and followed. They intercepted Linda, Rocky, and Jim.

"Sheriff Buchanan, can you tell us about this latest development in the Bitterroot Killer Case?" Julie Franklin shoved the microphone in Jim's face.

The group continued to weave its way toward Rocky's car. Jim looked back at his white truck and saw the word KILLER scrawled in fresh red paint across the tailgate.

"Who told you about this?" Linda asked.

"I can't reveal my sources," insisted Franklin.

Linda interjected, "We've got nothing to say. Let us pass."

Franklin continued, "Sheriff Buchanan, the last time we spoke you were investigating the bodies that were found by the Little Bitterroot River. Have you yourself now been implicated in these murders?"

"Let us pass!" screamed Rocky as he pulled Jim away.

Franklin followed and again jammed her microphone into Jim's face. "Sheriff, did you kill Jack Morton with you own knife?"

185

Linda grabbed the microphone from the reporter's hand, yanked it away and slammed it to the ground. "I don't know how you find out about these things so fast. Get the hell out of here."

Julie Franklin turned to her cameraman. "What did you get?"

Her associate shut down his camera and smiled. "I got everything."

Linda helped Jim into the back seat of Rocky's car, holding his head to ease him in. She and Rocky climbed in front and the three left for the sheriff's office.

Hank and Leon brought Morton's body to the FBI's temporary morgue. Inside the sheriff's office, Rocky fingerprinted, photographed, booked, and issued Jim an orange jumpsuit. He led Jim to the far end of the cellblock. Rocky made sure to keep Jim away from the handful of other prisoners who might try to harass him.

Jim spent the rest of the day alone in his cell and reflected on everything that had transpired. His lawyer, Vincent Cavalo, visited him at night and reviewed the facts of the case. He assured Jim that he would soon be out on bail but Jim knew otherwise.

·38·

On Saturday morning, June 15, Jim heard a voice at his cell door. At first he thought it was a dream but when it repeated not once but twice, Jim slowly opened his eyes.

Through a veil of murky half-awakened haze he noticed Rocky standing outside his cell door holding the keys to the cellblock.

"Hey boss, you got yourself a visitor."

Jim rolled over on his bunk and set his bare feet on the cement floor. "Is it my lawyer again? I thought I told him everything last night."

"No, it's Emily Cronin, the county prosecutor," said a tall, young woman with short black hair and briefcase in hand. The thin, gold-framed glasses on her face complimented her slight build.

Jim rubbed his sleep-filled eyes. "Emily, I expected to see you but not this soon."

"I know this is difficult but I have a job to do." Emily sat on a stool Rocky had placed in front of Jim's cell. She dropped the briefcase by her side, and pulled a pen from her suit jacket. "Would you like to answer some questions?"

Jim sighed, "Yeah… sure."

Emily pulled a folder from her briefcase and opened it to a bookmarked page. She glanced at Jim's bare feet. "I see they took your shoes and socks."

Jim rubbed his forehead. "You know the standard procedure for murder suspects. No socks, shoelaces, or belts… everyone's treated as a potential suicide."

Emily asked, "Do you want your lawyer present?"

Jim hesitated, and then said, "I've got nothing to hide."

"Do you want to confess?" asked the prosecutor.

Jim brushed a few sweaty strands of hair away from his eyes. "Confess to what?"

"How can I put this? They found you at the crime scene covered in the victim's blood, with your knife in Jack Morton's abdomen, and a defensive wound on your left arm."

"I didn't kill him."

Emily thumbed through her paperwork to a dog-eared page as her glasses slid from the bridge of her nose. She scribbled notes on the inside flap of her folder then continued her questioning. "Your fingerprints were all over the murder weapon."

"No kidding, it was my knife. It went missing days ago."

"A few of your deputies heard you threaten Jack Morton."

"When?"

Emily scanned her file. "On May 27 in your office you said that Jack will be in for a world of hurt."

"That was a figure of speech. I was upset with him but I wouldn't kill him."

"If you claim you're innocent where were you when Morton was murdered?"

"I made a promise to keep that in confidence."

Emily pushed her glasses back up to the bridge of her nose. "If you don't cooperate, my hands are tied. You leave me no choice but to schedule an arraignment."

"I know it looks bad but I'm innocent," Jim replied.

Emily laughed. "Looks bad? Morton's murder is a slam dunk. To be honest with you, my biggest challenge will be to pin the Bitterroot Murders on you."

"Emily, I've known you since you were an intern for Stuart Peabody. Do you really think I did this?"

Emily removed her eyeglasses. "The attorney general's office is pressing for a prosecution."

"That's no surprise. His political party always sides with anything that denies the rights of Native people," Jim said.

"So now you're a scapegoat? Please, save it for the judge."

Jim clutched the bars in his hands. "Emily, you know I couldn't have done this."

"Look Jim, I remain unbiased when I prosecute a case."

Jim sat on his bunk and hung his head. "I didn't kill Jack."

"If you see your lawyer before I do, tell him that I'm going to schedule an arraignment for Tuesday morning." Emily placed the folder in her briefcase. She lifted her bag off the floor and left the cellblock.

Rocky reassured Jim. "Don't worry about her. Let's get your mind off this stuff. Are you hungry?"

Jim nodded.

Rocky made some of Jia Li's Asian tea and poured a cup for himself and Jim. As they sat on opposite sides of the bars, they also shared a small platter of cake that Jia Li had made.

"This is pretty good. You said Jia Li made it?" Jim asked.

"Yeah. She said it's an old Chinese recipe."

"Is she taking good care of my house?" Jim asked.

Rocky tried to speak but his mouth was too dry from the cake.

Jim laughed. "Wash some of that down before you choke."

Rocky nodded, reached for his tea, and doused a big gulp. He coughed a few times and melon seed tea spilled from his nose. Jim pointed at Rocky and laughed again.

Rocky wiped himself with a napkin. "It's nice to see you laugh, boss. I wasn't supposed to tell you this but Kate called and said her and Alma Rose were boarding a flight home. They'll arrive later today."

"I called Kate last night. She wanted to return home but I told her to stay put. I guess she didn't listen to me. I'm trying to be less protective of her but now again I'm afraid for her safety."

"I know what you mean, boss. There's a murderer on the loose and it sure in hell isn't you."

·39·

Saturday turned into Sunday. The county jail's cold, darkened confines prevented an accurate estimation of day or night. When the outside door to the lockup opened, Jim sat upright on his bunk and rubbed his eyes.

Staring straight ahead, he saw a face bathed in the florescent light emanating from the office. Jim rubbed his forehead. For a moment, he thought it was a spectral vision, a visitor from an unearthly world. A second glance and he saw that the face belonged to Kate.

"Hey dolly, I heard you flew in yesterday."

"I couldn't stay away. I was worried sick about you."

Jim shrugged. "Now look who's worried about whom."

"I thought I'd drop by and see you. I brought you a tuna melt sandwich from Lucy's." Kate handed Jim a bag through the bars. "Rocky had to check the contents… procedures. I had to do all I could to keep him from eating it."

Jim laughed. "Thanks for the sandwich." He placed the bag on his bunk. Then he heard a voice near the cellblock door.

"How's the outlaw?"

Jim and Kate glanced at Linda entering the cellblock.

"Hey Linda, I don't blame you for doing your duty the other day," Jim said.

Linda confessed, "I had to go by the book." She walked up to Kate and whispered to her and Jim, "I know Jack Morton's killer is still out there."

Jim walked closer until his bare feet were against the bars of the cell. "Wish I was helping with the investigation."

Linda said, "What investigation? Emily's proceeding with you as the sole suspect. I heard a rumor that she's looking for a minimum of life without parole for Jack's murder, and if she can pin the Bitterroot killings on you, she'll turn that over to the Feds for a death penalty case."

Jim sat back down on his bunk and rested his head against the cement wall. "What am I going to do? There's someone killing people, we've got a bunch of racists in town, and I've got unfinished business to attend to."

"What business is that?" Kate asked.

Jim looked up at her. "I can't say. I made a promise."

"Is that what you were doing that morning? Martha said you didn't want anyone to know where you were going. Is that where you were when Jack was murdered?" Linda asked.

Jim covered his eyes with his hand.

Linda stamped her boot on the cement floor. "For God sakes, if you have witnesses who can testify where you were when Jack was murdered, tell us!"

Jim pulled his hand away from his face and leaned on his elbows. "I can't reveal where I was or who I was with."

"You goddamn stubborn horse," Linda yelled. "We're talking about your life here!"

Jim rolled onto his side, facing the wall of his cell. "The hell with it, as long as Kate's safe, what does anything else matter?"

"Stop! I may be safe but I'm lost without you," Kate said.

Linda rattled the cell bars with her nightstick. "What's the matter with you! You were my mentor," she said.

"Your mentor?" Jim asked.

"Why do you think I came back to Taylor after graduation?"

"You grew up here," reminded Jim.

Linda shook her head. "When I began studying Criminal Justice at the University of Montana, I had this dream of working for the FBI in Washington... or maybe the CIA... I don't know." She looked back at Jim. "Your pictures and trophies are all over the university. You're a legend there."

Jim frowned. "You turned down a dream to become an FBI agent because I played football at Montana?"

Kate rolled her eyes. "He's like that at home too."

Linda yelled. "Listen to me! It was more than that. You were successful at everything you did; football, the Air Force, the highway patrol, sheriff, and you did it the right way. I wanted to emulate that. I returned to Taylor to learn from someone who I hoped would share that professional vision with me."

Jim stood up and walked to his jail cell door. He stuck his arms through the bars. Kate took one hand and Linda the other. He whispered, "When I get out, we need to talk about cleaning up this town."

Linda nodded, let go of Jim's hand, then turned and walked to the cellblock door. She slammed her palm three times on the steel door until Rocky opened it.

Jim's eyes met Kate's. There was no need for words. Kate grasped his hand and kissed his lips between the bars, then left. Jim knew they were thinking the same thing. He sat down on his bunk, took a bite out of the tuna melt, and paused. Somehow, it didn't taste the way he remembered Lucy's sandwiches. It was different, it was better.

·40·

Jim spent the remainder of the day in solitude. Though he was in custody locked up in his own cellblock his mind remained busy evaluating who could have killed Jack Morton. His suspicion initially centered on Dave Anderson but there was no proof other than they appeared to be partners in the illegal liquor sales.

Jim's theories kept coming back full circle to Sam Clayton and that he could be the key to breaking this entire case wide open. Exhausted by his own thoughts, he fell asleep. Sunday evening, Rocky's voice awakened him.

"Boss, I had Tony at the dealership wipe off those nasty words that someone wrote on your tailgate and then had it repainted."

Jim stood up. "Thanks Rock. How much do I owe?"

"I took care of it. Can't have lyin' words like that for all to see." Rocky changed the subject. "Got yourself another visitor."

Jim looked up and saw Father Bongiorno from Saint Michael the Archangel at the cellblock door. He wore a black suit, black shirt, white collar, and held a bible in his hands.

He walked down the steps toward Jim's cell. "Rocky, may I sit inside the cell with Mr. Buchanan."

"I can't do that Father."

"Yes you can, my son. The Lord won't take no for an answer." Rocky hesitated and then as if mesmerized by the holy man, opened the cell door. Rocky locked the cell door behind them. Father Bongiorno held out his hand.

Jim wiped his hands on his jumpsuit and reached out to greet the white-haired clergyman. "Last Rights so soon?"

Father Bongiorno smiled. "I'm supposed to crack the jokes." The two men laughed and then the priest said, "Let's talk about your soul."

"My soul?"

Father Bongiorno continued, "The purpose of punishment is not for vindictiveness. Christ's healing love proves that human life is never beyond redemption."

"Look, Father..."

"Be still young man and have faith."

"Father, with all due respect, faith is to believe in something that has no tangible evidence. What I do requires evidence. Without evidence, I have no facts, without facts I have no belief, without belief I have no faith. Do you understand, Father?"

"What evidence do you need? Look at our world."

"Father, this world is going to put me to death. I'm an innocent man."

The priest sat on Jim's bunk and invited Jim to sit beside him. "An innocent man was executed two-thousand years ago." He continued, "They said that according to the law he must die. Jesus, was without sin and innocent of any crime, yet was judged to be guilty and executed. He suffered for our sins so that we would be free to rejoice in Heaven with the Father."

"So tell me now... who am I suffering for?"

The priest placed his hand on Jim's shoulder. "The Lord awakened me last night. He spoke to me and said that I must help save your soul."

"Are you saying I have sinned, Father?"

The priest stood up. "My son, we all carry sin."

Jim heard the cellblock door open and slam shut.

A voice yelled, "Let him out."

Jim looked past the priest and caught a glimpse of Hank waving a plastic bag with Dan and Emily following behind.

"Hank, what are you up to?" Jim stood up and met Hank at his cell door.

"We've got proof that you couldn't have killed Jack Morton." Hank held the plastic bag aloft containing a pair of forensic gloves. "We found this in Jack's wastebasket. It has Morton's blood all over it and the gloves can't possibly fit Jim's hands."

Emily shrugged. "This has nothing to do with why Jim was standing over a dead body, why his own knife protruded from what was left of the victim's stomach, and why he had a knife wound on his arm."

Hank smiled. "Jim was on the phone with Martha before he found the body. That was less than five minutes before Linda arrived on the scene and we found conclusive evidence that Jim wasn't at the scene when the murder occurred."

Emily folded her arms. "Exactly what is that evidence?"

Hank continued, "Jim's boots were bloody underfoot. He picked up blood from the floor but the top of his boots were dry."

"So?" Emily asked.

"So that means he didn't receive any blood spatters when the fatal knife thrusts occurred. The blood on his shoes, pants, and face were transfers from the blood that was already on the furniture and the floor."

Emily's brow wrinkled. "I'm not convinced."

"We have an imprint, a bare spot on the floor," Hank said. "We were able to isolate an area where Morton was killed. The blood spattered around what appears to be the shape of a shoe. I believe the killer received blood spatters on himself and that his shoe prevented those blood spatters from reaching the floor beneath his shoe."

"So?" challenged Emily.

Hank raised his voice. "The tops of Jim's shoes were clean and we have a bare floor imprint."

"Well, he must have changed shoes," Emily said.

"Jim wears a size sixteen. The imprint is of a shoe less than a foot in length."

"So what are you telling me?"

Dan McCoy interrupted, "I spoke with my girlfriend Esmeralda last night. She told me that her son saw Jim at his dad's old farm the day that Morton was murdered. He also said that he accidentally cut Jim on his arm with his jackknife."

Emily's eyes swooped toward Jim. "Is that true... is this what you've been hiding?"

197

Jim nodded. "I found stores of booze at my dad's farm. I believe Morton was involved in selling illegal liquor to the tribes on the Flathead Reservation."

"Do you have proof?" Emily asked.

"No, that's why I wanted to speak with Morton. There may be another person or two involved but I don't have all the proof right now that we need to make arrests."

Emily continued, "You're a stupid fool." She looked at Jim's bare feet. "Someone, bring him his personal belongings."

Rocky walked past Emily. "I got them right here."

Emily grabbed a clean pair of shoes, socks, and the rest of Jim's clothing. Then Rocky pulled a set of keys from his pocket and unlocked the cell door. Emily handed the clothes to Jim. "I owe you an apology."

Jim turned to Father Bongiorno. "I can't promise when I'll stop by."

The priest whispered to Jim. "Christ was falsely accused on a Friday just like you and then crucified. Then he was resurrected on Sunday. Today is Sunday, do you see the similarities?"

"Coincidence, Father."

"Not so, the Lord is speaking to you and you will continue to suffer until you respond to Him."

"Father, I have more pressing issues to deal with. My salvation will have to wait." Jim turned to Hank. "I have unfinished business with Sam Clayton. He's likely involved in the liquor sales and probably responsible for the fire at the morgue."

Everyone agreed with Jim. Clayton was still missing and the rest of the bums at Warehouse Row had not seen him in more than a week. The vacant factory where Sam lived with his fellow vagrants did not provide any clues.

The three Native boys' inability to identify other accomplices from mug shots that Jim brought to the reservation for the boys to examine stalled the case. However, Antonio Hightower and Abraham Sizemore positively identified the photographs of Jack Morton and Sam Clayton as the two individuals involved in the transportation of the alcohol.

Everyone speculated that Jack was the Bitterroot Killer but the case was left open because there were no suspects in Jack's murder. A fugitive warrant was issued for Sam Clayton but he was nowhere to be found.

However, there was still the matter of identifying the bodies. Hank encouraged the FBI to employ a forensic anthropologist to reconstruct the decomposed head found in the panel truck. Images of that reconstructed face, distributed throughout the region, in the hopes that someone would come forward and make a positive identification, were all they banked on for now.

As the days and weeks passed things settled down in Cedar County. However, something unsettling continued to gnaw at Jim's insides.

·41·

Summer turned to fall and fall became winter in Cedar County. The few deciduous trees shed their leaves. The small critters that lived in the valleys and mountains foraged for provisions that would assist them through the long, cold Montana winter. Snow had fallen and crews closed the high mountain roads for the winter season.

Jim discovered a new dedication to his work. Kate told him that living in fear is no way to go on with your life. His ongoing therapy sessions also convinced him of that.

Jim shared information with the FBI regarding the illegal liquor sales on the Flathead Indian Reservation, Jack Morton's involvement and Lucy's information regarding Jack's contact with that young man whose body may have been the one discovered near the Flathead River. After an investigation of nearly six months without any new leads the FBI put the Bitterroot Killer murder case on hold with Jack Morton the likely suspect.

The clay reconstructed head of the skull found in the panel truck and the DNA results did lead to its identification. Newspaper photos prompted the local police in Portland, Oregon to provide the name of Mario "The Wrench" DeFazio, a part-time hustler, part-time gambler, and full-time enforcer in the Brunazzi crime family of Portland.

Since Jack Morton was dead and Sam Clayton missing, the exact details of how DeFazio met his demise were unknown. What everyone did know was where and when he disappeared.

On May 15, 1996 DeFazio, decked in gold chains, bracelets and diamond rings, attended a Portland Trailblazers' basketball game with Julius "Sweetheart" Innamorato, a bookie for the Brunazzi family, Tony "The Bull" Ristoro, personal bodyguard for Luigi Brunazzi and finally, Mr. Brunazzi himself.

DeFazio left his courtside seat in the second half for a trip to the men's room. Caught on a security camera at a concession stand where he purchased a beer, he then disappeared and never returned to his seat.

After the FBI confirmed the identity of the head as DeFazio's, men in dark glasses and suits frequented the local businesses in and around Taylor. Some residents believed they were part of the west coast mafia while others said they were federal agents but no one knew for sure.

The new, state-of-the-art morgue, attached as a wing of the State Crime Lab, was finished. Hank processed the remainder of the corpses from the Bitterroot Killer murder case. The Native bodies were turned over to the Flathead Tribe and the others to their families.

The only body related to the Bitterroot Killer investigation that remained in the morgue's crypt was DeFazio's decomposed head. Hank needed to examine every shred of evidence before he could release it to DeFazio's mob brethren.

The Guardians of Doctrine continued their presence in Taylor and began to spread their influence to other parts of Cedar County. They stayed within the law while spreading their hateful speech to whoever offered an interested ear. They even gained a few converts by raising money for civic events and assisting those in need. Even so, Sheriff Jim Buchanan kept a watchful eye on their involvement in the community.

The Roy Lewis Show's popularity thrived resulting in the parent station of KCHM successfully promoting its syndication. Roy Lewis' influence spread beyond western Montana. Fans now stretched from Idaho to Wyoming, the Dakotas, Iowa, Nebraska and everywhere in-between. Roy Lewis was poised to become a national media figure.

It was past seven o'clock on Christmas Eve. The sheriff's office was empty except for one person pulling dispatcher duties. The door to the sheriff's office opened. A few snowflakes swirled through the doorway as a young woman entered the building. She walked up to the dispatcher's bulletproof glass window.

"Merry Christmas, I'm looking for Sheriff Buchanan."

"I'm Undersheriff Tom Hyde." He swiveled around in his chair and faced his visitor. "Buchanan's not here. I'm the only one working."

"That's awful you have to work on the eve of our Savior's birth."

"Bah humbug." Tom laughed.

The woman removed her green knit hat and shook her head as tumbling blond curls fell to her shoulders. "My name is Claire Hanley. I'm a social worker with the Western Montana Catholic Charities at the Flathead Reservation. Today, I learned there may be another victim in the Bitterroot Killer Murders."

"That's a closed case, ma'am."

"Someone gave me the name of a missing person." Claire looked around the office. "Do you expect Sheriff Buchanan back soon?"

"Who gave you his name?"

"Someone told me to see Sheriff Buchanan. He said to keep him out of it. I just want to provide the information to the sheriff and then I'll be on my way."

"I know exactly what you mean. Let me buzz you in. My office is at the end of this hallway. Let me show you where it is and then I'll call Sheriff Buchanan on the radio and tell him you're here. Would you like a coffee while you wait?"

Claire nodded. "It's so cold outside. I'm from New York but it never gets this cold in the city." She blew her warm breath into her cupped hands.

Tom flicked on the light switch in his office and Claire sat in one of his guest chairs. She watched him walk to the front of the building then heard him place the call. Looking around, she found Tom's office immaculately appointed. A neat worktable behind his desk, and above that, a row of shelving containing textbooks on criminology and veterinary medicine, finished the warm inviting space.

"Here's your coffee," Tom said returning to his office.

Claire faced him, smiled, and reached for the coffee cup. "Thank you."

"Checking out my books?" Tom asked.

"You have quite a collection."

"Have a seat."

Claire complied and sipped her coffee. "This is nice and warm, thank you."

"You're welcome." Tom reached for a pad and pencil. "Jim asked me to begin taking a statement from you."

"I really want to wait for Sheriff Buchanan."

"He said he'll be here in thirty minutes."

"Well, all right. I guess I should start from the beginning and give you a little background about me. I was living on the reservation with a Native American family."

"What did you do there?"

"I help families apply for food and housing assistance."

"Go on." Tom jotted down notes on a legal pad.

"There is such pain on the reservation."

Tom leaned back in his chair. "Just tell me what you know about the killings."

Claire put her coffee mug down and leaned forward in her chair. "One night, I received a phone call from a tribal woman whose husband was beating up their daughter."

"Go on."

"He was beating her because she stole some money."

"What were their names?"

"The family's name is Bear Cloud."

"What do you know about them?"

"Willow Bear Cloud told me that her husband Robert sells liquor to the other Indians on the Flathead Reservation."

"What else did she tell you?"

"This is why I didn't want to go to the police department. She said that once when her husband was drunk, he threatened her. He told her that all he had to do was tell someone in the Taylor Police Department that she knew all about the liquor sales."

"And what would happen if he did that?"

"He told her one of the policemen would kill her, just like he killed the others."

"What else?"

"That was a few weeks ago. Her husband disappeared the next day and she hasn't heard from him since."

Tom got up from his desk and stood beside Claire. "Would you mind if I record your statement?"

"No... not at all," Claire replied.

"We'll place you under protective custody until we can round up the suspects." Tom walked to the door. "I'll have to get my tape recorder from the storage closet."

"Okay," Claire replied as she took a final gulp of her coffee.

"Feel free to have another cup. I'll just be a couple three minutes," Tom said walking toward the back of the sheriff's office.

Claire heard the door to the storage closet creak open. She walked to the coffee station and was about to pour another cup when she noticed a pretty, green box with Chinese symbols imprinted on it.

She opened the box and removed a small foil bag. On the bag, written in English were the words, <u>Chinese Melon Seed Tea</u>. She noticed a pot of hot water on the coffee station and ripped open the foil pouch. With no metal tea basket to accommodate the loose tea leaves, Claire dumped the contents of the pouch into her cup and poured in the hot water.

The tea leaves swam about the cup as the hot water agitated the mixture and softened the leaves. She picked up a spoon lying at the coffee station and walked back to Tom's office. She stirred the tea, and placed the spoon on a bookshelf next to Tom's desk.

One errant tea leaf on the underside of the spoon adhered to the shelf. Claire raised the cup to her lips and sipped. The taste of this exotic tea surprised her and she took another sip. The quietness of the empty office and the warm beverage worked their calming ways.

Tom poked his head back in his office. "I forgot I moved the recorder equipment in the back. Would you help me retrieve it?" he asked, disappearing into the hallway.

Claire finished the tea, picked up the spoon and the cup, and carried them back to the coffee station.

"Sure," she said and followed Tom down the hall.

"The equipment is near the back door, behind the jail cells," Tom said.

"Jail cells... aren't there prisoners in there?" Claire asked.

"Not on Christmas Eve. We're the only ones here."

Claire breathed a sigh of relief. "Thank God, I feel safe now."

The two walked into the cellblock and back toward the solitary door at the end of the building.

·42·

At 7:34 p.m. on Christmas Eve, a series of persistent knocks brought Jim racing to the front door with Angel at his heels. Angel seated herself on the red welcome mat in anticipation of her usual greeting of jumping, twirling and wagging. Jim told her to stay and slowly opened the door keeping himself between Angel and the visitor.

"Merry Christmas!" Linda said sporting a dimpled smile.

Snowflakes from the sudden and unpredicted snowstorm that raged outside still hung onto Linda's short blond locks peeking out from under her red and white knit hat.

"Merry Christmas!" Jim replied.

"Aren't you going to invite her in?"

Jim turned to Kate and then glanced at Linda. "Yeah, come on in."

Linda walked into the living room where Angel greeted her with a nudge. The Christmas tree was adorned with lights, bulbs, and tinsel while the distinctive sound of bagpipes pumped out "Loch Lomond" on the stereo.

"The tree looks great," Linda stated, petting Angel on her head.

Jim excused himself and went to get his and Kate's coats.

Linda took Kate's hands in hers. "You look much better. I think your trip to New York did wonders for you."

Jim returned with the coats. "Kate, we should leave now. Come on Angel."

They departed for Hank's Christmas Eve house party amid a violent snowstorm that dashed over the Coeur D'Alene Mountain Range and roared into the Clark Fork River Valley. The Cabinet

Mountains slowed the easterly progress of the storm and caused it to stall and dump most of its precipitation on Taylor.

Jim's SUV slowed to a crawl as he navigated the snow covered roads. The wind-swept flakes battered his car but Jim finally arrived at Hank's house and parked in the spacious driveway alongside six other cars. They sat and watched the snowflakes smother the landscape.

Linda reached from the backseat and touched the shoulders of Jim and Kate. "Are you two okay?"

Jim turned to her as Angel stuck her head in-between the seats. "I've got a lot on my mind," he said.

Jim, Kate, Linda, and Angel trudged through the snow and up to Hank's porch.

The doorbell barely rang when Hank swung open the door and greeted them with a loud, "Merry Christmas!"

The room full of people resonated with the recorded sound of Glen Miller's "I'll Be Home for Christmas". There was Dan McCoy on the great room couch with his arm around Esmeralda Hightower. Her hair was long and she wore a traditional buckskin dress with a red coral necklace.

Paul Harris, in black dress slacks and a gray turtleneck sweater, stood in front of the fireplace. The flame's flickering warmth radiated throughout the room. A glass of wine in his hand, Paul chatted with his wife Sherrie and their three children, Jamal, Sharita, and Marcus.

Hank's two daughters, Kim and Kathryn, their husbands, Mark and Matt, and their young children, John, Joan, and Luke sat at the dining room table working on a 3-D jigsaw puzzle.

Hank's wife Mary stood in the area between the great room and the kitchen. She wore her legendary apron, using it to wipe her hands. Rocky stood next to her with a mouthful of food while Jia Li held a tray of assorted cookies.

On the floor was Antonio Hightower, Esmeralda's son. He played in the corner with an HO-scale electric train set whose tracks looped around the Kelly's Christmas tree.

Jim surveyed everyone in the room. He said to Hank, "It's nice to be in such a warm home with people I care about."

"I'm glad you and Kate could make it. Let me take your coats."

"We're going to have trouble getting back home in this storm," Kate said.

"Nonsense," Hank replied as he took Jim, Kate and Linda's coats. "They're now predicting two feet of snow. We're all sleeping in tonight. Mary's going to hand out pajamas and we'll throw all your washables in the machine if need be. I've got plenty of room upstairs and in the basement rec room. And don't forget Rocky helped me build those two bedrooms in the attic this fall. Plus we have a generator in case we lose power."

"Well then, Merry Christmas!" Jim handed Hank a gift-wrapped box while Kate and Linda piled two more onto his outstretched arms.

Kate turned to Jim, stepped closer to him, and pointed upwards. Jim looked at the ceiling and saw a twig of mistletoe hanging from the foyer chandelier. Gently grasping his shoulders, Kate pulled Jim's face down toward hers and planted a kiss on his cheek. "Merry Christmas." Jim returned the kiss and the greeting. Kate smiled then said, "You and Hank must have things to catch up on. I'll see if Mary needs help."

Jim watched Kate walk away. His gaze lingered longer than his thoughts. When she disappeared into the kitchen, he turned to Hank. "Anything on DeFazio?"

"No. The FBI investigated but so far, there are no leads. They tried to find out if there was any connection between DeFazio and either Jack Morton or Sam Clayton but they couldn't find anything."

Rocky overheard their exchange, excused himself from Linda's company, and joined the conversation. "I have a hunch he was supplying the booze to Morton. The mob must have covered their tracks."

"They're good at that," Hank said. "I saw firsthand their grip on people by threats and intimidation."

Rocky nodded. "When I lived in Brooklyn, DeFazio's second cousin, Salvatore lived around the corner from *la mia famiglia*. I knew his sons. I dated one of his daughters. The other daughter, her name was Regina DeFazio," Rocky laughed. "When we were singing a cappella on the street corner and she'd walk by we'd call to her, *ehi Gina Novena, ho un braciola grande per lei.*"

"I have no idea what you just said," Jim replied.

"You don't need to know," responded Hank.

Rocky continued, "She not only went to Mass every day but she did First Friday's every single month! I even sat in the same pew with her Uncle Patsy the morning after he had his thugs drive an ice pick through a snitch's ear."

Hank replied, "Rocky, you don't have to tell me stories like that. I've seen my share spending my days fishing the docks on the East River."

"We should keep our eyes and ears open in case anything comes of this guy DeFazio. If the mob was involved in the illegal liquor sales, then I'm sure we'll have visitors," Jim warned.

Kate walked into the great room with a tray of hors d'oeuvres and made a beeline for Jim, Hank, and Rocky. "Have some," she said.

Jim's busy fingers surveyed the tray. He selected a few treats. "They're good! Rock, try some."

Linda walked up to Rocky and tapped him on the back of his shoulder. "Yeah, have some Rocky." Rocky took a few and then Linda whispered to Jim, "A full mouth can't speak." Jim stifled a laugh.

Kate carried the tray of hors d'oeuvres around the room offering its contents to the other guests while Paul Harris and Dan McCoy joined the group.

Paul said, "It looks like Jack Morton was the Bitterroot Killer. Since his murder last summer no additional bodies have turned up in Cedar County and the bootlegging on the Flathead Reservation ended. We still have to discover who killed Morton but they had two similar cases over the past two months off Route 200, east of Sandpoint, Idaho. No suspects or motives. It appears those and Morton's murder may have been random acts by the same perp or copycat killings. The good news is there's no longer a murderer walking the streets of Taylor."

"Amen to that," Hank replied. "When I retired to Taylor… and I want to emphasize retired." The group laughed and Hank continued, "I never thought I'd get involved in another high profile case again. I saw enough of them in New York City."

Dan McCoy leaned back on the couch. "I hear ya. This was the crime of the century in these parts. Worse than that body part scheme that Jim solved last year. I hope we don't see anything like this ever again."

"All I can say is that I came this close to retiring myself," advised Linda as she measured a space between her thumb and index finger. "Finding Morton murdered was enough for me."

"Yeah, it affected me too," Rocky said. "I lost a few pounds running around worrying about the case."

"Really! You lost weight?" Linda said with a wink.

"Hey, that's muscle." Rocky patted his flat stomach.

"You're pretty quiet over there, Jim," Hank said.

Kate returned and placed the empty tray on a table. She sat next to Jim on the loveseat. He opened his mouth to speak but Kate stopped him by placing her hand on his knee. "Jim's got a lot on his mind."

Linda spoke next. "We're your friends Jim. I've learned that friends need to share not just the good times but the hardships as well."

"Jim, is there something bothering you... can we help?" Paul asked.

Jim scanned the faces of his friends. Five sets of eyes were upon him. He turned to look at Kate by his side who returned a smile. "Things are all right. Next week Kate and I are traveling to Billings to visit my sister and daughter."

"That's it?" Hank asked.

Jim barked, "I don't want to get into details."

A knock at the door quickly interrupted the lull that had fallen over the room.

"Now who can that be at the height of this storm?" Hank said walking toward the front door. Opening it, he met a burst of snowflakes that flew into the room. "Deputy Police Chief Anderson... Merry Christmas," Hank opened the door wider. "Would you like to join us?"

Dave Anderson gazed at the crowd of people in the house. "I was driving by and saw the lights on. I thought I'd wish everyone a Merry Christmas."

Angel growled and bared her teeth at Anderson. Jim commanded her, "Sit and stay!" Angel sat down, lifted her paw, and stroked empty space in front of her.

Hank took Anderson's coat as the deputy police chief weaved his way through the crowd and engaged in conversation with the guests.

While Hank had the closet door open to hang Anderson's coat, Jim grabbed his own and stuck one arm in a sleeve.

"Where are you going?" Hank asked.

"Angel has to go out," Jim replied as he grabbed her leash. He felt a hand lift the coat over his shoulders and turned to see Linda behind him. He said, "I don't need help."

Linda simply said, "I love the snow." She grabbed her coat and walked past Hank. "Let's get going."

Outside, Jim brushed the new-fallen snow off his shoulders while Linda walked alongside. "Enjoying the holidays?" he asked.

Linda answered, "They could be better."

"What's wrong?"

"It's just I don't speak much with my family anymore. So I've been working most of the time. How about you?"

"I'm taking a few days off next week to visit my sister and daughter. My counselor told me that would be the final part of my treatment."

"Kate told me that you've been going to therapy. Is it helping?"

"Yeah, it's helped a great deal."

There was silence for a few seconds as they traversed the snow-covered sidewalk away from Hank's house. Then Linda said, "That's not what's bothering you."

Jim sighed. "I can't talk about it yet. I have no evidence."

"Then let's talk about Anderson."

Jim stopped. "What's up?"

Amid the snowflakes, Linda blurted out her suspicions. "I think Anderson's mixed up in the Bitterroot Killings."

"Why do you say that?" Jim asked. "Everyone thinks it's pretty much a closed case."

Linda said carefully. "Hank spoke with me in confidence and told me to tell you when the time is right. He has evidence that he won't release because of the fear that the Bitterroot Killer is still on the loose and it may be someone in the Taylor Police Department. As you know the original evidence was conclusive that an unknown assailant is responsible for Jack's murder."

"The killer is still out there and that's what haunts me."

Linda explained, "I did research on Anderson, things that Chief Peters doesn't know about."

"Like what?"

"Anderson was involved in a couple of questionable arrests in Wisconsin. Four times he was brought up on charges of police brutality but nothing stuck. There were also other incidents."

"Tell me."

"I made a few phone calls and found out that on two separate occasions Anderson was the arresting officer where the suspect and the victim both died at the scene."

"That's regrettable but not uncommon."

"Both times, his partners were also killed and there were no other witnesses."

"Was there an investigation?"

"There was, that was standard procedure but…"

"But what?" Jim asked.

Linda paused while the snow draped across their shoulders. With determination, she said, "I found out there were no ballistics evidence on the two dead police officers."

Jim shook his head. "It smells like a cover-up."

"What are we going to do?" Linda asked.

Jim thought for a moment and then said, "Let's get back to Hank's. Keep this between you and me."

·43·

During the night, the unrelenting snowfall accumulated on the ground, on the trees and on the roofs of the houses. The storm raged on throughout the Clark Fork River Valley and coated everything with a pristine layer of snow. The storm continued into the bleak early morning hours. Already the fifth blizzard of a busy season, the landscape accepted twenty-nine inches of new fallen snow.

It was early Christmas morning in Taylor and the thick, overcast skies projected a muted appearance on the blanketed, snow-covered land. Drifts cascaded in carpet-like formation from the Cabinet Mountains. Where wind-swept snow could not continue their path, they gathered against walls, fences, fir trees, and buildings. Sometimes having reached rooftops where telltale wisps of persistent white smoke from red brick chimneys revealed human attempts to thwart the seeping bitter cold.

The White Christmas gift kept most of the Taylor residents inside, close to their warm fireplaces, oblivious to any activity that transpired outside.

It was in a certain darkened house near the high school at two in the morning when a teenage boy, suffering from Christmas Morning Insomnia pressed his nose against one of his bedroom windowpanes. Josh Nelson looked back at what had partially blocked his ability to visualize himself running for another imaginary touchdown on the snowy high school football field.

He saw two people standing next to a sled. They lifted an oblong black bag off the sled and carried it to one of the test pits excavated for the installation of next spring's new football field lighting system. They picked up the bag from the sled and dropped it into the hole. Retrieving shovels from the sled, the two buried the object with what appeared to be fresh, unfrozen topsoil from a tarp-covered pile dumped next to the test pit.

·44·

Tracy turned over in bed. The silence of the night and its veil of darkness plummeted upon her in an unsettling manner. When the cool air of the house assaulted her senses, she whispered to her spouse, "Matt, can you throw more wood on the fire?"

"What did you say?" Matt slowly nestled back to sleep.

Tracy heard a noise downstairs. "Who's there?" Tracy asked again, "Who's there?"

A young voice piped up, "It's me ma."

Tracy gazed at the alarm clock on her nightstand. It read 3:45. She rose from bed and covered herself in the bathrobe she snatched from the bedside chair. She raced downstairs in her bare feet, turned her head from side to side, and then walked into the kitchen. She saw Josh leaning against the countertop, phone in hand.

He spoke into the telephone. "Can I talk with Sheriff Buchanan?"

Tracy ran up to him, grabbed the receiver, and hung it up. "What are you doing?"

He ran past her. "Aw ma!"

Matt Nelson, stumbled into the living room. He caught Josh as the boy sprinted by. "Whoa, where are you off to? Tell your mother you're sorry."

Josh stopped and pulled his arm away. "I want to see Uncle Jim today."

"You what?" Matt asked.

"I want to see Uncle Jim."

"Don't ever mention his name in this house," Matt yelled.

"I want to see Uncle Jim or I'll tell mom what you do on Wednesday nights."

"Josh, what are you talking about?" Matt gave his son a sideways glare.

Josh tried to wriggle away from his father's grasp. "Kevin Peck said you and his dad belong to a club. He said you're going to get everyone together to fight the Indians, kick them off the reservations, and take the land back. He said the club will finish what Custer started."

"That's Jeb Peck's son! What's going on?" Tracy asked.

Matt looked at his wife. "I don't know what Josh is talking about."

"Are you saying Josh is lying?"

"I'm not lying momma."

"Matt?"

"All right, all right! I don't know how I ever got involved in this." Matt sat at the kitchen table and cradled his head in his hands.

"Josh," Tracy said harshly, "go upstairs right now and get back to bed."

"But what about Uncle Jim?"

"Go upstairs right now!" Tracy ordered.

Josh unwillingly trudged up the stairs.

The telephone rang. Matt got up and answered. "Hello? Yes, this is Matt Nelson... Oh that was Josh... No, he just wanted to wish everyone at the sheriff's office a Merry Christmas... Yes, I'll tell him that... Goodbye." Matt hung up the phone and looked at Tracy. "That was Tom Hyde, the undersheriff. It's all right."

"No it's not! What's going on Wednesday nights?"

Matt bowed his head and clasped his hands behind his neck. "A couple three years ago... I was invited..."

"Invited?"

Matt continued, "Yeah, invited. Some people in town wanted to form a group to address business and civic issues. I thought it was a great idea. You know, we buy in bulk... insurance, suppliers, and vendors. Then we got involved in community action issues; town beautification, neighborhood watch, charity work, gun safety. That's when things got crazy."

"What do you mean?" Tracy gathered Matt's hands in hers.

"Everyone was encouraged to bring their handguns and rifles to the downstairs meeting room at the Church of the Revelation. We had someone from Idaho present a lecture on gun safety." Matt took a deep breath. "Near the end of the meeting, he spoke of the Double Ds."

"What are the Double Ds?" Tracy asked.

Matt replied, "The Dark Dangers... the non-whites."

"Good Lord!"

Matt continued, "I was uncomfortable. But Cy Taylor said we were the town's business leaders and we were in this together. We had to first take back the town, then the county, then the state and..."

"Go on."

"The Absolute Conclusion would be to cleanse this country through armed resistance if necessary until the only ones left are of Aryan blood."

"You believed that crap?"

"You don't understand. There was pressure on me. If I didn't go along with them they said they wouldn't support the pharmacy and they wouldn't protect it."

"Who else is involved in this?"

"Jeb Peck, Reverend Scott Simmons, Harold Porter, about a dozen others and then there's this guy I never met. They call him the Supreme Divinity. He runs the whole show. And..." Matt paused.

"Who else?"

"He's dead now."

"Who else!"

"Jack Morton," Matt confessed.

"Oh my God! We've got to tell the police."

She picked up the telephone but Matt placed his hand on hers. "You don't want to do that," he said.

"Why not?"

"Because if the people in the group found out that we contacted the police, our lives would be in danger."

Tracy screamed, "What is this group!"

"They're called the Guardians of Doctrine."

"We're going to call Jim."

Matt held the receiver down. "You can't do that."

"Why not?"

"The group has plans to kill him. If he gets involved they'll just do it sooner."

"What has Jim ever done to anyone?"

"They call him a mud person, a non-white, a red heathen."

Tracy placed her hands on her husband's shoulders. "Look at me!" she commanded.

Matt's eyes inched upwards until they were even with hers. "I'm tired of sneaking around with this feeling of hatred," he said weakly.

"Release yourself. Ask God's forgiveness, do what's right."

"Tracy, you don't understand."

Tracy's voice grew louder, "Oh, I understand. I understand that I'm sick and tired of people condemning others because of where they were born or what language they speak or the color of their skin. When did judging people by how they treat others go out the window?"

Matt brushed Tracy's hair across her forehead with his hand. "You're right. I owe Jim an apology for how I've treated him. I'll speak with him."

Tracy corrected Matt. "We'll all speak with Jim."

·45·

B y mid-morning, the skies had cleared but the temperature
suddenly dropped to below zero. Common after storms in
the northwestern corner of Montana, the warmer Chinook
Winds then picked up and battled the cold weather. The air
currents swiftly drove eastward and increased in speed with some
isolated gusts reaching seventy miles per hour.

Jim struggled to keep his SUV on the road. Massive wind-
driven snowdrifts piled up against walls, fences, and homes
scattered about Taylor. Jim and his passengers, Rocky, Linda,
and Paul reached the sheriff's office unscathed.

The four law enforcement officials entered the building,
each stomping the snow from their shoes.

Jim noticed Josh outside the dispatcher's office sitting on
the hallway bench. "Merry Christmas, Josh."

Before Josh could answer, Martha got Jim's attention.
"Tracy and Matt are in Tom's office. Go right in."

"Why?" Jim asked.

"Just go in."

As Jim ran his cardkey through the reader, he felt a tug on
his arm.

"I have something to ask you," Josh said.

Jim took his hat off. "How's my favorite football player?"

Josh whispered in Jim's ear, "Last night, I saw people on
the football field."

Jim laughed. "You mean imaginary players."

"No sir. These were real people," assured Josh.

"No one should be on the high school field during a storm.
Are you sure?"

"Yes sir. They were real."

"Maybe you saw a grizzly and her young at the school dumpster?"

"No Uncle Jim. There were two people and they had a sled. They pulled something off that sled, dropped it in a hole, and then covered it up."

Jim's hat fell from his hand and onto the floor. He felt his face flush and then glanced at Martha. "Keep an eye on Josh." He spun around to Rocky. "Call Hank... pick him up and meet me outside the Nelson's home. Bring your gun." He picked up his hat and turned to Linda and Paul. "Let's talk to Tracy and Matt."

Jim brought Josh inside the dispatcher's office and seated him in a chair next to Martha's desk. Jim, Linda, and Paul stomped into Tom's office just as Tracy and Matt were putting on their coats.

"We're finished in here," Tom said.

Jim stared at Matt. "What you know about the high school football field."

"It's behind our house."

Tom Hyde raised his voice. "Jim, the Nelson's are leaving with me to speak with some townsfolk regarding the Guardians of Doctrine."

"Matt, did you see any people on the high school ballfield last night?" Jim asked.

"I don't know anything about any people on any field. I went to bed early."

"I'm leaving with the Nelson's now," Tom said.

Jim stepped in front of Matt blocking his way to the door. "No one is leaving until someone explains to me what Josh saw on the football field last night."

"Josh said he saw people drop something in a hole. Is it a crime for people to be out in a storm?" Matt asked.

"I'm sure no one saw anything. There was a blizzard last night." Tom grabbed his hat and put on his coat. "I've got a search warrant for the Church of the Revelation."

"Tom, forget about that warrant for now. We're going to the Nelson's home. I want Josh to show us where he saw the people on that field."

"Sounds like a wild goose chase." Tom turned to the Nelsons. "Let's go."

Tracy interrupted, "Captain Stevens, I'm sure that Matt will cooperate if you're involved." Matt nodded.

"Of course I will," Linda said. "What Josh saw on the field may have something to do with the Bitterroot Killings."

"That's an open and shut case and I'm not going to trample around a snowy field," Tom argued. "Matt, are you going with me or not?"

Tracy spoke up. "I don't like the idea that what Josh saw might have something to do with the murders. That's too close to our home."

Matt stood up and faced Jim. After a pause, he said, "We may have had our differences, but if anything were to happen to Tracy or Josh I couldn't live with myself." He stared at Tracy. "We'll cooperate."

Jim held out his hand to Matt who grasped it firmly.

Tom put his hat on and walked to the door. "Jim, I've been on shift now for more than sixteen hours. If you don't mind, I'll catch up with you later."

Jim nodded to Tom who turned and left. Jim, Linda, and Paul followed Josh and his family back to their home. Once there with Rocky aboard, Paul drove Jim's SUV to the high school field and waited for Jim's instructions. Jim and Linda joined Hank and went upstairs to Josh's bedroom.

"Josh, show us where you saw the people," Jim asked.

"Right there." Josh pointed to the goal line at the south end of the field.

Jim contacted Rocky on his cellphone and directed him to where Josh had pointed. He could clearly see Rocky and Paul, loaded down with emergency gear from Jim's SUV, trudging through the snow across the football field.

Putting his phone on speaker, Jim asked, "See anything?"

Rocky headed for the spot. "The winds are tough... if anyone was here last night; their footprints are now covered by the snow drifts."

When Rocky reached the snow-covered mound of soil, Jim issued an order. "Mark it."

Rocky sunk a five-foot surveyor's stake with an attached orange flag in the snow.

"Ask Paul if the FBI can dispatch a digging crew. I don't want the area disturbed until they get here."

"Right," Rocky said.

"And Rock."

"Yeah boss?"

"You and Paul have boots, a thermal coat, gloves, and a shovel. Until the crews arrive, grab a couple deputies and have them dig a spot a few feet from the stake and open that flip-over shelter you have. Use the portable flameless heater to keep warm."

"Harris just said the crew won't be here for seven hours," Rocky said.

"You have any firepower in case of trouble?" Jim asked.

"We each have our service sidearm and I'll have the deputies bring a couple of shotguns."

"Good, see you in a few hours," Jim replied.

Hank said, "I'll phone Leon and have him prepare the morgue to receive a body."

Jim whispered to Linda, "Make sure Anderson doesn't find out about this until after we know what's in that field."

·46·

As the sun set in the western sky, an FBI dump truck with a plow attachment arrived hauling a backhoe on a flatbed trailer. The truck driver unhitched the trailer and plowed his way onto the field. He then cleared a staging area complete with lighting next to the stake that Rocky had placed in the ground.

Jim, Hank and Leon met them on the scene and after an hour of careful digging by the FBI crew under Hank's watchful eyes, they exposed a layer of black plastic. The FBI crew jumped into the shallow pit and manually handled the extraction.

Inside the bag was a partially frozen and badly mutilated body. They removed the corpse and placed it in the State Medical Examiner's van. Jim saw the expression on Hank's face. It clearly explained to him that the Bitterroot Killer was still on the prowl.

"Linda said you have some info you're holding back about the Bitterroot Killings. Want to tell me what it is?" Jim asked.

Hank laughed. "You and Linda are as thick as thieves."

"It comes with the territory. That's how we trust one another."

"We'll go over it in the morgue."

Leon wheeled the body from the high school football field into the new state of the art mortuary facility. In front of Hank and Jim, Leon pulled the sheet from the corpse.

Leon turned to Hank. "Doc, it looks like there's not enough meat in the stew."

Hank nodded. "We only have a torso, just like the others." Hank examined the body's exterior and spoke into his tape recorder as he moved about the corpse. "The body is that of a young woman who seems to have been in relatively good physical condition."

Hank set the tape on pause and remarked, "Jim, listen carefully. This body has the same characteristics that lead me to believe that the killer is still out there. Except for the missing extremities and frozen tissue in a few places, it's in the best shape of any we've found. I'd estimate this victim has been dead only a few days, maybe less."

"Josh told me two people buried the body," Jim said.

Hank pointed to the areas of interest. "See how the arms and legs were severed. These were precise, deliberate cuts. We would expect to see evidence of pulling and tugging on the flesh, muscles, ligaments, and tendons if this was done by an amateur or someone in a hurry. The killer dissected the body in a deliberate manner."

"What do you make of it," Jim asked.

"Whoever this victim is, it was not a random killing. I also don't think this victim was killed in a conspicuous location. I think this person was led to where she would be murdered and I think it had to be done in a safe place." Hank looked down at the body. "I don't know... a doctor? Maybe someone with advanced medical training did this. Regardless the killer is still out there."

Splaying the abdominal wall, Hank used scissors to open the stomach. After suctioning away residual fluids, he noticed something. He scooped up a few dark green particles with a pair of toothless forceps and placed them on a flat plate. With the forceps, he pushed the particles back and forth. As they made further contact with the forceps, one began to disintegrate. Hank carefully dropped the two remaining intact samples in a solution laden laboratory specimen dish and closed the plastic lid.

"What do you think they are?" Leon asked.

"It appears our victim had something to eat before she met her demise," Hank said. "Leon, contact Agent Paul Harris... he's still at the high school."

It only took Paul a matter of minutes to arrive at the morgue, and with a curious Rocky rejoining the group in the autopsy room, there were now five sets of eyes staring at the specimen.

"What do you make of it?" Paul asked.

"It appears to be a piece of partially digested salad," Leon said.

"It's more than that." Hank said clinically, "It will tell us what she ate, when she ate, and perhaps where she ate."

Paul photographed the dark green particles and advised everyone that the FBI would take this very seriously since the particles could determine the last movements of the victim. Working until the wee hours of December 25, Hank finally shut the lights to the morgue and the group bundled themselves against the cold Montana winter and slipped into the darkness.

·47·

The next morning under sunny skies with a warming trend engulfing the Clark Fork River Valley, Jim arrived at the sheriff's office. Martha and Tom seemed to be the only people in the building. "How was your holiday, Tom?"

"Not bad. What did you find out about that body from the high school field?" Tom asked.

"Not much."

"That's too bad. Probably a copycat killing… right?"

"I don't know."

"But that's a possibility."

"It could be." Jim sought to change the subject. "Hank identified the body we found by the Flathead River."

"He did?"

"Yeah, some kid from Ohio who graduated college last June. His name was Steve Clancy. He was a scientist working for a nonprofit in and around the Flathead Lake area."

"How did Hank ID him?"

"He had an old high school football injury. Broke his ribs a few times and they had to insert a small metal plate to stabilize them. The plate was supposed to come out next year. We're lucky it was still intact with the manufacturer's name and serial number inscribed on it. We were able to trace it back to the hospital where they performed the surgery. From there it was easy to track down the surgeon and then the patient."

"How about that?" Tom said flatly.

Jim excused himself, and headed toward the cellblock. He heard Tom's chair scrape across the floor and sensed him following, but made no motion to acknowledge him.

After the discovery of the body and the possible resurgence of the Bitterroot Killer, Jim wanted to make certain everything was in order before getting on with his day. Opening the cellblock door, Jim stopped in his tracks. A trail of blood led to the back door. He turned to Tom. "What do you know about this?"

Tom did not speak a word as Jim walked into the cellblock, drew his revolver, sidestepped the blood, and opened the back door. He cocked the hammer on his gun and slipped around the corner. The blood ran from the cellblock door straight to Tom's cruiser, a deer carcass splayed across the top of the trunk.

"I planned to clean it up today," Tom apologized.

"What happened?" Jim asked as he holstered his revolver.

"There was a deer strike on 228. I'm dropping it off at Dr. Larson's later today for burial."

"How did blood get in the jail?"

"I'm sorry. I found the carcass in such a mess and I struggled trying to get it up on the cruiser. I got blood all over my clothes and then I tried to clean the blood off the deer with the water hose in the back. Then I had to come in the office to call the vet. That's how I got blood all over the place. It won't ever happen again."

"Clean up this mess right now. I want that deer delivered for burial this morning."

"I'll take care of it."

Jim turned his back to Tom and followed the trail of blood back into the building.

·48·

It was a cold morning on December 31 as most Taylor residents prepared for the New Year's festivities. However, at the sheriff's office it was anything but fun and merriment. Paul Harris and a man in a black trench coat, buzzed inside by Martha, approached the front desk. "Are you here to see the sheriff?" Tom asked.

Before either of the men could answer, Jim walked out of his office.

"Hey, Paul who's your friend?"

"This here's Special Agent Emmanuel Costa. He heads our western interdiction efforts. Drugs, stolen money, illegal arms. The riskier it is, the more he's up to it. Hank invited him."

Costa was a husky, middle-aged man with a shaven head. A deep scar across his left cheek from eye socket to jawbone dominated his face. The bottom half of the disfigurement disappeared into an ugly mass of composite skin grafts.

Jim held out his hand. "Nice to meet you, Emmanuel."

"Call me Manny," the agent said. Folding his arms across his chest, he added, "I heard you have some shit out here that you can't solve."

Jim raised his eyebrows. "You have no idea what it means to live in Montana. Trouble comes with the territory."

Manny laughed. "Cry me a goddamn river why don't ya."

"I'll take you for a tour so you can see firsthand how we survive out here. But we gotta make it fast. I'm leaving with my family for Billings later today."

Manny Costa stared at the sheriff without blinking, and then laughed. "Hey, take it easy there big fellow. Yeah, maybe this big city cop don't know some shit that takes place in this freaking wilderness but I've still got a job to do and I get it done any way I can… even if it means doing it the unconventional way."

Scrutinizing the FBI agent, Jim felt satisfied with the end of the exchange and smiled. "Let's get down to business. We'll go in the conference room. Hank's already in there waiting for us. I've got a metal wall map that we can mark up with colored magnets." Jim turned to Tom who had watched the proceedings and said to him, "Make sure we're not disturbed."

As Jim, Paul and Manny entered the conference room Hank immediately clasped Manny's hand. "Costa, it's been what, twenty years?" he asked.

"Doc, you old bastard," laughed Manny.

Hank kept shaking Manny's hand and said smiling, "I've worked with this guy on many cases. He's got a third eye, a sixth sense. You don't question what or why Manny does what he does, you just let him lead and go with the flow." He reminded Manny, "Remember our fishing expeditions in the East River?"

Manny laughed again. "A few times I was sure you'd be pulling me out of that cesspool someday."

They all sat at the conference table and every set of eyes were on Jim. He held two small magnets and displayed them to the group. "Blue for male and red for female."

They all nodded in agreement and Jim grabbed four small, round blue magnets and positioned them on the wall map alongside Route 28 near Lonepine. He took another blue magnet and covered a spot near where they had found the head in the panel truck near the railroad bridge. One blue magnet identified a spot near the southern end of Flathead Lake on a line that represented the Flathead River. Jim placed a seventh and final magnet, a red one, on the map where the town of Taylor was located. That magnet corresponded to the recent body they found at the high school football field.

Jim looked at the map and asked, "All right, what do we have here?"

"It's obvious," Hank said, examining the configuration. "Since we have DeFazio's head in custody, so to speak, and the killings are still ongoing, I've rethought my mob theory and have now come to the conclusion that this is a serial killer who lives in

Taylor. This information, plus the green particles found in the final victim's stomach are keys to finding this beast."

Hank pointed to the various locations where they found bodies. He placed a series of magnets with attached strings on top of the original magnets. By doing so, he drew a perimeter and connected the reference points.

Manny put his head down. "This is bullshit. It's goddamn bullshit." He pulled a cigarette from a pack in his shirt pocket and placed it between his lips. He then flicked on his lighter.

"You can't smoke in here," Jim said.

Manny let the unlit cigarette dance as he spoke. "I don't give a crap whether or not the killer lives in this town. I've spent fifteen years investigating serial killers. They don't go to these lengths to conceal their victims."

"How do you know that?" Paul asked.

Manny explained, "If they bury their victims they bury them in shallow graves, they leave clues behind, they wanna be found. They get a high when they kill and an adrenalin rush when they toy with law enforcement. It's a cat and mouse game to them."

Paul asked, "What if this serial killer doesn't want to be found?"

"That doesn't make sense. It's not a serial killer per se," Manny replied as he walked over to Jim. "Sheriff, who else knows about the stuff Doc found in the stomach of the last victim?"

"Just us in this room and Leon, Rocky, and Linda."

"Good, let's keep it that way," Manny replied. "Look, I don't know if your killer is from these parts but just suppose that he was and just suppose that he didn't know about the stomach contents."

"You're sure it was a he?" Hank asked.

"Yeah," Manny replied.

Paul took a few steps. "What else are you sure of?"

"Manny, just tell us what you think you know," Jim said.

Paul interjected, "Manny, I'm heading up the Bitterroot Killer Case. If you have any ideas that can help, tell us now."

Manny thought for a moment and then said, "You all better sit down." Everyone sat at the table and Manny began his story. "Doc, this broad that's been sleeping in your cooler, she probably happened to be in the wrong place at the wrong time."

"So what do we have here?" Paul asked.

Manny addressed Hank. "When would you pinpoint the time of death?"

Hank leaned back in his chair. "It's in my report. We think she was killed between the twentieth and twenty-fourth."

Manny stood up and walked around the room. "Okay, you found the body on Christmas Day, so the killer's had about a week or more to cover his tracks." He turned and faced Hank. "We've got to account for the time before the murder. I want to know everyone's whereabouts in this freaking town since a week prior to Christmas... residents, visitors, migrant workers, bums! I want to know about every freaking person that set foot in Taylor and if there's no leads locally, then I want to know what's going on in the goddamn county." Manny pulled out his lighter as he walked toward the door. "I'll shut down the whole goddamn state if I have to."

Manny slammed the door shut. Jim turned to Paul. "I thought you said you were running this investigation?"

Paul confessed, "Manny's got a lot of pull with the Bureau. Rumor has it that he may end up working in Washington. Some even say a cabinet post."

Suddenly, Manny burst into the conference room. "What's this?" He held an opened foil packet. "These look like the leaves I saw in Doc's evidence drawer." He placed the foil packet down and let the contents spill onto the table. Chinese melon seed tea leaves settled in a small pile next to the reports and pictures of the evidence.

Hank looked at the tea leaves and the evidence photos. "They could be similar. I'll need to perform a few tests."

"Where did this come from?" Manny asked.

Jim replied, "Jia Li gave me a box of this tea."

"Who's this Jia Li person?"

"She's my housekeeper, not your killer."

"Let me decide after I speak with her," Manny said.

"What do you mean?" Jim asked.

"I'm saying that the victim may have shared some tea with this Jia Li girl or right here in this office."

"So, you want to see this girl?" Paul asked.

Manny picked up a single tealeaf and held it up to the light. "Especially now."

·49·

The first day of the New Year presented the residents of Taylor with a bitter cold and wintry evening. Swirling snow wrestled with nearly every crevice in every building in town.

A knock on the back door of a faded brick building on Warehouse Row interrupted the persistent sound of the rustling wind.

Sam Clayton walked up to the door. "Who is it?"

"It's me... Anderson."

"What do you want?"

"Open up. We need to talk."

"Here?"

"Hell yeah! Here and now."

When Sam opened the door partway Anderson stuck his foot on the threshold preventing Sam from closing the door.

"I didn't sign up for no murders just some money for helping sell booze. You promised me that no one would be in the old morgue when I set the explosives on that Saturday," Sam said.

"No one got killed that day," Anderson said.

"Yeah but you guys have been killing everyone that got in your way and I want no part of it."

"I've got your money."

Sam fully opened the door and let Anderson in from the cold. "I see the money was a ruse. What brings you here? I thought you said we need to lay low through the spring."

"Something came up."

Sam waved him in. "Follow me." They walked into the deep recesses of the warehouse toward a hidden room that Sam called home. It had a bed, a couple of chairs and a table, a pot belly stove next to a stack of firewood, four hurricane lamps, a sink, toilet, a battery-operated radio and a cupboard stocked with food and booze. "Have a seat. Now what's this all about?"

"We've got a problem," Anderson said.

"What problem?"

"Did you hear they pulled that body out of the test pit in the football field?"

"Yeah I heard. The boss said not to worry. He said there's no evidence that'll link the body to anyone in Taylor. With that idiot Morton gone now we're in the clear."

Anderson tossed his hat on the table and laughed. "Jack was more interested in accepting bribes for construction work than selling booze to the Flatheads. He was sloppy and had to be eliminated." He sat down.

"Sloppy?"

"Yeah, Jack was a nuisance. Couldn't keep a low profile and left all kinds of evidence to tie him to the booze and bodies."

"Are you going to tell me how that went down?"

Anderson leaned back in the chair. "The boss was worried about him. He said Jack couldn't be trusted."

"So you stole Buchanan's own knife to kill him?"

"Hell no, I had to improvise. Stealing the knife was Jack's idea. I have to give him credit though. The boss said if he was a little smarter, we could have let things be. Jack would still be in with us. He never knew what happened. It was like putting an old dog to sleep." Anderson laughed. "Clean and easy... the only prints they found were Jack's."

Sam shook his head. "I told you, I want no part in this operation if murder is involved. Besides, the boss gave me a little demolition job to do up at old man Buchanan's farm. That'll be a pretty payout for me."

Anderson leaned over to Sam. "I got plans to take over the operation. I'll be the new boss and we'll be swimming in cash."

"Only if you promise me that they'll be no more killing."

"Sam, I don't make promises."

·50·

U nder a moonless sky just before midnight, January 3,
Deputy Police Chief Dave Anderson parked his personal
car, a black, 1993 Chevy Blazer behind one of the
abandoned buildings on Warehouse Row across the street
from the brand new morgue building. He shut down the engine
and turned the headlights off. Anderson and Sam sat in the car for
a few minutes as the cold night air slowly infiltrated the
automobile's interior.

After reviewing their plans, both men, dressed from head
to toe in black, exited the vehicle, and then crossed the street.
They scurried up to the backdoor of the morgue. Anderson
removed two pairs of gloves from his pocket and handed one to
Sam.

"Stay close to me and don't do anything or touch anything
unless I say so." Anderson took a set of keys from his pocket,
showed them to Sam, and laughed. "They'll think it was an inside
job. I had an extra set of keys made that no one knows about.
That Med Ex and the coroner are going to get screwed not to
mention what happens to Buchanan."

They quickly gained entry to the building and Anderson
skulked to the alarm system box. He shined his flashlight on the
keypad and typed in the security code. The blinking red light
turned to green and the silent alarm switched off.

"You knew the code?" Sam asked.

Anderson turned and smiled at his accomplice. "The police
department has the security codes for every municipal, county,
and state building in Taylor."

Sam glanced at the dark shadows that permeated every corner of the morgue. Reflections in the moving glow of Anderson's standard issue tactical flashlight resembled shape-changing apparitions. A chill shot up his spine and he tapped Anderson on the arm. "Hurry up so we can get the hell out of here."

Anderson inserted another key into the lock of the door that sealed the entrance to the crypt. They were halfway inside when Anderson grabbed Sam by the back of the arm.

Sam jumped. "Shit! Don't scare me like that," he yelled. "I heard about that Indian legend where the soul rips apart anything in its way."

"Shut up!" Anderson shined his flashlight along the labels of the individual doors. "Here it is."

Anderson opened a vault door labeled Jane Doe, Christmas Day. That drawer held the extracted body from the high school football field. The men placed it onto one of the fresh body bags that Hank kept in the morgue, carried it across the street, and placed it into the back of the Blazer. Anderson returned to the morgue and checked all the doors. Ensuring that everything was in order, he reset the security system.

They climbed into the car and drove away. Sam began to remove his gloves. "Where we dumping the body before it rots?"

"Keep those gloves on." Anderson smiled at his passenger and laughed. "Buchanan's house... it's cold enough outside to keep if from smelling up the place."

"You're what?" screamed Sam.

Anderson laughed again, "Don't worry, no one's home. I found out him and his wife are in Billings visiting the rest of his Indian family. That mutt of his is staying with Captain Stevens. That Chinese housekeeper is only there during the day."

"What's your plan?"

"You'll see." Anderson smiled.

The dark night sky was a perfect cover for his plan. Anderson shut the car's headlights as they approached the entrance to Jim's home. They parked a few hundred feet from the house and carried the body to the white pickup truck that Jim parked outside in the back.

"Are you going to dump the body in this pickup?"

"Right in the bed."

Sam nodded, "What a great idea. It'll look like he was planning to dispose of it."

Anderson climbed into the bed of the vehicle and Sam handed him the body bag.

"Throw me those new digging tools from my car. I want to lay them next to the body. This way it'll look convincing."

Sam handed Anderson the shovel and pickaxe from the trunk and Anderson placed the morgue's spare set of keys next to the corpse. They cleaned the area of tracks and then drove down the mountain and back to Taylor.

Anderson returned to Warehouse Row, drove to the back of the building that Sam was living in and parked the car. The two men walked up to a second floor room that faced the road. Anderson positioned a chair in front of a window. There he had a clear view of the morgue.

"What's the plan now?" whispered Sam.

"I want you to sit in this chair and watch the morgue." He handed Sam a notebook and pen. "Make a list of everyone who goes in and out and the times that they do."

"Hey, it's cold as a bitch in here."

"Anderson threw him two blankets. Cover yourself with one and warm up the other by the stove in your room downstairs, then switch off every half hour."

"What about that body we just dumped at Buchanan's?"

"The morgue's closed for the weekend but Buchanan should be back by Sunday. On Monday morning, after they discover the body's gone, they'll accuse him of stealing it to hide the evidence."

"How is he going to get in trouble if he finds the body?" Sam asked.

"I've got a plan to make sure a certain someone is at his house on Monday morning. They'll have no trouble finding the body." Anderson snickered and continued, "All hell will break loose across the street. I just need you to tell me who's doing the investigating."

"You can count on me," Sam replied.

·51·

It was late Sunday evening and the white knuckled drive in the snowstorm from Taylor International Airport to his home provided Jim with a chance for reflection. A few days away from the office were all that Jim could spare but it was therapeutic. Tomorrow he would dive back into the Bitterroot Killer investigation with a renewed perspective.

Jim's therapy sessions with Teresa Merrick were nearing an end. He couldn't wait to tell her about his newfound confidence and the renewed trust he had in Kate's decision making.

While Jim was away, he kept in daily contact with Hank who told him that Paul Harris and Agent Costa questioned Jia Li. However, they soon came to realize that in spite of the Chinese melon tea leaves in the stomach of the body found buried in the football field, Jia Li was not involved.

He and Kate had just returned from Billings where they visited Jim's sister, Sarah Whispers Two Elk and his daughter, Alma Rose. Jim squinted at the rear view mirror and spotted Alma Rose fast asleep in the backseat. She decided to accompany Jim and Kate back home.

Jim's thoughts drifted back to Sarah's life-saving, liver transplant surgery more than a year ago. It had been such a revelation for all. Alma Rose learned for the first time that Jim was her father. They were still sorting out their relationship and it would be a long emotional recovery.

Jim glanced at Kate asleep in the passenger seat as he drove her Volkswagen Samba Bus up the winding road that climbed into the hills. The snowstorm was waning as Jim pulled into the garage. Alma Rose helped get Kate out of the car and then into the house while Jim removed the snow chains off the tires. Jim put her to bed right away and then walked into the kitchen where Alma Rose was microwaving a cup of milk.

"Dad, I can stay home tomorrow and take care of Kate."

"Thanks, Alma Rose. I'll call Captain Stevens and find out when she wants to drop off Angel."

Jim received a 3-beep error tone and an automated message that said, "The number you have reached has been disconnected, please check the number and try again." He turned to Alma Rose. "The storm must have knocked out her phone service. She'll probably drop off Angel before work tomorrow. Can you let her in? I plan to leave early and get a head start."

"Sure dad, no problem."

After a quick breakfast the next morning, Jim arrived at the Sheriff's office at 6 a.m. sharp. An hour later the full office crew arrived and Jim immersed himself in the exhilarating freshness of the New Year.

"You're in a good mood," Rocky said.

Jim looked up from the early morning paperwork. "Kate and I just got back last night. Alma Rose is visiting us for a few days. It was good to spend time with my family."

Expecting Manny Costa to grill his staff relentlessly, Jim spent the next two hours with Rocky preparing a list of talking points. He had just finished when the outside door opened and a procession of officials, Leon, Linda, Dave Anderson, and FBI Agents Paul Harris and Manny Costa followed Hank inside. Martha buzzed them in.

Jim stood at his door and stared at the crowd gathered at the front desk. "What's going on?"

Hank spoke first. "Jim, the morgue was broken into over the weekend."

"What?" Jim asked.

Hank continued, "Linda waited for you to call when you got back last night but this morning she found her phone line was cut. Then she went to your house to drop off your dog. She watched Angel tear around to the back of your house. When Linda caught up to her, Angel was sitting beside your truck. Inside the truck bed under yesterday's snowfall was the body of that girl we found in the football field along with a set of keys to the morgue."

"That's impossible!"

Anderson spoke. "It looks like an inside job. No forced entry."

Jim walked to the back of his desk. "Are Kate and Alma Rose all right?"

Manny Costa sat on the corner of Jim's desk. "They're fine. We hoped you'd fill us in on what happened."

Jim raised his palms. "I didn't have anything to do with this."

"You had a spare key to the morgue," Manny said.

"Where were you going to hide the body?" Anderson asked.

Rocky stepped in front of Jim. "He had nothing to do with this."

"How do you know that?" Harris asked.

"He was in Billings," Rocky said.

"This weekend?" Costa stepped past Rocky.

"I got home Sunday evening."

"What time?" Costa continued to grill Jim.

"I don't know... about ten, I guess."

"Can someone vouch for that?"

"Kate was tired. I put her to bed. She slept like a log all night. After I tried to call Captain Stevens I went to bed. I think my daughter went to bed later after she had a cup of warm milk."

"Can anyone verify that you didn't leave the house?"

"I don't know... why don't you ask my daughter."

Manny continued, "We did."

"What did she say?"

"She said she couldn't be sure. Did any of them see you get up for work this morning or hear anything suspicious outside the house?"

"They were both sleeping when I left."

Anderson dove into the questioning and was relentless. "There were no signs of a break-in at the morgue, the body was in your truck and you have no alibi from about eleven last night until when you arrived for work this morning."

Jim turned to Linda. "You don't think I had anything to do with this?"

243

Anderson glanced at Linda. "I'll tell him." He turned to Jim. "We found a shovel and a pickaxe next to the body. Where did you plan to bury it?"

Manny Costa said, "Jim, you have some explaining to do."

Sweat beaded up on Jim's face and neck. He looked first at Hank and then Linda. "I didn't do this," he said.

Anderson barked, "Buchanan, that tea at the coffee station was from your housekeeper. That dead girl had tea leaves in her stomach. Did you give that poor girl a cup of tea before you killed her?"

Jim noticed Manny turn to stare at Anderson. He returned his glance to Jim and winked.

Distracted for a second, Jim then said, "Hank, I was with you when we found the leaves in that girl's stomach. I didn't have anything to do with that."

"I sampled a few tea leaves from the box in your office. I simulated a partial digestive process and compared the cellular structures of the sample and the original specimen from the victim's stomach. They're an exact match," Hank replied.

"Jim, come clean. We'll make sure the federal prosecutor considers your cooperative confession," Paul Harris said.

Jim knew by the looks on everyone's faces that they had their minds made up. Only their suspicions needed confirmation. "I didn't have anything to do with what you're accusing me of. We arrived home last night and went to bed. I don't know how the corpse got from the morgue to my house. I also didn't give that girl any tea. I never met her."

Manny held his hand out to Jim. "Come with me, we just need to talk."

Jim pushed Manny's hand away. "I didn't have anything to do with this. We went through this already, remember?" Jim pointed at Hank. "I sat in a jail cell because everyone thought I killed Jack. Someone set me up then and someone is setting me up now, probably the same person who shot at me near my home earlier this year. Tell them, Hank." Hank stood silent while Jim felt his heart pound.

Anderson said, "We're reopening the Jack Morton murder investigation. We also have a court order to exhume Jack's body."

Jim stared across the room. "What makes you all think I did this?"

Manny alerted the others. "Let me handle this." He turned back to Jim. "I want to take you to where you found the first bodies so that you can show us how you buried them. Let's go get your coat."

Jim watched Manny pull his gun out from under his coat, handle first and then present it to Jim out of sight of the others. He went along with the ploy. "I didn't kill anyone," argued Jim as he walked with Manny toward his coat.

Anderson continued, "He should come with me to the police station right now and answer some questions."

Jim put on his heavy coat and hat and then quickly grabbed the gun from Manny. In one motion, he pulled Manny toward him and then locked his arm around the agent's neck. Jim pointed the gun at the others. "I had nothing to do with this."

"Then stop acting guilty," Linda fingered the butt of her revolver.

"Don't anyone do anything foolish," advised Manny who gasped for air as he remained in the firm grasp of Jim's headlock.

Releasing his hold on Manny, Jim raised his right leg and gave the agent a solid push with his boot. As Manny tumbled across the floor, Jim dropped Manny's pistol, turned, tucked his chin against his chest, and dove headfirst through the window.

As his legs disappeared through the broken glass and wooden window frame, he heard a firearm discharge but the bullet missed. Jim somersaulted outside amid a shower of broken glass and pieces of window frame. A four-inch cut across his neck drew a trickle of blood that slowly drenched his shoulder and chest. A longer cut, six to eight inches, through his tattered pants leg saturated his right thigh.

Jim reached his SUV, and with the keys already in the ignition, he started the engine. The tires squealed and smoke swirled from the wheel wells in the car's wake.

Glancing in his rear view mirror, Jim saw Paul Harris' vehicle careen and fishtail behind him as they raced through the streets of Taylor heading east toward U.S. Highway 228. They flew by the towns of Big Stump and Horace and then north on State Highway 28.

Entering the Flathead Indian Reservation proper, Jim turned down a road marked by a sign that identified the trail as belonging to the Bitterroot Salish Tribe. Familiar with the road, Jim was able to put considerable distance between himself and Paul's car.

Jim drove by many house trailers and a few ranch homes interspersed alongside the road. He parked his SUV near the entrance to the community center building and ran inside. He dashed down a hallway past a longtime friend, Jaypee Brown Bird who called out to Jim as he sprinted by. Jim didn't answer.

Running by an open classroom door, a familiar voice hollered, "Little Hawk!"

Jim stopped and retraced his steps. When he saw Elijah Sizemore, he pulled his jacket over his blood-drenched uniform and stood sideways to hide the one bloody pants leg. They shook hands. Noticing the children's inquisitive faces, Jim smiled at them in an attempt to disguise his agitation.

The class replied in unison, "Good morning Little Hawk."

Jim smiled and waved to the children.

"Elijah, I need your help. You have to get rid of the men who are looking for me."

Three loud knocks on the outside door reverberated throughout the community center. Elijah spotted Jim's blood-drenched shirt and pants. "Come with me." He turned to his class. "Students, continue with today's lesson. I'll return." Elijah looked at the children. "Johnny, Billy, bring Little Hawk to the great hiding place. Quickly now. And find Miss Martin. I have to answer the door."

Two boys, older than the others, walked past Jim. One called to him, "Come."

Jim nodded to Elijah, turned, and followed the boys down the hallway.

They led Jim to the back of the building and down a flight of stairs to a basement door marked <u>Fallout Shelter</u>. Down another set of stairs in the bunker, Jim sat wounded and exhausted on one of the many cots in the large room. The boys, as if trained, immediately went to his aid. One brought Jim a fresh set of clothes and a blanket; the other supplied a basin of water and towels.

Jim removed his coat, then stripped off his bloody shirt and pants leaving them on the floor and donned the pair of blue gym shorts. Wrapping his body in the brown blanket, he leaned back on the cot. A woman entered the shelter and began treating Jim's wounds with antiseptic. The sheriff grimaced each time she patted the cuts and abrasions with a soaked absorbent pad.

Just moments later, Elijah entered. He asked the woman, "How bad is it Miss Martin?"

The young, attractive woman with long black hair, dressed in jeans, a flannel shirt, and cowboy boots glanced up at Elijah. "I already removed as much glass and wood as I could find. He'll need stitches but he'll survive."

"Miss Martin is our nurse. She's part Bitterroot Salish and part white. She's a Mixed-blood Native, just like you, Little Hawk. Her great, great grandfather was Wounded Bear," Elijah said.

Jim stared at the pretty woman washing his wounds. "Wounded Bear?"

She nodded, "Yes."

Jim remarked, "My grandfather always speaks of him in praise."

"Are you Salish?" Miss Martin asked.

"No, I'm Crow."

Miss Martin turned to Elijah. "The Crow were enemies of Wounded Bear."

"We are all one. Little Hawk is my friend," Elijah said.

She turned back to Jim, injected a local anesthetic, and then sewed his wounds.

Elijah gestured to the two boys. "Leave now and be silent about this."

The two boys ran up the steps and the first boy opened the door. A large man stood in the doorway and the boys screamed. At the top of the steps was Jacob Walkabout. The two boys pushed past him disappearing out the door. The Flathead Tribal Police Chief closed the door and walked down the steps.

"What's going on here?" Jacob's voice boomed and reverberated throughout the fallout shelter.

Jim glanced at the three pairs of eyes and explained, "There was a break-in at the morgue in Taylor. Someone moved a corpse to my house while I was away visiting my sister. They think

I'm responsible. I need a place to stay for a few days until I can sort things out."

The tribal police chief approached Jim and knelt on one knee.

"This is the work of the *ṁalyè es šeýiłk*."

Jim shook his head. "That's a superstition."

"How do you explain all the bodies and the destruction of your morgue."

"Evil people," Jim replied.

"Look at me," commanded Jacob.

The two stared into each other's eyes. Neither man blinked for more than a minute. Then Jacob stood up and reached for Jim's hand.

"Well?" Elijah asked.

Jim placed his hand in Jacob's and the police chief said, "I believe you Little Hawk. It's not *ṁalyè es šeýiłk*. I'll help you."

Elijah said to Jim, "Creator sent me a vision last night. In that vision, you came here. You are always welcome, Little Hawk."

While Miss Martin continued to stitch Jim's wounds, Jacob said to Elijah, "Pleasant words won't stop a warrant. Jim needs to decide what to do."

"Jacob's right," Elijah agreed. "You must rest. Ask Creator for the strength to make a wise decision. You can stay as long as you need. Miss Martin can help."

Jim held out his hand and clasped Elijah's arm. "Thank you my friend but I don't know how much longer I can stay."

"I can delay them with a few tricks. The white man's law is full of loopholes," Jacob replied, folding his arms. "I will bring Little Hawk new clothes."

"Done!" Miss Martin cut the extra length of thread from Jim's leg and smiled at the three men. They each stared at her without saying a word. She returned their stare and then remembered the last words she heard Elijah speak. "Oh no. I can't help. I mean I won't. My trailer's not big enough. No, he has to go somewhere else. I can't do this."

Elijah pleaded, "For a little while. The law won't find him if he stays with you."

Miss Martin looked at the three men and sighed, "All right."

·52·

The ensuing week proved fruitless for various law enforcement agencies, both local and state. At the request of Deputy Police Chief Anderson, Chief Peters assigned the task of coordinating local law enforcement activities to the Taylor Police Department under Deputy Chief Anderson's directive.

Anderson drew up a resisting arrest and suspicion of murder warrant for Jim but the Tribal Council of the Flathead Nation refused to accept it because it was a local charge and the police were outside their jurisdiction.

Emily Cronin then contacted the local state attorney who issued a similar warrant but with an added fugitive from prosecution charge with the support of the State Attorney General.

They attempted to serve it with the assistance of Taylor's IX District Office of the Montana Highway Patrol. Again, the tribal council denied them passage on reservation land because they were not subject to local and state laws.

It took pulling strings within the FBI hierarchy but Paul Harris obtained a warrant for Jim's arrest under Title 18 of the United States Code, chapter 7, section 111 with the help of the Bureau of Indian Affairs (BIA).

Because the warrant stated that Jim committed a federal crime when he assaulted a federal officer while that officer was engaged in the performance of his official duties, it was enough to provide teeth to that document. Ironically, FBI Special Agent Costa who was the officer assaulted by Jim wanted no part of serving the warrant and insisted to Harris that he was using the wrong tactic.

Then as part of an elaborate plan, on the cold, clear morning of January 11, a helicopter piloted by a U.S. Marshals Service Aviation Enforcement Officer along with a U.S. Federal Marshal and two FBI Agents, hovered above a car displaying a BIA insignia.

Inside the car were two FBI agents, two representatives of the BIA, and Jim's cousin, Tribal Police Chief Preacher Running Wolf of the Crow Nation. The FBI flew in Preacher, to provide Jim one last chance to peacefully leave the Flathead Reservation and surrender to the waiting U.S. Marshals. With Preacher on board, Paul Harris' plan was in full-on mode.

As the car turned toward the trailer where agents were certain Jim was hiding out, the helicopter veered off. Hovering around the periphery of the reservation, the rotary-winged aircraft perched in wait. Far enough away to be out of human eyesight of the trailer, the federal agents in the helicopter were able to observe the car through their long-range binoculars.

The car pulled alongside the trailer, and three men appeared at the front door. Two BIA reps, two FBI agents, and Preacher got out of the car. After a brief exchange, all eight men retreated into the trailer.

Moments later, agents spied a person wearing a white Stetson and brown jacket backing out of the doorway aiming a rifle at the inside of the house. The person jumped into the car with the BIA insignia and sped away.

Heading west off the reservation, the car traveled in the same direction it originated from. The helicopter picked up the movement of the car and followed. The vehicle traveled at a high rate of speed but the chopper roared in hot pursuit.

The U.S. Federal Marshal sitting next to the pilot radioed his commander on the ground, "Delta-4 to Bravo-1, we have the vehicle in view." The marshal listened to the instructions. "Yes sir... we spotted Buchanan. He left the house armed. No communication from the house? Don't worry sir, we'll get an ID."

The helicopter swooped down and the marshal got a visual on the driver. Gray Stetson, sheriff's issue jacket, long dark hair protruding from under the hat. "We have an affirmative on the driver." He glanced at the two FBI agents seated behind him in the chopper. "We'll wait until he's off the reservation, just to be safe and not start a confrontation with the Flatheads." They followed the car for another twenty minutes until it crossed the border that separated the Flathead Nation from the State of Montana. The marshal then signaled, "Okay... let's end this parade." He tapped the arm of the pilot and pointed to the vehicle on the road.

"Yes sir," the pilot said.

A voice boomed from the helicopter loudspeaker, "Federal agents... stop your vehicle."

The car continued its easterly progress and increased its speed. The marshal aimed a rifle through the open cockpit door and fired a warning shot in front of the vehicle. The car swerved away from the round's impact on the road. The marshal waved the pilot down, so that he could get a closer shot. He aimed for the rear tire and fired. It was a direct hit and the car weaved back and forth. It hit the snow bank on one side of the road, fishtailed, and hit the snow bank on the other side. The car finally came to a stop and the pilot brought the helicopter down on the road forty yards in front of the vehicle. The three agents exited the helicopter and ran to the car with guns drawn.

"Exit the vehicle with your hands up," shouted the marshal, dressed in a brown field jacket. He saw the driver open the door and step out, hands raised. "Do it nice and slow. Keep your hands up where we can see them." The driver stood head down, the brim of the Stetson blocking their face. "On the ground, get on the ground! Face down!" screamed the marshal.

The driver, dressed in the uniform of the Cedar County Sheriff's Office complied with the command while one FBI agent radioed his commander. "We have the suspect on the ground and under control."

One FBI agent sat on the suspect, pulled the fugitive's wrists back locking them in a pair of handcuffs. The marshal barked an order. "Turn him over. Let's see if he's as ugly as his photos."

The FBI agent complied and when he did, Miss Martin's beautiful face smiled up at them.

"Do you men have passports to visit Turtle Island?" she asked.

The men looked at one another. The marshal slammed his fist on the hood of the car while the other FBI agent radioed back to his command center. "Scratch that capture. Do you read? We are a negative here."

·53·

With Miss Martin occupying the interest of the lone helicopter, Jacob Walkabout and Preacher Running Wolf escorted the four federal agents from Miss Martin's house trailer off the Flathead Indian Reservation and then guarded the main entrance with double barrel shotguns.

One cloudy night during the standoff retired Cedar County Sheriff Dan McCoy drove onto the reservation with Jim's dog Angel for a secret meeting.

Far from danger and unnoticed, Miss Martin's 1978 Oldsmobile headed unimpeded north along the Hubbart Dam Road. It ran parallel to the old logging road that followed the course of the Little Bitterroot River slicing through the Flathead National Forest.

At the wheel, McCoy avoided the roadblocks the FBI had set up at each entrance to the reservation. Although the car often hit bottom on the one-pass plowed road, the chained tires kept the car gripped to the snowy surface. Jim lay on the back seat covered by an assortment of colorful Native blankets. He kept a good grip on Angel, who was hiding with him.

"I'm not familiar with this road. How will I see the turnoff?" Dan asked.

Jim lifted his head from under the makeshift canopy. "Take a right onto Route 2. Then after the bridge over the Little Bitterroot River, turn left onto a gravel road. That will take you around Little Bitterroot Lake. My dad's farm abuts the northeast corner of the lake."

"Okay," Dan said.

Jim felt and heard the car's wheels hit pavement on U.S. Highway 2. A few minutes later, the vehicle turned onto the gravel road. As they headed north, Jim spotted the Cabinet Mountains on the left and the Salish Mountains on the right.

"How's Kate?" Jim asked.

"She's doing all right. Alma Rose decided to stay with her."

"She was supposed to go back to school after a few days."

"Alma Rose said this is a teaching experience for her and far more important than anything she'll ever learn in school."

Jim sighed. "That's my girl." He felt the car slow down, and then asked, "Are we here?"

"Yep."

Jim threw off the blankets and sat up. There was the old barn, the silo and the farmhouse. The dilapidated structures looked different in the snow-laden landscape. Dan parked the car in front. Dressed in jeans and a flannel shirt, Jim saw that the driveway had been plowed. He drew his gun. "Dan, stay in the car."

"Bullshit!" Dan slowly opened his door.

Not bothering to look back, Jim ran to the house, opened the front door, and slowly walked inside. Jim's eyes canvassed the living room and for a split second, he imagined the furniture that used to reside in the house. After what seemed like a lifetime of reminiscing, he heard the back door swing open and the familiar whistling of "Scotland the Brave". He watched Dan walk inside with a stack of firewood.

"I told you to stay in the car." A few barks and then Angel leaped, throwing her front paws onto Jim's legs. He knelt down and petted Angel while she wagged her stumpy tail and fussed over him. Jim then heard a car drive up. He looked out the window and saw Kate's Samba bus. Alma Rose was driving.

"Now what?" Jim went outside and confronted them. "What are you doing here?"

Kate ran to Jim and hugged him. "I didn't know if I would ever see you again."

Jim wiped the tears from her eyes and kissed her. "I'll never leave you." He turned to Alma Rose. "Do I have you to blame for this?"

"No, you have me to thank for this."

254

Jim whispered to Alma Rose. "This is dangerous. You and Kate should not be here."

"I'm here because it is dangerous. There is something inside the house that needs to be discovered."

"Like what?" Jim asked.

"A long lost history that will resolve everything."

"Another vision of yours?"

Alma Rose shook her head. "A dream I had... the ṁalyè es šeyiłk, she's inside the house."

"Alma Rose, that's just a fable."

"Dad, not this time."

Jim carefully weighed everything and then said, "I want you and Kate to stay in the car... and lock the doors."

Once they complied, Jim went inside the house. Dan got a flicker going in the fireplace.

"As soon as it's nice and warm, we'll look for evidence."

"Why wait?" Jim stood up and brushed off his pants. The men descended into the basement with Dan directing their way with a flashlight. Angel boldly accompanied them. Jim and Dan inspected every bin and storage area. They couldn't find enough that had survived through time and the elements.

"Do you know how long this illegal liquor operation was going on?"

Dan removed his Stetson and scratched his balding head. "I asked around. It seems like at least three years. No one remembers exactly when it started." Dan rubbed his chin and then snapped his fingers. "When did your daddy die?"

"About five years ago, why?"

"That's when he donated the farm to the county, right?"

"He lived in a nursing home for four years. The farm donation was in his will. What are you getting at?"

"Maybe someone involved with the county decided to use this place back then. Maybe Anderson and Jack worked for them?"

"You think more people were involved in the bootlegging?" Jim asked.

"We know that Sam was probably involved in the explosion at the morgue and we know that mob guy was also involved.

That's at least four people. If we look around maybe we'll find evidence pinning others to the booze and the murders."

Jim shook his head. "Sam's not a serial killer."

The men heard a loud banging as if someone just ran up or down a stairway.

"What was that?" Jim asked.

An old red lantern fell off a shelf and crashed to the ground, its globe shattered into pieces.

"This place gives me the creeps," Dan said hunching his shoulders as he shivered where he stood.

"The first noise sounded like someone's in the house. We're done here, let's go upstairs." Jim took the lead and climbed the basement steps with Angel at his heels.

The two men, guns drawn looked for loose boards or secret compartments where anyone could have stashed paperwork, money, or invoices. Nothing turned up on the first or second floors.

"Looks like a dead end," confessed Dan.

Jim glanced at the second floor ceiling. "Let's check the attic."

"Damn, I was hoping you wouldn't say that." Dan shook his head and opened the hallway door that led to the attic stairs.

When Jim was a boy, the stairs were in good condition. Jim's father always kept the house in impeccable shape when he was in good health. Now, after more than nine years of neglect, the stairs creaked with every step.

When they reached the door at the top of the stairs Jim tried the handle. "It won't budge."

"It's jammed, lay your shoulder into it," suggested Dan.

Jim pushed on the door but it still refused to open. "It's locked."

"Got a key?" Dan asked.

"Hell no, I don't have keys to the house."

"Good!" Dan pushed Jim aside and kicked the door in with his boot, slicing off a part of the doorframe in the process. He looked at Jim, smiled, and then shrugged. "New door and frame is on me."

They walked into the darkened attic and poked around the spacious and barren floor. Even in those dark hidden spaces the area appeared clean. They were about to leave when something caught Jim's eye.

"Dan, see that… the wall's not even with the house."

"What do you mean?"

With a puzzled expression, Jim pointed to the far wall. "That wall is only about fifteen feet past the chimney."

"Yeah… so what?" Dan said.

"Outside, the chimney is at least thirty feet from the edge of the house."

"You're right. It looks like a false outside wall, studs, and horizontal wall boards like 1920s construction."

Jim walked to the interior wall that extended from the front to the back of the house. He felt along the wall, inch by inch, looking for a loosened board or two.

Then Jim heard Dan call to him. "Hey, over here."

Jim stopped his search and rushed over to Dan. There was a hole in the floor near the back outside wall. It wasn't a broken floorboard, a gap in the floor, or a cavity caused by pest infestation. It appeared to be a perfectly drilled two-inch diameter hole.

Dan took his flashlight, turned it on, and placed it over the hole in the floorboards. "Let's go to the second floor and find the other side of this peephole. Someone was using this hole to observe something or someone."

On the second floor they searched for where Dan thought the hole might be. Their bearings brought them to a closet in a second floor bedroom.

"The hole in the ceiling should be right here." Jim searched for the glow from the flashlight.

"Look over there," Dan said, pointing to a spot in the corner of the closet where a sliver of light flashed between a gap in the wall and the ceiling right next to an overhead light fixture. "It appears that if this closet light were turned on anyone up in the attic could see the beam of light and know that someone was down here."

Jim tapped along the bottom wall, in the dark recesses of the closet. Moving from right to left, his tapping only revealed hollow reverberations. Balling his fingers into a fist, Jim swung and punched a hole in the sheetrock. With Dan's help, the two pried the panel free. Between the sheetrock and a second wall, Jim noticed a small door. He unlatched it and a four-foot insulated square panel swung open.

"Bingo!" Dan said. "Let me get my flashlight."

When Dan returned they crawled into the newly found space and spied the surrounding area. A window illuminated the room with natural light. However, the stagnant air seemed to stabilize the room's environment. Thick foam, insulated panels covered every wall and even the ceiling. A wood stove sat in the corner of the room, its stovepipe climbing the wall. Heat from the house began to circulate through the opening in the wall and warm the secret room. Angel joined them.

Jim spotted an overhead trap door, reached up and pulled on the string. A retractable ladder descended. Jim climbed up the ladder and entered the secret attic space. The dryness of the windowless and insulated hidden room accompanied by a fleeting memory of the *ṁalyè es šeẏiłk* drew the warmth from his flesh.

"Dan, hand me the flashlight."

Dan stood on the ladder and complied. "What do you see up there?"

Jim shined the flashlight around the small room. On one side, a desk, chair, and a bookcase while in the corner on a bed, was a fluffed up blanket. Jim walked toward the blanket, pulled it off the bed, and cast the flashlight beam upon the mattress.

A spectral apparition hurtled toward him and assaulted him like a thousand tiny pinpricks. Gasping, Jim fell backwards and dropped the flashlight.

·54·

Angel barked from the bottom of the ladder as Jim, lying against one wall watched Dan first poke his head through the trap door and then enter the room. There, lying on a tattered bed was a nude mummified body whose remains depicted a long delayed, welcoming pose to its visitors.

"I think that's Sam's missing wife."

"How can you be sure?" Dan asked.

"We'll let Hank confirm that but I'm sure it's her. She just told me."

"She told you?" Dan shivered. "Let's get the hell out of here."

Jim again thought of the ṁalyè es šeýiłk and recited an impromptu prayer over the body. "Great Spirit, beneath this flesh all things are alike. Gaze upon the spirit before me and grant her peace. Let her face the four winds and walk among those who came before her along the good road to the day of quiet. In this physical world our bodies are but earthly vessels and our spirits yearn to rejoin You in the wondrous eternal journey of Your creation." Jim took the blanket, folded it in half and covered Olivia's body.

Dan took the flashlight from Jim and walked to the desk and file cabinet. He opened drawers and pulled out a pile of papers. He examined the paperwork, took a deep breath, and rubbed his forehead. "Jim, take a look at this."

By the flashlight's glow, Jim read the sticker on a folder that Dan had extracted. "It says, <u>Guardians of Doctrine</u>." Jim opened the folder and thumbed through a pile of paperwork. "They're all dated within five years after the county took over the farm." Jim glanced at Dan and then continued, "It has dates and amounts... here's an invoice for liquor. It's addressed from Mario DeFazio."

"That guy from the Brunazzi crime family," Dan replied.

Jim resumed reading, "It's signed by Jack Morton and received by Doug White Bear of the Flathead Nation." Jim looked at Dan. "Doug disappeared off the reservation two years ago."

"I bet you found him at the Little Bitterroot. What else is inside that folder?"

Jim noticed a few other members of the Flathead tribe listed on various pages. On the bottom of one of the pages it all sunk in. He looked at Dan and said, "There's an initial... WI."

"Jim, it must stand for White Bear... Indian, right? We know that he was involved."

"Chief Peters told me that Dave Anderson was from Wisconsin. WI is the postal abbreviation for that state."

"Then Anderson must be using WI as a code name for himself. Jim, one thing I learned in more than thirty years of police work is that some people will do just about anything if the price is right."

Jim handed the folder to Dan. "Bring this to the sheriff's office and submit it for evidence."

"Once we get you cleared, we'll request Hank and Leon do a thorough investigation of this crime scene."

"I don't get it."

"What don't you get?" Dan asked.

"What does Sam Clayton's wife have to do with this and why was she left here to rot?"

Jim and Dan heard Angel's barks of distress and anger. They quickly climbed down the ladder, through the opening in the hidden room and over to a window overlooking the front yard.

The sun glistened on the snowpack as Angel chased a man with a canvas sack headed toward Kate's Samba bus. Jim raced downstairs, through the front door and called Angel off.

He measured his angle of pursuit and for a split second, his innate football instincts clicked into action. He experienced the adrenalin rush and the sensation of seeing the whole field, filling in the gap, and tracking down the ball carrier.

Jim caught up to the intruder, flung himself airborne at the man, and drove his shoulder into the intruder's side. The man tumbled onto the snow-covered ground a few feet in front of Kate's car. The canvas bag separated from the man's grasp. Jim's forward progress caused him to pancake the trespasser who screamed in pain. Jim stood on his knees, turned the man over and came face-to-face with the county's most wanted criminal.

"Clayton? Where the hell have you been and what the hell are you doing here?"

"I think you broke my ribs," Sam painfully moaned through blood-smeared lips.

"Answer the question!"

"I haven't had a drink in two days. There's supposed to be booze here, where'd it go?" Sam began to shake and broke out in a cold sweat.

Dan reached out to Jim. "Damn, they don't hit like that in the NFL anymore."

Jim grabbed Dan's hand and got up. He looked at the canvas bag that was on the ground, ten feet away.

"What's in the bag, Sam?" Jim asked.

Sam sat up and struggled to breathe. "That's none of your goddamn business."

Jim retrieved the bag, examined its contents, and then rushed back to Sam. "You've got enough RDX here to blow the farm sky high!"

"Fuck you." The words slid through Sam's bloodied lips.

"Are you working for Dave Anderson?"

Sam spat blood. "I ain't talking unless I get a lawyer."

"Jim has to offer you a lawyer but I don't." Dan stood over Sam, pointed his gun at him, and cocked the hammer.

Sam cringed. "All right... I'll talk." He looked at Jim. "But I still want a lawyer and I didn't kill nobody."

Jim helped Sam to his feet, dragged him into the farmhouse and sat him in front of the fireplace.

Jim grilled him. "What happened to your wife?"

Sam wiped blood from his lips. "Have you seen Olivia?"

Jim and Dan shared quizzical looks then Jim turned back to Sam. "When was the last time you saw her?"

"I dunno, maybe three years ago?"

"Did she say where she was going?" Jim asked.

"Yeah… Murphys, California."

"Where's that?"

"Outside Sacramento."

"Can you get in touch with someone there?"

"She lived in the Heaven's Oasis commune. I contacted the only person I knew and she said Olivia was traveling home for the summer in '93. They said she never returned."

"Did you see her when she got to Montana?"

"Yeah, for a couple three days and then she said she had business to take care of. That's the last I saw or heard of her, I swear."

"Why didn't you get the police involved?" Jim asked.

Jim noticed Sam stare at Dan. Then Sam said, "Aw hell, I was in so much trouble with the law I didn't want them to think I had anything to do with her disappearance."

"Did you?"

"Hell no… I loved her. She was the most beautiful woman I ever saw. I was still trying to sort out how I could convince her to stay with me. It broke my heart every time she left Taylor."

"Then why couldn't the two of you make a go of it?"

Sam's eyes began to tear. "It was the damn drugs. It was my way of coping with the shit I saw in 'Nam."

"Tell us about your wife," Jim said.

"When Olivia and me first got married everyone knew I was seeing a shrink because of the war so no one would hire me. To earn money I did light woodworking out of our garage. To cope with the shit I started smoking pot again, just like in 'Nam."

"And Olivia put up with that?"

"No sir, she even tried to get me to quit… went with me to a new shrink and all that."

"Did it help?"

"For a while. I even got a steady job but then some of the guys I worked with got me into heavier shit like cocaine and heroin. If I didn't get arrested for injuring that cop a couple three years back I would've been dead by now."

"What happened to your marriage once you got arrested?"

"Olivia visited me every week in jail but once I got out she couldn't support both of us. We lost the house and had to move to an apartment. When the landlord found out I was an ex-con he kicked us out. That's when Olivia moved to California. I tried to get a job but no one would hire me so... I lived off the streets."

"How did you support yourself?"

Sam hung his head. "Olivia was giving me money."

"Was she working?"

Sam looked up. "I don't really know if she had a job or what she was doing in California. I was just so glad that she would come back to visit with me. I didn't ask her no questions about the money. But when she disappeared I had to improvise."

"What's that mean?"

"Look, I'll tell you anything you want to know about me but if I'm going to rat on someone else I want a lawyer."

"Are you doing drugs now?" Jim asked.

"No, I know Olivia won't take me back if she hears I'm on that shit. I just need a drink a couple three times a day. Hell, if she took me back I'd even quit the boozing for her."

"Were you ever upstairs in this house?"

"I was only allowed on the first floor and in the basement. That's where we stacked the booze."

"Sam, I think we found your wife." Jim watched the look on Sam's face turn from bewilderment to joy.

"Olivia? Where is she?"

"Upstairs, she's been there a while, probably the whole three years since she's been missing."

"You mean she's dead?"

"You didn't know?"

Sam hung his head and began to sob. "No, I didn't know. I thought she was done with me. If I knew she was still around I would have changed my ways." Sam cradled his head in his hands. "I loved her." He looked up at Jim. "She's in the house? I think I know who killed her... goddammit! She was only thirty-nine years old when she disappeared. She didn't deserve that. I'll cooperate. I'll do it for Olivia. Can I see her?"

"You will, in time. Did Anderson kill her?"

"No... get me that lawyer but I want protective custody."

Jim turned to Dan. "Bring the evidence to the sheriff's office. Call Rocky and have him bring Sam to the hospital."

Sam piped up. "You mean Deputy Salentino?"

"Do you have a problem with that?" Jim asked.

"No… he's a good guy. I don't want anyone else."

Jim continued, "Dan, have Rocky get Sam in a detox program. Then have him process Sam's arrest. And contact Public Defender Blair." Jim took a pair of handcuffs from Dan, flopped Sam onto his stomach, and locked the cuffs on his wrists. Jim turned to Angel. "Keep an eye on him girl."

Angel walked up to Sam, sat next to him, and placed her paws on his legs.

Jim pulled Dan aside and when they were out of earshot of Sam, he said, "I'm going to pay Anderson a visit. Make sure Alma Rose drives Kate back home."

"Please don't do this without backup."

Jim faced his mentor. "Until you show Hank what we found in that attic and can convince Harris and Costa that I had nothing to do with that woman we found in the football field, I'm a wanted man. I need to do this alone."

Dan shook his head. "This isn't wise."

"I have to bring Anderson in. I need to find out what he knows and learn if he's really WI."

·55·

It had been a long day with no progress on the standoff at the Flathead Indian Reservation. The squawk of two-way radios electrified the air as scores of operatives in overcoats, battle dress uniforms, and work clothes scurried between the half-dozen tents on the makeshift parking lot just outside the reservation.

As a result, the patience and tempers between the FBI, U.S. Marshals Service, BIA and the local authorities in opposing camps had nearly reached their boiling point. Amid all this tension and anxiety positive and negative vibrations clashed among two law enforcement officers, supposedly working together.

FBI Agent Manny Costa stared at Deputy Police Chief Dave Anderson and spied his every move as the Taylor policeman stood next to his patrol car across the parking lot.

Hank walked up to Manny. "Are you all right?"

"Never been better," Manny said as he composed himself and took a final drag on his cigarette, then snuffed it out with his heel.

"I haven't been able to say this to you before. Thanks for what you did for Jim," Hank said.

"What did I do?" Manny asked as smoke billowed from his mouth.

Hank snickered. "The Manny Costa I knew would never let a suspect take his gun from him."

Manny returned the chuckle. "Don't you ever tell anyone."

"Why did you do it?"

265

"This damn investigation is going nowhere fast. Buchanan is innocent, you and I know that. Whoever's responsible will try to get to Buchanan. They'll find each other."

"Oh I get it... you're using Jim for bait. Think that's right?"

"Buchanan's a big boy. I thought that headlock he caught me in was a little too tight based upon the opportunity I presented to him." Manny reached up and massaged his throat. "Yeah, he can take care of himself." Manny noticed Deputy Police Chief Dave Anderson and Agent Paul Harris walking toward him and Hank. "Keep it down, we got company."

Harris said to everyone, "It's starting to get dark. Why don't you all go home and get some sleep?"

"I want to be here when Buchanan gets his ass nailed," Anderson replied.

"Like you backwater cops didn't have your chance?" Manny said with a sly grin.

Anderson scowled at the crusty FBI agent. "What's that supposed to mean?"

"It means you ain't worth that tin badge on your shirt."

Anderson rushed up to Costa and met him face-to-face. Manny assumed a defensive posture but Paul Harris forced himself between the two combatants. "Take it somewhere else," he ordered.

Anderson screamed, "But the son of a..."

Harris interrupted, "I said break it off."

Anderson removed his hat and pointed it at Manny as he backed up toward his car. "Why won't the FBI pay for more plastic surgery on your damn face?"

Harris pulled Manny aside. "I don't want you alienating the locals."

Manny fingered the scar along his jawbone. He turned away from Harris and watched Anderson climb into his car.

"There's something I don't like about him."

"Manny!" Harris continued, "Forget about him. That Indian woman the U.S. Marshal picked up is at the State Crime Lab and eventually, she'll talk. We're going to serve Walkabout a new warrant. This one should cover all the bases." Paul put his hand on Manny's shoulder. "Why don't you head back to the motel? It's been a long day. I'll call you when the warrants are ready."

"Something's gnawing at my insides telling me Buchanan isn't who we should be after," Manny said.

"If not Buchanan, then who."

"We just spoke to him."

Harris wheeled around and caught a glimpse of Anderson driving away. "Him? He's just an ego with a badge."

Manny turned to Hank and winked.

·56·

Anderson accelerated in his black and white as he headed for Taylor. He made the turn onto U.S. Highway 228 and dialed a number on his cellphone. "Where will you be in a half-hour? Good, good... we need to talk. I need to split and lay low for a while. Yeah, okay. I'll stop at my house and grab the rest of the money. Then we can split what we have."

Anderson ended the call and put the phone down. He grinned to himself and checked the revolving cylinder of his handgun. It was fully loaded.

A few minutes past nine in the evening, Anderson drove up to his modest four-room ranch and turned off his headlights. He swung his car into the driveway and parked close to the door. He stepped through the front doorway, stuck a Marlboro between his lips, struck a match, and lit the cigarette. He took a deep drag, exhaled, and opened the hallway closet door.

Reaching toward the ceiling, he pushed aside a piece of plywood above a gaping hole, brought down a brown metal box and walked into the living room. He sat down and counted and recounted the money, his smile broadening each time that he did.

Nearly an hour later the front door burst open. Anderson stood up holding the box and faced the barrel of Jim's revolver. Anderson backed up. "Hey, wait a minute."

"Drop your gun."

Anderson complied. "What's this all about?"

"I know about your involvement. Are you WI?"

"I don't know what you're talking about." Anderson backed up deeper into the living room.

Jim followed and glanced behind the front door to ensure no one was there. He explained to Anderson, "I've got your name on an invoice for illegal liquor sales. Were you mixed up with Jack Morton... did you kill him?"

"I could have killed you when you dived out your office window. That excuse for a woman police captain saved your life by hitting my arm as I fired."

Jim asked again, "Did you kill Jack Morton?"

"Look, we can come to an understanding. Just let me go and I'll tell you everything I know." Anderson offered the box to Jim. "Take this. There's money and information about who ran the whole thing. Let me go. You'll never hear from me again."

Anderson continued to back up into the kitchen. "Stop!" Jim ordered.

Standing next to the back door, Jim said, "Sam's in custody. If you're involved, it'll come out in the investigation."

The back door burst open and a shot rang out. A bullet tore through the back of Anderson's head. Jim flinched as his face was spattered with blood. Anderson lurched forward and to the left, then toppled facedown onto the kitchen floor as the box crashed against the wall.

·57·

The wispy smoke from the barrel of a 92-FS Berretta pistol rode in on the cold outside breeze invading the house. For a lingering second, the weapon pointed at Jim from between the partially open door and the doorframe. Jim dropped behind the refrigerator and aimed his gun at the door.

"It's me, Tom. I thought he had a gun trained on you." Tom stepped inside the kitchen and glanced at the floor. "Hell, it was just a box. Dan told me what happened at the farm and that you were coming here without backup."

Jim took a deep breath then holstered his handgun. He knelt next to Anderson and felt for a pulse. Finding none, he turned to Tom. "We could have closed the case with Anderson's testimony."

"Did you check Anderson for any concealed weapons? If you find one you'll thank me for what I just did."

Jim retrieved Anderson's service revolver. "Someone else is involved, someone who goes by the name of WI."

"Come on Jim, we all know what was going on. Dan filled me in at the sheriff's office. Anderson, Sam and Jack sold booze to the Indians. They killed anyone who tried to stop or report them."

Jim stood over the kitchen sink and washed the blood off his face. He then watched Tom pick up the box that had fallen from Anderson's grasp. "Anderson said there's information in that box."

Tom said, "We'll process it at the office. We can talk to Sam too."

"We need officers here, I'll call Linda to secure the scene," Jim suggested.

He placed a call to Linda's cellphone. After three rings, she answered.

"Linda, it's me, Jim. Where are you... the reservation? I'm at Anderson's house in Taylor... what new warrant? Anderson's dead... listen to me! I don't have time to explain. Dan and I broke the case. Sam, Anderson, and Jack were involved in the illegal liquor sales. They may have had something to do with the killings. Tom and I are going to interrogate Sam at the sheriff's office... well, make sure the FBI stays at the Rez until after they serve the warrant. That should give me enough time to find out what Sam knows." Jim looked at his watch. "It's 10:05 now. Give me until midnight, and then meet me at the sheriff's office."

Jim ended the call and said to Tom, "Linda is going to send two officers to secure this house. After they get here, we'll pay Sam a visit. He'll talk when he hears that Anderson is dead."

Tom scoffed. "If he won't talk, we'll make him."

·58·

As January's cloudless evening sky dropped its cool, crisp temperatures on Taylor, Jim climbed into Miss Martin's sedan. After the officers arrived and Tom filled them in on what happened, Jim followed Tom's patrol car to the sheriff's office. As soon as Jim stepped out of the car the greenish dazzling glow of the Northern Lights waltzing above the Cabinet Mountains caught his attention. He walked up to the front door and stood next to Tom.

"You think Sam was involved?" Tom asked, still carrying the box.

Jim bypassed him and stepped inside. "I think so. I knew it was too clean to think Jack was the only one involved." Jim continued as Tom followed him. "We caught Sam at the farm with explosives. His wife's mummified corpse was at the farm."

"Really... you think he killed her?" Tom asked closing the outside door.

"No, he was pretty upset. Seemed that he didn't even know where she was."

"Then Anderson must have killed her. He was a real prick. I never liked him."

"Anderson was in Wisconsin until last year and Sam's wife has been dead for years. Jack probably killed her."

"Right... makes sense now."

Jim noticed no one was on duty at the dispatcher's desk. "Who's working second shift dispatcher?"

"Helen had an emergency so I routed the calls through the Taylor Police Department. Jenny is taking calls tonight."

"Where's Bill? There should be a deputy in the office."

"Bill got called out. We're shorthanded but Rocky is in back with Dan."

"Good. For a moment you got me worried." Jim heard a dog bark from the cellblocks. "Is that Angel?"

"Yeah, Dan said he wanted to take her for a walk. Maybe they just got back."

Jim walked up to his desk. "I need to gather a pad and a pen for Sam's statement. Tell Dan I'll be right in and have Rocky sit in on this."

"All right," Tom said.

Jim opened his bottom desk drawer and removed a lined note pad. As he looked up, he saw the blinking red light on his telephone. He opened the middle drawer of his desk and grabbed a pen. Again, he noticed the blinking light. He placed the pad and pen on the desk and reached for the phone.

"Anything wrong?" Tom asked.

Jim felt Tom hovering around his desk. "Before we begin Sam's interrogation, let me take this message and get it out of the way."

Jim retrieved the message and listened to the caller's voice. "Sheriff Buchanan, this is Doctor Larson over at the Veterinary Clinic. I just wanted to relay some information about that deer strike last week. Tom delivered the deer to me for burial. After he left, I realized the deer's injury didn't look like a car impact. There were no broken bones and there was a clean cut on the animal's body from where it bled. Then I noticed a small hole in the carcass, so I did some investigating. I found two more holes and pulled three slugs from its body. I think Tom may have surprised a couple of hunters. They probably dropped the deer by the side of the road and took off when they heard Tom's car approach. You may have a problem with poachers..."

Jim pulled the receiver away from his ear. He thought about the fourth A. The Northern Lights... the Aurora!

Tom asked, "Something wrong?"

Jim glanced at the empty dispatcher's desk. He dropped his hand to his side and his fingers slid onto the handle of his revolver.

Tom raised his pistol and pointed it at Jim. "Get your hand away from your weapon." Tom walked over to the desk and pulled

Jim's revolver from his holster. He stuck it between his shirt and pants.

"Tom… you're WI."

"No, WI for the Western Imperium… the new world empire. Shut up and get to the cellblocks."

·59·

They walked past Tom's office. Jim looked inside and noticed the leather briefcase in the middle of the desktop. A solitary tealeaf sat on a bookshelf and Jim thought back to the tea leaves that Hank had found and the box of tea Jia Li had given to him.

"You killed that girl."

"How did you figure that one out?"

"She must have been here with you and drank Jia Li's tea from the coffee station."

"I gave her a cup of coffee. I guess she went and got herself a cup of that Oriental tea. Is that how she got those tea leaves in her stomach? I should have killed Hank too. Big city medical examiner, I knew when he got here that old man would be a pain in the ass."

"And you killed the deer to mask her blood spatters in the cellblock. You knew no one would dig any deeper if they saw you cleaning deer blood from the floor. Then you buried her in the high school football field. Who helped you, Anderson or Sam?"

Tom pushed the barrel of his pistol against Jim's back. "Sam's a coward and Anderson would do anything for money."

"Blind man's dreams. That innocent girl's been speaking to me but I only heard her voice now," Jim said as they approached the cellblock door.

Jim opened the heavy door that led to the row of jail cells deep inside the building. Sam Clayton was in one cell hunched over in pain from alcohol withdrawal. Dan McCoy and Rocky sat in another cell. All were handcuffed with duct tape covering their mouths. Angel was in a third locked cell. She wagged and barked when she saw Jim. Helen, the evening dispatcher was in another cell and two prisoners were in the cell next to her. All were similarly bound and gagged.

Jim locked eyes with Dan and Rocky, and then snarled at Tom. "What the hell did you do?"

"Shut up and get in that empty cell," he jabbed at Jim with his gun directing him to the cell next to Sam.

Jim complied and Tom threw one loop of a set of handcuffs on Jim's wrist and the other loop on one of the bars of the jail cell.

Jim looked at his friends and then at Tom. "Why?"

Tom closed the cell door and sat on a stool outside the bars. He pointed his pistol at Jim. "Before you became sheriff, I was selling liquor to the Indians all by myself. You fucked up my plans with your high moral code." He waved his gun at Dan McCoy. "He didn't know what I was doing. He didn't snoop around like you. As long as I did my job, that's all Dan cared about." He pulled back the hammer on his pistol. "Over the years, I found others who shared the same values that I did."

"Jack and Sam?"

"Yeah, but then the operation got to be unwieldy. I contacted Anderson in Wisconsin and convinced Peters to hire him. I knew Anderson growing up. We did a lot of shit as teenagers. I needed him to thin the herd. But I also needed him to keep things from stampeding out of control. He failed that part."

"You had Anderson kill Jack but why all the other bodies?" Jim asked.

"They weren't all innocent. Some of them wanted a piece of the action or threatened to turn me in. I had to take care of the problem."

"What about the innocent ones?"

"That blond social worker and the environmentalist?" Tom laughed. "They learned what was going on. I couldn't allow them to expose the operation."

"How does DeFazio fit into all this?"

"He was my supplier. I killed him as a favor for the mob."

"What happened to Olivia Clayton?"

Tom smiled. "Hey Sam, listen up. You'll want to hear this." He turned back to Jim. "Olivia needed money for Sam and I was happy to oblige as long as I got some lovin' out of the deal. We'd meet at your dad's farmhouse every weekend she was in town. I gave her cash and she passed some of it on to Sam. She felt sorry for him and wanted to make sure he was taken care of... hey Sam, she was still in love with you."

"Did you kill her?" Jim asked.

"When she found out that Sam was involved in the reservation liquor sales she threatened to expose me. She said she wanted to save Sam before he got deeper into it. I had no choice. I was merciful."

"And you left her in that room to rot?"

"Why not? It was hidden and served its purpose. After I killed Olivia, I only needed the farm to hide booze. No one except my people knew the stuff was there and no one knew Olivia was there until you stuck your big nose in my business."

Sam yanked on his handcuffs against the cell bars and tried to yell through the duct tape. Tom unlocked the cell door, walked up to him and clobbered him on the head with the butt of his gun. Sam fell to the floor unconscious.

Jim yelled, "You son of a bitch... he's going through the DTs. You could've killed him."

"I don't give a shit. It's you and your friends that you should be worried about."

"What do you plan to do with us?" Jim asked.

"Kill you first, then everyone else with your gun. I'll tell the FBI that you broke in here to steal weapons and ammo from the arsenal. Dan and Rocky tried to stop you and you killed them and you killed Sam, Helen and the prisoners so there wouldn't be any witnesses. Then I came in and shot you in self-defense."

"We recovered paperwork at the farm and it lists contacts at the tribe."

"Oh that? Dan showed that to me before he suspected I was involved. Now it's a pile of ash in Martha's wastebasket. Anderson's box is the last piece. I just have to grab the cash, destroy the documents and my tracks are covered."

"You've got it all figured out, haven't you?"

"That call you made to Linda complicates things. After I'm done here, I'll wait for Linda to show up, kill her and then go back to Anderson's place and take care of those officers there. I'll use your gun then come back here, finish you off with my gun and then leave your gun by your side. The news will portray it as a massacre by a crazed sheriff but after I produce new evidence that implicates you in the liquor sales, it'll be a closed case." Tom laughed, "Hey, I guess I'll end up being the new sheriff. I'll really be able to control the county now."

"You carved up your victims with your skills from veterinary school?"

Tom laughed. "Why do you think I went to vet school in the first place? What I learned I put to good use."

"Who's your contact with the tribe?"

"Robert Bear Cloud. He's got two bullets in his head and he's lying at the bottom of Gold's Well."

"Why did you do it?"

"Hey, I'm the Supreme Divinity of the Guardians of Doctrine. I can do what I damn please. I run the whole show."

"What does that damn club have to do with anything?"

"I can assure you it was not a club. It was a secret organization me and Anderson formulated when we were growing up. He was the only one that knew I was the leader. It served my purpose. I wanted to throw the Flathead Reservation into chaos, the way it will be for all the mud people when they go to hell. I knew some kids would drink themselves to death. I knew some men would beat and kill their wives because of the booze. I wanted to eliminate them one by one. Over the years, I grossed over a half-million from the liquor sales. Then there was the money from DeFazio. The mob paid me a quarter-million to whack him. He was screwing the mob boss' mistress."

"What's in the briefcase?" Jim asked.

"Money from the liquor sales plus my payoff for DeFazio."

Jim heard the front door buzz open. He watched Kate, Alma Rose and Linda walk into the cell block.

"Jim, Kate and Alma Rose told me everything so I thought I'd stop by early to see…" Linda's voice went silent when she saw Tom holding a gun on Jim and Rocky, Dan and Sam handcuffed inside the jail cells. "Tom, what's going on here?' she asked.

Tom wheeled around and faced them with his gun. "Linda, I'm glad you're here to help."

Alma Rose stepped in front of Linda and addressed Tom. "The *ḿalyè es šeýiⱡk* is behind you."

·60·

ilence seemed to hang in the cellblock's stale air. Even the constant hum of a solitary ceiling fan could not disburse the oddly tinged odor that suddenly arrived and overtook every corner of the lockup. A greenish hue supplanted the smell and enveloped the building along with a numbing cold that penetrated everyone's senses.

Alma warned Tom again. "The *ḿalyè es šeýiłk* will get her revenge tonight."

He laughed at her. "What are you talking about girly? Some mumbo-jumbo from your Indian ways or did you release some hocus-pocus smelly gas to distract me?" He turned to Jim. "Are you going to pray to God before I kill you?" Tom aimed the revolver at Jim. "You're a mud person. You and your kind are going straight to hell. We'll rid of all of you one by one until there's only white people left in this country. Animals like you are the reason for the crime, lewdness, and wickedness we have today. When you're gone, we'll have peace and total order."

"You won't live past tonight," Alma Rose said.

Tom was distracted by her outburst. "Girly, I won't live? You've got it all wrong." He laughed then asked Jim, "What in the hell is your daughter talking about?"

"She sees things that we cannot. We fear what we do not understand."

"So, who is she supposed to be seeing that I can't?"

Alma Rose stepped toward Tom. "Her name was Olivia Clayton. Now she is known as the *ḿalyè es šeýiłk.*"

Tom's jaw dropped as he swiveled his head and stared in all directions.

281

Kate rushed up to Tom even as he responded to her actions by sticking the barrel of his gun against her forehead. "Release them all," she said.

Jim yanked on his handcuffs but didn't say a word. He let Kate speak and trusted her decision to confront Tom.

"Mrs. Fucking Buchanan I'm about to put a bullet through your goddamn head."

"I'm not afraid to die."

Tom laughed loud and hard. "I haven't killed one person who wasn't afraid to die."

A stoic Kate spoke with conviction. "I already died once. I would do it again especially for good people. Now drop your gun."

"Do as she says," Linda yelled and drew her weapon. "Tom, drop the gun."

He turned and met her face to face. "I can't. You're not a mud person. Look at yourself." Tom stared at the blond, blue-eyed woman. "Manifest Destiny, Linda you're part of the Aryan race. We have to purify the land. It starts tonight, right here," he said, emphatically pointing to the ground.

"I said, put the gun down."

Tom kept his gun trained on her. "Linda, join me. We can do this together. I've got over seven-hundred grand. I'll split it with you."

"Tom, murder isn't a solution for anything."

"Seven-hundred grand, Linda. That's three-fifty apiece. It's high time we took back this country and built the Western Imperium."

"Drop it!" demanded Linda.

Tom shrugged his shoulders. "I'm sorry." Tom fired a round that plowed through Linda's jacket, into her abdomen just above her left hip and exited through her side.

As she fell backward, she squeezed the trigger of her revolver. An errant bullet from Linda's gun ricocheted against one of the cell bars and struck Tom above his left breast pocket.

Tom's gun flew from his grasp as he slumped into a crumpled heap. He grasped his left side with one hand and tried to loosen his collar with the other. Tom then tugged on his collar with both hands and let out a piercing scream. After a long moment,

Tom's body stiffened and then went limp. He lay sprawled on his back bleeding from the bullet wound.

Linda crawled over, pushed Tom's weapon away, pulled Jim's revolver away from Tom and then slid it between the bars into Jim's cell.

As Linda's wound saturated her shirt and pants, her bloody hand grabbed a set of keys from Tom's pocket as he lay there dying. She handed them to Kate who unlocked Jim's jail cell door and then Jim's handcuffs.

Alma ran to Linda's side, laid her hands on her and spoke a few words in her Native tongue. Jim recognized them as asking for the grace of *Apsáalooke* ancestors to give Linda the strength to survive.

Jim picked Linda up and placed her down on the cell bunk as Kate dialed 911 and got Jenny at the Taylor Police Department where she was serving as temporary dispatcher. Medics were on their way.

Linda glanced at Tom on the floor and with a growing weakness in her voice, said to Jim, "If I don't make it, promise me one thing?"

"What is it?" Jim asked.

"Don't tell anyone about that day you escaped from your office to the reservation and I stopped Anderson from shooting you. I wouldn't want anyone to think I'd let a suspect get away."

·61·

The February days and nights were still cold and a dense snowpack covered the ground, but an uplifting of spirits had occurred in Taylor and on the Flathead Reservation. No longer would people be living in fear. The demons of a twisted few would forever be banished.

Linda sat up in her hospital bed at the Taylor University Medical Center, still recovering from the bullet wound. It had been touch and go for a few days. She had suffered a significant blood loss but the quick work of skillful doctors, kept her vital signs from deteriorating. It also helped that Alma made a few hospital visits along with spiritual offerings.

There were a few loose ends regarding the illegal liquor sales, comprised mostly of low-level accomplices in the local area. They were more interested in cooperating with the authorities for leniency than trying to avoid prosecution. They were the only local remnants of the far-reaching bootlegging conspiracy.

The Montana Attorney General's Office with the assistance of the U.S. Justice Department completed the investigation while the U.S. Marshals Service presented charges in federal court.

Manny Costa alerted his superiors at the FBI of the operation. They contacted ATF who rounded up significant players in the Northwest who were associated with organized crime. The authorities uncovered a regional network and as a result, the government shut down similar operations in two other states. With information from Jim and the confession from the Brunazzi Family bookie Julius "Sweetheart" Innamorato they were also able to bring charges against Luigi Brunazzi for the torture and murder for hire of Mario "The Wrench" DeFazio despite only having his decomposed head as evidence.

Sam was headed back to the big house but because he cooperated and was not involved in the killings his charges were reduced to arson and bootleg liquor sales. Jim petitioned for a shorter sentence and a promise that when Sam got out that a job, an apartment and a support network would be waiting for him. Even so, Prosecutor Emily Cronin was pushing for a fifteen year sentence. If it stuck, Sam would be nearly sixty years old when he got out.

With three dead members who were involved in murder and illegal liquor sales, Police Chief Peters issued an order to disband the Guardians of Doctrine. The Taylor Police Department filed charges against its organizers with the help of a statement from Matt Nelson.

The Nelson family was back together and Matt gained a newfound appreciation of Jim's integrity. They invited Jim and Kate over to their house for dinner and enjoyed a belated holiday gathering.

Paul Harris and Manny Costa were able to get their superiors to authorize a reward from Tom Hyde's confiscated funds for Jim's efforts in solving the case. With Jim's insistence, the check was earmarked for the Flathead Nation for their help in finding the Bitterroot Killer.

On a snowy day inside the Flathead Community Center Chapel, Father Bongiorno held an early morning Mass. At the end of the sermon in front of more than two hundred smiling children and adults, he stepped aside at the lectern and introduced Jim, Kate, Alma Rose and Elijah Sizemore. As they walked toward the front of the chapel, Jim carried the FBI reward check and an envelope in his hand.

"Elijah, first of all it gives me great pleasure to turn over this one-hundred-thousand dollar check from the FBI to the Confederated Salish and Kootenai Tribes. Congratulations," Jim said as he shook Elijah's hand. Elijah was about to speak but Jim cautioned him. "Hold on, I have something else." Jim opened the envelope and removed a sheet of paper. He said to the audience, "I received this remarkable letter the other day, and I want to read it to you. Please listen carefully."

Jim recited aloud...

Dear Sheriff James Buchanan,

Last month I received a letter from Steve Clancy. He mailed it to my son just hours before he died at the hands of Tom Hyde, the Bitterroot Killer. In it, he describes what life is like on a Native American reservation in the United States. The letter touched me and in my heart of hearts; I cannot fathom how such conditions can exist within the borders of this great country of ours. These conditions which were explained to me and which I have verified, rival what we see on TV in third-world countries. The only difference is that our government sends billions of dollars in relief aid to these third-world countries while providing a small fraction of that amount to our own, Native citizens. These people live on reservations, pay their taxes, and fight in our wars. This neglect is unacceptable and as long as I am a United States Senator, I will do everything in my power to right these injustices. I am introducing legislation today to establish a committee to investigate atrocities perpetuated by individuals, agencies, and local, state, and federal offices that abuse, interfere with, and deny the rights and privileges due to these first but often forgotten citizens of our country. I stand with you today, Little Hawk, to say to you and your people, Never Again!

> *Sincerely,*
> *Honorable Clark Lewis,*
> *United States Senator, State of Ohio*

Jim wiped his eyes and hugged Elijah.

With tears streaming down his cheeks, Elijah addressed the crowd. "This check will feed our people and pay for our children's education and for those of future generations so they will not forget the regalia, the customs, the songs, and most importantly, the words handed down to us by our elders." Elijah continued, "May Creator bless this Senator who heard our cries and decided to help rather than look away." Elijah took Jim's hand and held it aloft with the check to the cheers of the crowd.

Jim felt a nudge and looked down at Alma Rose. He whispered, "What is it?"

"The *ńalyè es šeýiłk* is here with us," Alma said quietly. "She's followed me everywhere I've gone since we left the farm. She's pure white spirit now. She's smiling and thanking you for releasing her."

"Can you tell her I only did my duty?"

"I don't have to... she understands. She said once she crosses over she will pray for you and Kate and for the baby you and Kate always wanted."

Jim remained silent for the rest of the service and then drove Kate and Alma Rose back home. He told them he had business in town. Something compelled him to go to the State Crime Lab in Taylor. Jim made a beeline right to Hank's office.

"Did you gather additional information from the autopsies?" Jim asked. From the smile on Hank's face, Jim knew something was up.

"I'm glad you stopped by. Maybe you can explain something to me." Hank waved Jim toward the door. "Follow me."

The two men walked the short distance to the morgue. There, Leon wheeled out Olivia and Tom's bodies.

Hank pulled the sheets off the corpses. "As you know, a few rambling notes we found in Tom's home seemed to suggest that passion was the main reason for his lust of Olivia. He also had her between a rock and a hard place when it came to Sam." He continued while Jim listened. "So was it lust that prompted Tom to let her mummify in the dry environment of the farmhouse's secret room so that her body wouldn't rot like all the others?"

"Everyone assumed that version," Jim said.

Hank nodded. "I have my own theory. It was obsession and not love that drew Tom to Olivia. She gave herself to Tom and in return got money from him and turned it over to Sam. Tom controlled her and in turn also controlled Sam. Leaving her body to secretly mummify in the hidden room was an alternative to burial which could have led to identification if her body was ever unearthed. Everyone stopped looking for Olivia when they thought she went back to the commune. If her body was found, Sam would have put two and two together and Tom couldn't risk Sam identifying her even if her head, hands and feet were missing."

Jim looked at the bodies on the tables. "Makes sense but why did you bring out Tom and Olivia?"

Hank pointed to Olivia's mummified body. "See here."

Jim stared at Olivia's dissected neck. "What?"

"Dislocation of several cervical vertebras... strangulation. Tom choked her to death. But during my autopsy of Tom's body, I had to reexamine my findings multiple times."

"Explain."

"Tom suffered a gunshot wound to the upper chest that severed his left subclavian artery." Hank paused. "It wasn't fatal."

"What do you mean?"

"Look here." Hank pointed to Tom's face and raised the corpse's eyelids. "See, he has subconjunctival hemorrhages in his eyes in addition to scratches and bruising around his neck. They point to strangulation."

"No one touched him from the time he threw handcuffs on me until the medics arrived."

"I was worried you'd say that."

"I'm confused. You mean they were both strangled?"

"That's what my findings point to." Hank said.

"I get it that Olivia was strangled but how was Tom? Could it have happened in the ambulance... resuscitation efforts... or after he died?"

"Absolutely not. We know he was dead when the medics arrived less than ten minutes after he was shot. The damage to the blood vessels in his eyes couldn't have happened after death."

"Are you saying..."

"I'm not. In fact, if I report that he was strangled I'd either get run out of town or be cast in a Twilight Zone sequel. My report will say that Tom bled to death from the gunshot wound. Just keep this between us."

Jim sat down. Over the next few minutes he considered what Hank just told him. After Leon put the bodies away, Jim had a clearer mind.

"I know what really happened."

"Justice from beyond the grave?" Hank asked.

"No... revenge of the *ńalyè es šeýiłk*."

End